Kanaka Blues

by
Mike Farris

Savant Books
Honolulu, HI, USA
2010

Published in the USA by Savant Books and Publications
2630 Kapiolani Blvd #1601
Honolulu, HI 96826
http://www.savantbooksandpublications.com

Printed in the USA

Edited by Jonathan Marcantoni
Cover Design by Mike Farris and Daniel S. Janik
Proofread by Zachary M. Oliver

13-digit ISBN: 978-0-9845552-1-5
10 digit ISBN: 0-9845552-1-8

Dedication

To Susan: my wife, best friend, and biggest fan.

Acknowledgements

A number of years ago, I first became interested in the Hawaiian sovereignty movement, and out of that fascination came this story. For helping me finally see it in print, I have to thank Dan Janik at Savant Books and my editor, Jonathan Marcantoni, whose keen eye and sharp story sense refined the novel beyond what I could have possibly done myself.

I also must thank friends and family who helped me throughout the process by reading and critiquing or simply offering support. They include my agents Donna Eastman and Gloria Koehler, Pat Davis, Steve Davis, Susan Farris, Cindy Grunwald, Rob Landers, Grey LeCuyer, Bill Morgan, and Katie Sessler.

A Glossary of Hawaiian Terms

a'a: stony lava
aina: land; earth
ali'i: chiefs or royalty
aloha: love; a common greeting
haole: white person
heiau: ancient place of worship
huhu: angry; offended
kahuna pule: priest
kanaka: Hawaiian
kapu: taboo; forbidden
keiki: child
lanai: porch; veranda
mahalo: thanks; gratitude
makai: towards the ocean
mana: supernatural or divine power
ohana: family
pakalolo: marijuana
pupule: crazy; insane
pu'uhonua: place of refuge
shaka: hand signal with fingers clenched, thumb and pinky finger extended
tutu: grandmother
wiki wiki: to hurry or be quick

CHAPTER ONE

A shroud of darkness draped itself around the coast of the Big Island of Hawaii. Far out to sea, a finger of moonlight peeked through gathering clouds spotlighting Pacific waters so deeply blue as to appear black. Closer to shore, those same waters attacked the *a'a,* the sharp-edged lava rock that guarded the island's interior. With each surge, pale fingers of foam stretched inward, pointing toward an ancient temple silhouetted against the night sky.

This is *Pu'uhonua O'Honaunau.* The City of Refuge.

A beautiful place.

A sacred place.

And tonight, a dangerous place.

*****

Seventy-nine-year-old Charlie Cain headed west from Hilo, pointing his blue rental Nissan Altima over the Saddle Road that bisected the island, the road that rental car agencies cautioned tourists against taking. Although he wore the trademark ensemble of a Hawaiian tourist – a red aloha shirt festooned with brightly-colored hibiscus flowers and wrinkled khaki slacks – his body language betrayed that status. He sat rigidly upright, with his hands clenched tightly around the steering wheel. Wrinkles spider-webbed from tired eyes, his mind lost in dark thoughts. He shivered, though the night was warm.

It had been two weeks since he first stumbled onto it. He didn't believe it at first – wouldn't believe it, even though it stared him in the face from the dusty pages. But now he had confirmed it, tracing the line back to its historical origin. There was no more escaping the facts. The man deserved to know, no matter the consequences. And there would be consequences, make no mistake about it.

He passed through Mauna Kea State Park and a United States military base, heading to an elevation of 6,500 feet on this rough road slashing through the Big Island between the peaks of Mauna Kea to the north and Mauna Loa to the south. If it were daylight, he would have enjoyed one of the finest views on the island. But tonight he saw only blackness.

Just past the military base, he began a descent through a scattering of eucalyptus trees before heading into the Waimea cattle country, then picked up Route 190 south to the tourist-filled town of Kailua-Kona. From there, it was only a few more miles to Kealakekua where he turned south from Kealakekua Bay onto a dirt road for the last stretch. He pushed his glasses up on his nose and peered ahead into the night.

The lights of his Nissan illuminated the entrance to The City of Refuge's parking lot, which appeared deserted except for a shadow at the far side, near the Visitor's Center. As he drew closer, the shadow took on the shape of a vehicle. Squinting, he saw what looked like Manu Pokui's Jeep near the front gate. He removed his foot from the gas and flipped off the brights. Yes, that was Manu's, the original paint long since eaten away by the salt air, orange rust rotting through the fender on the driver's side.

Charlie coasted to a stop, eased up next to the Jeep, and killed his engine. He checked his watch: 7:49. He punched a number on his cell phone, waited for the cue, and then left yet another message on the same answering machine in Texas.

"Erin, it's Charlie again. Please come quickly."

He put the cell in his shirt pocket, grabbed a file folder from the seat beside him, and got out. With the rumpled cloth hat covering his bald pate, the aloha shirt, and the khaki slacks, he might have appeared like any other tourist but for the hour, not to mention the death grip with which he held the file folder.

He stood frozen for a moment, doubts gnawing at him. But the man had a right to know.

He cocked his head to listen. Only the crash of breakers on the shore greeted him.

A breeze caressed his cheek, sultry and warm. Yet he shivered.

He tugged his shirt closed at the collar, bowed slightly at the waist, and walked to the entry. As promised, the gate was unlocked. He lifted the latch and pushed it open. Rusty hinges squeaked as it swung inward.

"Mr. Pokui?" Charlie called.

Again, only ocean sounds answered.

He stepped inside and looked around. No signs of movement. All he could see in the dimness was sand, coconut trees, and the small sheds and structures that made up the displays on the grounds. The ancient Hawaiians were controlled by *mana* – spiritual power – and *kapu* – the sacred rules of life. The high chief had lived here, guarded by his loincloth-clad warriors. Because of that, the grounds were sacred. Commoners were forbidden to walk in his footsteps or touch his possessions, or even to cast their shadows upon these grounds. To do so was *kapu*, and the penalty was death.

"Mr. Pokui?" Charlie called again.

Still nothing.

Across the way, he saw the great stone wall. Seventeen feet wide, ten feet tall, and one thousand feet long, the wall made of lava stone separated the palace grounds from the *pu'uhonua* – the sanctuary. To break the sacred law was to offend the gods, who were believed to react violently to insult. The people protected themselves from deific calamity by pursuing the *kapu*-breakers and killing them. The doomed malefactors might find absolution only if they reached the sanctuary first.

Charlie took a hesitant step, the folder clutched in his grasp. He cleared his throat, but his voice still quivered. "Mr. Pokui, it's Charlie Cain."

He continued across the sand, past a canoe-making display, past a large shadowy lump – probably a lava rock – then weaved his way between two fishponds until he found himself standing in the gateway of the wall. On the threshold of the sanctuary. Ahead lay the thatched-roof temple, the *Hale o Keawe Heiau*, where the high priest, the *kahuna pule*, would perform the ceremony of absolution for the *kapu*-breaker. The original temple also doubled as a mausoleum; the bones of twenty-three chiefs had rested there.

4

The spiritual power in those bones gave additional protection to the sanctuary. A fitting place, Charlie thought, to meet Manu Pokui.

Charlie inched forward, then peered around the wall to the right. No one in sight.

He waited for a moment then stepped inside the sanctuary. He took a deep breath as he approached the temple. When he was within thirty feet, a shadow moved just to the left of the temple's raised platform, and then it vanished.

Charlie froze. His heartbeat crescendoed, echoing in his own ears.

"Mr. Pokui? It's Charlie Cain."

The shadow flitted into view again and just as quickly disappeared, blending into the darkness. Charlie squinted, seeking vainly for the shadow or its owner. If the shadow belonged to Manu Pokui, what the hell was he doing?

"Mr. Pokui, please answer me."

Nothing. Something was not right. If Mr. Pokui said he'd be here, he'd be here. Then a thought struck him: If, indeed, that was Mr. Pokui on the phone.

A sound to his left snatched his attention. A shifting, shuffling sound. Like footsteps in sand. Then nothing. Charlie gripped his collar, abruptly turned on his heel, and retraced his steps back across the sanctuary, out through the gateway in the stone wall.

Sounds behind him, following. Footsteps. Most definitely footsteps. More than one set. Moving quickly.

Gasping for breath, Charlie accelerated into a broken-gaited, old man's run. His feet clomped heavily in the loose sand. The footsteps drew closer. He glanced over his shoulder but saw only his own shadow. He flinched. Casting a shadow on the palace grounds – *kapu*. Was his imagination playing tricks on him? Was that it, the imaginary footsteps of ancient warriors pursuing a *kapu*-breaker? Had he insulted the gods by coming to this place?

He pulled his cell from his shirt pocket and squinted at the numbers on its face. With a quivering thumb, he pushed the redial button.

"Erin, it's Charlie –"

Suddenly he found himself flying through the air. He dropped the phone and his glasses pitched to the sand, but he never loosened his grip on the folder. He scrambled to his hands and knees and looked back to see what he had tripped over. A Hawaiian man's body, lying facedown.

He lurched to his feet and stumbled through the front gate. Frantic. Past the Visitor's Center and out into the parking lot, the sanctuary of his car just ahead. He reached the door and fumbled for his keys. The footsteps sounded louder, echoing on concrete now.

He grabbed the door handle then turned to look.

His eyes widened as he dropped the folder, its pages scattering in the wind.

CHAPTER TWO

Manu Pokui rolled over in the soft sand. He rubbed his temple, and his hands came away wet and sticky. He looked at them, the blood almost tar-black in the moonlight. He worked his way to his hands and knees, pausing to let a wave of nausea pass. Then he inclined his six-foot six-inch, two-hundred-fifty-pound frame upright. He paused again as yet another wave of nausea passed, like the tide rolling in then receding. He looked around to get his bearings.

The great stone wall loomed nearby. He was at *Pu'uhonua O'Hononau.*

But he had found no refuge. And what was he even doing there?

He vaguely remembered the telephone call from Professor Cain but not its substance. Was that why he was there, to meet with Mr. Charlie? If so, where was he?

He looked around but saw only shadows. Heard only silence. Felt only stillness. It didn't take a genius to know things were not right. Better to just get the hell out of there and try to figure out the whys and wherefores the next day. He turned toward the parking lot and took one staggering step. Something crunched beneath his feet, ground into the sand by his rubber slipper. Clenching his teeth, fighting another wave of nausea, he bent down and grasped the object. A broken pair of glasses. Wire frames. Just like the glasses Mr. Charlie wore. But where was Mr. Charlie?

Next to the glasses lay a cell phone.

He tucked the glasses and phone into the pocket of his aloha shirt then staggered toward the front gate. Each step seemed to jar his brain. He stopped, took a deep breath, and plodded forward again. After what seemed like an eternity, he reached the gate. He leaned against the entryway and wiped the sweat from his brow. It took a bit of effort to concentrate, his eyesight cloudy, his vision blurred. There were two vehicles in the parking lot: his rusty old Jeep and a blue Nissan Altima.

He had seen that Nissan before. But where?

He willed himself to think clearly, the synapses of his brain handicapped by constant electrical impulses of pain. Of course. Mr. Charlie drove a car like that. Mr. Charlie had been there, all right. No doubt about it.

But where was he now?

Manu lurched toward the Nissan. Off balance, he stumbled forward, bracing himself with his hands against the driver's window to halt his momentum. He peered inside, but nothing jumped out at him. No papers, no personal items.

He grabbed the door handle and tried it. Locked.

He turned toward his Jeep when something caught his eye beneath the rear tire of the Nissan. Something white, blowing in the breeze, accompanied by a soft rustling sound. Papers. He shuffled to the tire, braced himself with one hand on the rear of the car, and bent over to grab the stapled pages. Using only the moonlight, he tried to read what was written on them. The letters all rushed together in a blur. He folded the papers and shoved them into his back pocket. He lurched to his Jeep.

Once behind the wheel, he checked himself in the mirror. His heart seemed to skip a beat as he realized how much blood covered his face, coursing from a gaping wound just above his left eye. He swiped his hand across his face to clear his eyes. He pulled the cell phone from his pocket as he cranked the Jeep and screeched out of the parking lot, then pushed the re-dial button on the phone.

CHAPTER THREE

The fresh aroma of Kona coffee tickled Erin Hanna's senses. She rolled onto her back and breathed deeply, drinking in the rich scent. Sunshine streamed through the window, bathing the bedroom with light that filtered through the towering palm trees. Outside lay a garden sprinkled with bougainvillea, hibiscus, and bird of paradise, surrounded by a lush lawn sloping to a salt-and-pepper beach. The bluest of oceans lapped gently at its edges.

Erin sat up and yawned, listening for the sounds of the surf. She ran her hand through her dark hair, stood, and stretched to her nearly six feet. Clad only in boxer shorts and an oversized Southern Methodist University T-shirt, her long legs rippling with muscles from hours of running, she pulled open the screen door and stepped onto a thatch-covered *lanai*.

Chris was waiting for her, cup in hand, already enjoying the morning. A tropical breeze gusted in from the Pacific, caressing her face and rustling her hair in its wake. She pushed a strand aside as she smiled at Chris.

"Hey, Sleepyhead," he said.

He poured a cup of steaming coffee from the insulated pot on the wicker table and handed it to her as she joined him. They sat silently, soaking in the morning.

Then the soft tones of Bruddah Iz's "Somewhere over the Rainbow" filtered into Erin's consciousness.

She awoke with a start. She shook the cobwebs away and looked around wildly to regain her bearings. Across the way stood Chris's dresser, its top still decorated with his red Texas Rangers baseball cap and his teak jewelry box. Things so familiar, yet so strange.

The ukulele tones continued to play on her cell phone. She looked at the clock – almost 2:30 in the morning – and realized that she was not on the Kona Coast of the Big Island but was still home in Dallas. Chris was not waiting for her on the *lanai* with a cup of Kona coffee. Not today. Not for a long time now. The house would be empty when she went searching for her morning cup.

She sat on the edge of the bed for a brief moment and gripped the mattress hard. A familiar lump rose in her throat. She swallowed hard to push it back down. She wasn't prepared for it that day. Not for the feelings it would produce if she gave in to it. She closed her eyes tightly as the phone continued to ring, willing the lump back down her throat. Back to her heart where it belonged. After a few seconds, it passed.

Having once again fought loneliness to a draw, she snatched up the phone and peered at the caller I.D. readout – CHARLIE CAIN.

"Charlie?"

She heard only deep breathing on the other end, along with what she swore were sounds of waves crashing on a beach.

"Charlie, are you there?" she asked.

A male voice answered in a rhythmic lilt. "Whozit?"

"Is Charlie Cain there? This is his phone."

Another long silence of deep breathing and crashing waves, then the phone disconnected.

Erin stared at the phone in disbelief and saw that she had three missed messages. They must have come in earlier, while she was charging it before going to bed. She played them back and listened to Charlie's panicky voice on each.

The first: "Erin, it's Charlie. I've whipped up a tsunami here, and I need you to come to Hilo."

The second: "Erin, it's Charlie again. Please come quickly."

But it was the third message that left her cold. "Erin, it's Charlie –"

There was a scuffling sound, followed by what might have been an exhale of breath. After that, silence.

*****

Less than fifteen hours later, wearing jeans, tennis shoes, and a blue SMU golf shirt, Erin sat in a window seat on a Hawaiian Airlines flight connecting between Honolulu and Hilo, gazing at the rich blue Pacific. Long black hair framed her Mediterranean face, with piercing, narrow-set blue eyes over high cheekbones that sloped down to a tapered chin. It was a face that seemed older than her thirty-six years, with eyes that had already seen a lifetime of pain.

Even with the four-hour time change from Texas, it was already mid-afternoon by the time the plane broached shore over the Kona Coast of the Big Island and headed across the divide between Mauna Loa and Mauna Kea. The land below looked nothing like what one normally envisions when thinking of Hawaii. Instead, this real estate more closely resembled the surface of the moon, with thousands of acres of black lava rock sweeping down from the volcanoes that had given birth to the island. Patches of green along the coast, heading north, represented a series of oases carved out by resort developers, the only testament on this side of the island to the promises by travel agents that this was, indeed, a tropical paradise.

Erin remembered the last time she made this trip, two years ago, sitting next to Chris, hands entwined as they looked out the window in search of their ultimate destination, the luxurious Kona Coast Cottages. Even now, she recalled her reaction at first setting foot on the resort grounds, as if stepping back in time to ancient Hawaii with its acreage of lush foliage and thatched-roof bungalows, the air sweet with the fragrance of plumeria. She and Chris had spent hours on the beach at Kahuwai Bay, sleeping or reading as its aquamarine waters gently lapped at the salt-and-pepper beach. They strolled hand-in-hand around the palm tree-shaded lagoons, snorkeled with giant sea turtles on the reef, and braved the mid-day sun by venturing onto the boardwalk through the petroglyph field. A belated honeymoon well worth the wait.

The helicopter tour over the volcanic craters that still spit, sputtered, and spewed endless waves of lava seemed like the perfect end to a perfect vacation.

She pushed aside her bangs and scratched the jagged six-inch scar on her forehead, remembering the shimmy of the chopper as it swept low over the living lava flow that poured into the ocean, sending a spiral of steam into the sky. Then came the realization that there was more than steam outside the Plexiglas window; there was also smoke trailing from the helicopter's engine. The pilot's frantic cry of "*Mayday, mayday, mayday,*" rang in her ears. She remembered Chris squeezing her hand, as if he could keep them in the air by the mere strength of his grip. Then she remembered falling. Beyond that, all memory failed her.

By sheer force of will, she shook the images from her head. That was then and this was now. There was no Chris sitting beside her, squeezing her hand, nor would he ever be beside her again. She was here alone this time, coming back to the place that held her most beautiful and her most horrific memories. The place to which she swore she would never return.

And yet here she was again. Because someone else she loved was in trouble and needed her.

*****

After the plane landed at the Hilo airport, she gathered her bags and headed for the rental car facilities. Less than thirty minutes later, she wheeled her rented red Ford Focus down Kanoelehua Avenue and its trappings of western civilization: grocery and discount stores, gas stations, and fast food restaurants. Not even Paradise had escaped the encroachment of capitalism. There was, of course, the ubiquitous Hilo Hattie, home of one-stop Hawaiian shopping for everything from aloha attire to music, food, jewelry, or souvenirs, but even that was a Madison Avenue special, targeting tourists and their dollars.

A light rain misted on the windshield, and the gathering clouds promised more and heavier later. At the intersection with Highway 19, which led into downtown Hilo, she continued straight onto the aptly named Banyan Drive, lined on both sides by giant banyan trees and home to virtually the only tourist hotels on the windward side of the island.

At the start of the row of hotels, she turned right onto a narrow side street that separated the Hilo Seasurf Hotel, on her right, from Reed's Bay – an arm of Hilo Bay – on her left. The charming hotel had been there for decades, and its owners successfully resisted the temptation to renovate and update. It offered a bit of old Hawaii just up the road from the new.

Erin parked on the street by a rambling carp pond, complete with footbridge, which fronted the building and wrapped around on the side nearest Banyan Drive. She entered an open-air lobby decorated with bamboo and Hawaiian quilt squares, still more vestiges of a Hawaii that once was. To her left, she heard the clatter of silverware and the chatter of diners in an attached restaurant. Straight ahead was the front desk.

A giant of a man stood behind the counter, in front of a honeycomb of pigeonholes that held room keys. He wore a bright red aloha shirt festooned with hibiscus and anthuriums. About thirty-years-old, he had thick black hair, a scraggly mustache, and the wide nose and swarthy complexion common to Polynesians. Erin pegged his height at perhaps six feet, but he weighed 350 pounds if he weighed an ounce. A nametag pinned to his shirt identified him only as "Harry."

He greeted her with a toothy smile as she approached the

desk. "Checking in, miss?"

"Actually, I'm looking for one of your guests. Charlie Cain."

His smile disappeared. "Mistah Chawlie know you?"

"I'm Erin Hanna."

His smile returned. "Oh, yeah? Mistah Chawlie talk 'bout you all time." She recognized a Hawaiian lilt to his voice. Every sentence seemed to play a melody.

"He in two-twenty, but he not here. Mistah Chawlie nevah come back las' night after he lef'."

The scuffling sound and exhaling Erin had heard from Charlie's cell replayed itself in her head, followed by the mysterious voice: "Whozit?" Not much of a voice sample, but probably not the desk clerk.

"Did you call me last night on Charlie's cell phone?" Erin asked.

"No, Missy."

"What time did he leave?"

"I don't know. Six o'clock, mebbe. Could have been six-thirty. I just remembah was already dark, but it gets dark early on dis side of the island."

Erin did a quick calculation in her head. With the four-hour time difference, that would have been around ten o'clock her time. According to the time on her cell phone, the last message – the aborted call – had come in at just before midnight. What had Charlie done in the intervening time?

"Do you know where he went?" she asked.

"He said he go to the City of Refuge. It's a tourist attraction on the other side of the island."

"Did he say why he was going there?"

"No."

"How long would it have taken him to get there?"

"Depends how fast he drive. Could be hour-and-a-half, could be two."

Erin nodded. The time fit.

"Can I see his room?" she asked.

"Sure. I show you."

Harry the desk clerk grabbed a key from its pigeonhole, rounded the end of the counter, and did the fat man shuffle down a nearby passageway, his flip-flops slapping against his heels. Erin followed, anxious to hurry him along but not wanting to antagonize him. As of right now, he was the only connection she had to Charlie, and she didn't want to lose it.

Harry led her down a short hall, past ice and vending machines, then up a half-flight of stairs to an open-air passageway that ran alongside a row of rooms. It overlooked a branch of the carp pond that snaked its way around the various wings of the hotel, giving almost every room either an ocean or a pond view. Erin glanced down at the fat orange and white fish milling about, mouths pressed to the water's surface as they waited for guests with handfuls of bread. Rain began falling more heavily, beating out a rhythm on the rooftop above and creating hundreds of concentric ripples on the surface of the pond below.

They stopped in front of room 220. Harry unlocked the door and opened it, then stepped aside. "There you go, sistah."

Erin entered and stood in the doorway, taking it all in. At first blush, nothing seemed out of order. The bed appeared freshly made. On the far wall, slacks and shirts hung neatly in a row on a clothes rack. A red cloth suitcase stood on the floor beneath them.

Erin recognized the clothes immediately as Charlie's – lots of dark slacks and multi-colored short-sleeve dress shirts. His uniform, Erin called it. And Charlie always buttoned the top button of his shirts. The only thing missing was his rumpled cloth hat.

"Has anyone else been in here today?" Erin asked.

"Maid not even go here today."

"The bed's been made."

"Mistah Chawlie ask fo' maid service only every two day. Today not his day."

"So his bed hasn't been slept in."

"He could have made it hisself but, like I said, he nevah come back las' night."

"How long has he been staying here?" Erin asked.

"Coupla weeks or so. Mebbe more."

"Do you know if he ever went away overnight?"

"Sometimes. He always tells me when he does, though." He pointed at the red suitcase. "And he always takes that with him."

"Where does he go?"

"Honolulu, sometimes, just fo' a day. He got an apartment there. I don't know where else."

Erin ventured into the room, scanning for any signs that might tell her where Charlie had gone. She opened the drawers in the dresser. Charlie's socks, T-shirts, and underwear lay neatly folded and stacked inside. A shaving kit was open on the counter in the bathroom. Toothbrush and toothpaste lay alongside a razor on the sink.

She picked up the toothbrush and ran her thumb along the bristles. Dry. She studied the blade of the razor. A few whisker remnants but nothing to provide any clue as to when it had last been used. Charlie wouldn't have left these things if he intended to be gone overnight.

She turned and looked at Harry. "You're sure he hasn't been back?"

"All I know is that he lef' las' night, and I don't see him come back. I was on duty 'til midnight, and his car not here this morning. I guess he could come and go, but unless he made up his own bed, he didn't sleep here las' night."

"What kind of car was he driving?"

"Blue Nissan Altima. I got the license numbah on his guest card."

She nodded, still scanning the room. Her eye fell on the small worktable, void of paper. That didn't seem like Charlie, who routinely left his research scattered on every surface he occupied. She zeroed in on an oversized briefcase on the floor in the corner. Black leather, battered beyond belief by years of abuse, his gold monogram only faintly visible beneath the handle: *CRC* – Charles Robert Cain.

She opened the briefcase and looked inside. Empty. Not a single page to be found. Also not like Charlie. If he had his work with him, it would be encased in this briefcase, and this briefcase would be in Charlie's right hand.

"What happened to his papers?" Erin asked.

"Got me. He had somethin' wif' him when he lef' las' night. Just a folder, I tink."

"You said he left about six?"

"Six, six-thirty, something like that. I put a call tru' to his room, then he come by a few minutes later with this folder. He say he had to go meet wit' someone."

"Who was the call from?"

"Don't know. Sound like a *kanaka* though." When Erin frowned, he added, "A Hawaiian, like me."

"Tell me again where Charlie said he was going?"

Harry nodded, worry lines creasing his forehead. Erin wondered if her frantic tone was starting to have its effect on him.

"*Pu'uhonua o Hononau*. The City of Refuge."

"I've been there before. That's where the ancient Hawaiians went for absolution, isn't it?"

"Das right. If a *kanaka* break *kapu*, the *ali'i* – the chiefs – punish him unless he got to the kahuna before they can catch him."

"And what if he didn't make it?" she asked.

"Den they kill him."

Kanaka Blues

CHAPTER FOUR

Erin took the same route Charlie had taken across the Saddle Road. By the mid-point of the trek between Mauna Loa and Mauna Kea, the rain ended, only to be replaced along the Mamalahoa Highway by the vog – a sulfuric mist of volcanic gases, Hawaii's answer to smog – which left Erin with a headache. Past the resort town of Kailua-Kona, she raced through the Kona coffee country with its slopes of coffee trees, rich with red berries, and expansive views of the Pacific.

She finally turned off at the town of Captain Cook toward Kealakekua Bay, where legend had it that the real Captain James Cook was killed and eaten by the natives, under the leadership of Kamehameha the First, in the Eighteenth Century. From there, she followed a rough road the remaining miles to the City of Refuge's parking lot and Visitor's Center.

The parking lot was half-empty, and the sun was already starting its descent. Erin bought a ticket despite a warning from the ticket seller that the City would close in a half-hour. Inside, on the white sand of the palace grounds, native Hawaiians put finishing touches on their craft-making displays for the aloha-shirt-and-baggy-shorts-wearing tourists. Some of the craftsmen were already closing up shop for the day.

Erin remembered coming here with Chris two years earlier. It was the day before the helicopter tour. She retraced the steps they had taken across the grounds, past the royal fishpond where commoners placed certain types of fish strictly for use by the chiefs. Not that different, she thought, from the downtown dinner clubs and executive dining rooms in Dallas, where the elite dined off the services of the great unwashed. Those who served, rather than those who were served, made up her client base during her days of active law practice. Evictions and protecting the rights of the homeless consumed many of her non-billable hours. She envisioned herself in this very spot, in Hawaii, during ancient days, arguing with the chiefs for admission to the sanctuary for the *kapu*-breakers who made their way there.

She continued on through the Great Wall that separated the sanctuary from the palace grounds. She stopped for a moment and looked at the Ka'ahumanu Stone, a large flat rock near a *heiau*, or temple, platform. Legend had it that Queen Ka'ahumanu once left her husband, King Kamehameha the First, after a lovers' quarrel, swam across Honaunau Bay, and hid under this rock in fear for her life. The king's men discovered her when her pet dog barked until she was found. There was a happy ending to the story, though, as the king and queen made up and lived a fairy tale "happily ever after." Erin and Chris had laughed at the legend, joking that they didn't need a big rock to live happily ever after.

Erin swept past the Ka'ahumanu Stone, past the thatched-roof temple and carved wooden statues of *Hale o Keawe Heiau*. She stood on the shore of the Bay on a smooth lava beach on which, amazingly, coconut trees sprouted like weeds in a concrete parking lot. She lingered for a moment, gazing seaward, letting the warm ocean breezes tickle her. The setting sun heated her face, and her dark hair swirled gently about her shoulders. On any other day, under any other circumstances, this might be a perfect day in Paradise.

Not sure what to do or where to look, or even what she was looking for, Erin spun and walked quickly back across the sand to the entrance, as if she had a purpose. As she passed the front gate into the parking lot, she found herself staring at a blue Nissan Altima. Just like the car Charlie had rented.

She stepped closer to the car and then froze.

Two very faint bloody handprints stared at her from the driver's window.

Kanaka Blues

CHAPTER FIVE

Erin stood impatiently near the Nissan as a silver Jeep cut across the parking lot, a flashing blue light attached to the roof. It seemed like an eternity since the ticket seller had called the police in Kailua-Kona, barely fifteen miles away, but the roads weren't conducive to speed, and the skeptical cops who answered the call apparently saw no need to hurry. She had spent the frustrating last half-hour shooing departing tourists from getting too close to the Nissan, earning a disapproving look or two, and watching the sun slowly slip toward the horizon over Honaunau Bay. Darkness would impede any processing of the crime scene, and she certainly viewed it as a crime scene, although she had no real proof that a crime had been committed. But to her lawyer's mind, blood and a missing Charlie left no uncertainty.

Only a handful of cars remained in the lot when the Jeep pulled up behind the Nissan. Two men stepped out, a tall Anglo with close-cropped brown hair and a movie star's rugged good looks, and a compact Hawaiian with a weightlifter's build. Both men wore jeans, black T-shirts, and black "Kona PD" baseball caps, and had badges and holsters clipped to their belts. They looked around for a moment before settling on Erin, who headed their way.

"I'm Erin Hanna," she said, then pointed at the Nissan. "And this is the car."

"I'm Detective Kanahele," the Anglo said, "and this is Detective Montgomery."

Interesting reversal of names, Erin thought. Anglo with a Hawaiian name and Hawaiian with an Anglo name. The Hawaiian had attitude written all over him, one hand on his hip, the other on his gun, as if he expected to draw and shoot at any moment. Erin had heard that some natives resented whites, as if the pale-skinned interlopers had broken a sacred trust by merely stepping foot on Hawaiian soil. In fact, that had a lot to do with why Charlie was over here in the first place.

"Whose car is this?" Detective Kanahele asked.

"It's a rental. Dr. Charles Cain, from Texas, rented it." Erin looked over the detective's shoulder. "Is Crime Scene coming?"

"Let's not jump the gun on this," Kanahele said. "How do you know we've even got a crime?"

"Charlie called me last night and left a message that he needed me here."

"Called you where?"

"At my home, in Texas."

"Last night? In Texas?"

"Yeah. Dallas."

"And today you're here."

"That should tell you how seriously I'm taking this."

"Okay," Kanahele said, "go on."

"The desk clerk at the hotel where he was staying in Hilo said he came out here to meet someone and never made it back.

But this is his car. And look –"

She pointed at the driver's window. "Bloody handprints on the window. Blood on the door handle." She pointed at the ground. "And on the concrete. That's at least a little suspicious, don't you think?"

She had gotten Kanahele's attention, but the Hawaiian remained in his gunslinger stance, apparently unimpressed by the obvious. Kanahele leaned close to the car and studied the window and door handle, then squatted and looked at the blood on the ground. He touched the spot but the blood was dry. He straightened back up and circled the car, inspecting for other traces, then cupped his hands and peered inside.

"You sure this is his car?" he asked.

"License plate matches the number the hotel clerk gave me," Erin said. "The last phone message Charlie left got cut off. All I heard was some noise, like a kinda thud, then some heavy breathing, and then the phone went dead. And early this morning, I got this real weird call. My caller I.D. said it was from Charlie's phone, but it wasn't Charlie."

"Who was it?"

"I don't know. He sounded Hawaiian. All he said was, 'Who is this?' or something like that. Then he hung up."

"What do you mean he sounded Hawaiian?" Detective Montgomery asked. Attitude oozed from every pore. "What, we sound different?"

Erin stared at him for a moment, never breaking eye contact. "Yeah, you do."

Montgomery bristled, his nostrils flaring. He put on his best frown and tightened his grip on his gun.

The two continued to stare at each other, like fighters in the ring before a championship bout. Kanahele regarded both of them with what could be described only as amusement, fighting a smile that threatened to break into a laugh.

He looked at Montgomery. "Go call it in, Joe, and get Crime Scene out here. *Wiki wiki*."

Montgomery kept his eyes locked with Erin's, his feet set as if in concrete.

"Joe," Kanahele said, "just do it."

At last Montgomery tore his eyes from Erin, glanced at Kanahele, and then walked back to the Jeep.

Erin took a better look at Kanahele, his face tanned and leathery from exposure to the sun. It probably aged him beyond his years, but she put him at about forty. Despite the "cop look" he wore when he first got out of the Jeep, she saw it for the façade that it was. Laugh lines crinkled outward from his eyes when he smiled, which he was doing now.

"I don't think he likes me," Erin said.

"You don't got the right blood in your veins."

"And he thinks *I'm* a racist."

"Race has got nothing to do with it. It's all about land and who took what from whom."

"From *whom*?"

"Never underestimate a Kamehameha Schools education. And I got some college, too."

"Well, the land and who took what from whom is why Charlie was here in the first place."

Kanahele crossed his arms and leaned against the hood of the Jeep, while Montgomery finished his radio call. "Maybe you better start at the beginning. Who's Charlie and what specifically is he doing here?"

"He's a retired law professor from Texas. SMU, which is where I teach."

"So you're a lawyer. That explains some things."

Erin refused to take the bait. "Yeah. I don't practice anymore, though. Just teach at the law school. Anyway, Charlie's over here doing some research as part of a Senate investigation into the sovereignty movement."

Montgomery finished his call and got out of the Jeep. "They'll be here in fifteen."

Kanahele nodded. "Miss . . . what did you say your name was?"

"Erin Hanna."

"Joe, Miss Hanna was just saying this Charlie's over here looking into sovereignty for the United States Senate."

Now Erin had Montgomery's attention, as well. He looked at her with newfound interest. "The *United States Senate*, huh?" He said it like it was a four-letter word. "Doing what?"

"How much do you know about the Apology Bill that President Clinton signed?" Erin asked.

"I know it was supposed to apologize to the Hawaiian people for the U.S. helping overthrow Queen Lili'uokalani and stealing our land in 1893."

"Right," Erin said, realizing she had touched a raw nerve. Was it the same kind of raw nerve, she wondered, that resulted in

Charlie's disappearance? "Charlie was researching a book on the overthrow when he got interested in the sovereignty movement and all the competing groups trying to reclaim Hawaii as a sovereign nation. He got involved with Congress in helping structure the Apology Bill. He even helped draft the language."

"But they still haven't given us our country back," Montgomery said.

"Well, that's what Charlie was doing over here. Now Congress is considering some bill to recognize the rights of native Hawaiians –"

"That's Senator Hasegawa's brainchild," Kanahele said.

"You know about it?"

"Over here we know about stuff that affects us. Just like you Texans would probably know about it if some politician was trying to take away your guns. Believe me, it's the number one topic of conversation in the islands these days."

"The Senate Indian Affairs Committee appointed Charlie to review the claims by the different sovereignty groups and report back. He may even have been asked to make recommendations on which groups should take the lead if the Hasegawa Bill passes."

Erin went silent as a Japanese family with four kids, ranging in ages from about three to nine, piled into a Subaru station wagon parked in front of Charlie's Nissan. She watched as the frazzled daddy strapped his kids into seat belts, tuned out his chattering wife, cranked the car, and pulled away. Erin looked at the pavement the car vacated, her senses immediately on alert. She walked over quickly, knelt, and studied the surface. Kanahele and Montgomery watched in bemused silence, Montgomery rolling his eyes for his partner's benefit.

"I think you need to see this," Erin said.

Both detectives stiffened then came up behind her. The sun was now gone and the dim lighting from the Visitor's Center was barely sufficient for them to make out what Erin had found, but there was no mistaking it: a bloody shoeprint.

Erin pointed to the black streaks of a tire track leading away. "Somebody left in a hurry." She rubbed her hand over the surface. "Feels like new rubber."

"You a cop?" Montgomery asked.

"I'm a lawyer."

"Then you know not to touch anything," he replied. "Leave it for the techs."

She nodded, duly chastened. When her eyes met Kanahele's, he smiled. "We watch *CSI*, too," he said. "Only difference is, we turn on the lights instead of just using flashlights."

She smiled back. She hadn't lost him yet.

"What was I saying?" she asked.

"You said your Professor Charlie was looking into Hawaiian sovereignty claims. Then what? Like Joe said, the government gonna give us our land back?"

Erin scrutinized Kanahele, running her eyes over the exposed skin of his arms. "Us?"

"Don't let this *haole* skin fool you, sistah," he said. "My great-grandfather was pure Hawaiian. The blood of chiefs runs through my veins."

"Yours and everybody else's," Montgomery snorted. It was obviously an inside joke between the two detectives and represented the first sign of a sense of humor Erin had seen in the sour Hawaiian.

"All I know is that Charlie was supposed to report back his findings," she said. "It would be up to Congress after that."

"He could make a lotta people *huhu* if he say the wrong thing," Montgomery said.

At Erin's quizzical look, Kanahele added, "Pissed off."

Erin looked at the bloody footprint on the concrete, then at the bloody handprints on Charlie's car. "Looks like somebody's already plenty *huhu*."

CHAPTER SIX

The night sky was velvety black, speckled with brilliantly intense stars. Erin had never seen stars so clearly in Texas, where the ever-present ambient light of city life washed out the sky, even in the suburbs. She arrived back at the Seasurf with a heavy heart, convinced that foul play had befallen Charlie and with no confidence that the local police would even thoroughly investigate, much less actually find him. Maybe that's just as well, she thought. If he were merely missing, she could continue to entertain the fantasy that he was still alive. The same fantasy she nursed two years ago about Chris for a week, until a fishing boat netted his rotting body in the waters off the coast of Punalu'u.

Erin wheeled her rental car to the curb just as a new rain began to fall. For the first time all day, she realized that she was hungry. Amazingly, more hungry than tired, even though she had been up for nearly twenty-four hours. Erin got out and went inside the lobby. Gentle Hawaiian music wafted on the night air, falsetto voices singing "Lovely Hula Hands" coming from the hotel restaurant. She barely cast a glance at Harry the desk clerk as she breezed past and entered the dining room. Though the hour was late, aloha-clad diners nearly filled the room, chatting casually. A trio of native men strummed guitars and sang on a low stage at the far end of the room, accompanied by two teen-age hula girls whose weaving hips and undulating arms visually told the story of the hands the men sang about. The singers smiled but the dancers kept their faces neutral, concentrating on each move.

An elderly hostess escorted Erin to a glass-top bamboo table next to a window, gave her a menu, and then retreated. Erin opened the menu, but her attention wandered out the open window to the vast ocean that lurked just beyond Hilo Bay. She heard the ripples of gentle waves, protected from the harsher ocean by a mile-long breakwater jetty that curved across the mouth of the bay. Where the hell was Charlie?

The sound of shuffling and flip-flopping pulled her mind back inside. A huge shadow overtook her table. She looked up into the concerned face of Harry the desk clerk.

"How you doing?" he asked.

The first thing she noticed was that he seemed to have lost his Hawaiian lilt.

"You sound different," she said.

He smiled, his chubby cheeks nearly squeezing his eyes completely shut. "That Hawaiian shtick's for the tourists. I just don't feel like it tonight."

"You do it very well."

"Not too bad for a farm boy from Eugene, Oregon, huh? Believe it or not, my name's Harry Johnson."

They both laughed, and the mood lightened for a brief moment.

"May I sit down?" he asked.

"Sure."

He slid a bamboo chair back and squeezed his bulk into the seat, barely fitting between the arms.

"Looks like my diet's not working," he said.

"You're on a diet?"

"No. Guess that's why it's not working."

He laughed again, a nervous laugh, like that of a small boy uncomfortable around girls. He leaned forward, elbows on the table, and regarded Erin for a few seconds. She felt the intensity of his scrutiny as he studied her features. Then he leaned back.

"You're even prettier than Mister Charlie said you were."

She felt her face flush with embarrassment, heat rising in her cheeks. "Thank you."

"He said you were the prettiest lawyer in Texas," Harry added. "I think I'd amend that and say in the whole continental United States."

"Just the continental U.S.?"

"I've got a cousin who's a lawyer in Kahului, over on Maui. She's family, so I've got to give her top billing. And I've never been to Alaska."

"Apology accepted."

He laughed again. "Mister Charlie also said there's a mind like a spring-loaded trap hidden behind that façade."

"I don't know what that means, but it sounds like vintage Charlie. Probably some Texas-ism he dug up from somewhere."

"He did love Texas. I gotta admit I didn't know what he was saying half the time. He kept talking about dogs that won't hunt and saying things like 'fixing to.' It's worse than our pidgin. You need a dictionary just to keep up."

Erin smiled at the memories Harry's description brought to mind. Yeah, that was Charlie all right – Texas through and through. Born and bred in Sweetwater, he had spent his entire adult life in Dallas but never completely got the west Texas red dirt out of his clothes. She'd give anything to hear one of those stupid expressions right now. The thought that she might not ever hear them again in Charlie's twang sobered her; her smile vanished.

The trio on the stage launched into an upbeat version of "My Little Grass Shack in Kealakekua, Hawaii," and the hula girls matched the tempo with their hips. Erin and Harry sat silently and watched for a few minutes before Erin said, "I drove through Kealakekua today."

"Did you see any little grass shacks?"

"No. I didn't see Charlie, either."

Harry nodded. "I could tell by your face as soon as I saw you come in that you didn't have good news to report. But I kept hoping if I sat here long enough, he'd walk in the door to join us and say something in Texan, and we'd all laugh and everything would be okay."

"I don't think he's ever going to do that again."

"Why do you say that?"

"I found his car in the parking lot. There was blood on it."

"Mister Charlie's blood?"

"I don't know."

Harry thought about that for a moment, then muttered, "Damn."

He took a small envelope, folded in half, from his shirt

pocket and held it in front of him on the table. His thumbs played with the flap, as if he was debating whether to open it. Erin waited for his decision.

He opened the envelope and dumped a small key onto the tabletop. Erin looked at it, then back at Harry.

"What's that?"

He slid the key across to Erin. "Mister Charlie kept this in the hotel safe. I thought maybe you'd know what to do with it."

Erin picked up the key and looked at it. It was much smaller than the usual door key, with no markings as identifiers. "Do you know what it's to?"

"You got me. Looks like a locker key or something. Airport, maybe, or a safe deposit box."

"There's no number on it."

"Maybe he kept some kind of storage locker at his apartment in Honolulu."

"Why keep it in the hotel safe if it's just to a storage locker?"

"I guess it depends on what he kept in that locker."

Erin palmed the key and squeezed her fist shut. "Can you book me on a flight to Honolulu in the morning? First one out."

"I'll make the call right now."

Harry extricated himself from his chair and stood. "Mister Charlie was a good man, Miss Erin. He treated us all good here at the hotel. You find him, okay? You bring him back."

"I will."

*****

Though her body was exhausted, Erin's mind refused to allow her a restful sleep. The day had brought back images and sounds that she thought she had finally banished from her nightmares. Now, as she slept, those images and sounds once again haunted her dreams. Not even the white noise of rain falling on the carp pond below her window could drown out the pilot's urgent *"Mayday, mayday, mayday,"* that filled her unconscious mind.

They had just completed a sweep over the Kilauea Caldera when the Hawaiian Paradise Tours ASTAR helicopter made a pass down the Chain of Craters Road, following the remnants of past lava flows. As they passed over the chimney of steam where an active river of bright orange dropped into the waters of the Pacific, they first noticed the smoke from the engines. The pilot swung out over the ocean in an attempt to turn around and find a safe landing spot. About a quarter-mile offshore, the helicopter began to pitch and buck. The pilot fought the controls, trying to steady the flight, but the only constant direction was down.

Chris squeezed her hand and whispered reassurances in her ear, but she knew he didn't believe them. She could see it in his face, hear it in his voice. Maybe the first, and only, time she had ever seen him afraid.

The pilot looked over his shoulder at them, his own face white with fear. "Life vests," he said. "Under your seats."

Chris let go of her hand and dug out a vest. He spun Erin around by the shoulders and slid it over her arms. Just as she was fastening it into place, the helicopter suddenly jerked over on its side. She felt Chris's hands leave her shoulders and assumed he was grabbing for his own vest. From her vantage point on what was now the top of the cabin, she looked down, horrified to see the door fly open behind him. At that same instant, his seat belt failed. Erin watched him slide across the leather seat toward the blue waters below. At the last second, he grabbed hold of the edge of the doorway. Veins bulged in his muscular forearms as he squeezed for purchase with his fingers.

Erin loosened her seat belt and shifted toward him, but gravity threatened to tear her from the cabin as she hung limply.

"Tighten it," he yelled. "Your seat belt."

"Chris, no." With her back now facing up, she reached straight down. "Grab hold."

He let go of the doorway with one hand and pulled with the other in a one-armed, five-fingered pull-up. He stretched his hand toward hers, closing the distance. Then she felt his skin as their fingertips touched. He inched his hand upward, as if climbing a rope, until his palm rested in hers. She clasped her hand shut and squeezed.

Suddenly the helicopter bucked again, and then spun over in a spiral. Chris's legs snapped out as if some godless giant had played crack-the-whip with his body. His hand slipped from her grasp, and he hung precariously from the edge of the doorway by the other.

Then his fingers let go, and he disappeared from view.

*****

Erin bolted up, bathed in sweat. She threw the thin covers aside and clambered out of bed. Full of nervous energy, she felt as if her heart were about to burst from her chest. She walked to the sliding glass door to the lanai, opened it, and felt the cool air on her face. She stepped outside and hugged herself. The rain continued its pitter-patter assault on the carp pond as the first tear fell onto her cheek.

CHAPTER SEVEN

As she had the day before, Erin sat in the window seat of a Hawaiian Airlines plane and looked down at the moonscape that made up the Big Island's Kona Coast. Dark circles punctuated her eyes, testimony to nearly thirty-six hours of sleeplessness. She wondered what she would find when she reached Charlie's apartment near the University of Hawaii campus in Manoa. Would there be any hint as to where he might have disappeared? Or as to what had befallen him? Or would the apartment be as devoid of clues as his hotel room at the Seasurf? She wasn't sure if she really wanted to find out but knew that she must.

Below, black lava rock dropped away to the rich blue of the ocean. She looked for the string of oases that made up the resort strip northward toward Waikoloa and envied the carefree day the tourists there faced. She spotted the lush treetops of the Kona Coast Cottages, south of that was the Hualalai Resort and, adjacent to that, construction activity. Yet one more resort destined to spring up and reclaim a portion of the Big Island for the god of tourism.

As she looked closer, it appeared that this bit of land wasn't going to go without a struggle. Two groups of people stood on a black sand beach. One row had their backs to the ocean, forming a protective line in front of a homeless city of tents and lean-tos; the other row, composed of blue-suited police officers, fronted a line of construction equipment. Erin thought she could almost hear the revving engines of the bulldozers.

*****

The hapless army of Hawaiians knew what was coming as they stood in front of their homes of canvas and cardboard, facing helmeted cops with nightsticks drawn. They, and others like them, had been through this before. They had been born and raised here, as had their parents before them and their parents before that, yet they couldn't afford homes of their own in the face of spiraling real estate prices and encroaching mainlanders. They found themselves relegated to the beaches and their pitiful excuses for houses.

But homelessness was a blight on the landscape, and over the past decade, they had been evicted from beach after beach in the name of tourism. Those same beaches were then reclaimed for gaudy resorts and hotels that trivialized the Hawaiians and their customs. The once-proud people were relegated to cleaning toilets, washing dishes, vacuuming floors, and serving tropical drinks to the here-today-gone-tomorrow invaders with money to burn.

Determined to reclaim this small sliver of beach for themselves, the ragtag army carried signs and banners bearing slogans such as HAOLES GO HOME, HAWAII IS FOR HAWAIIANS, and THIS LAND IS OUR LAND. Off to one side, eagerly awaiting the battle, stood the ever-present members of the media, notepads at the ready, cameras on shoulders. Most of their attention was focused on the large man leading the homeless. He strutted back and forth like a modern-day Goliath. In reality, this man was more of a David, facing down the Philistine hordes of police, construction crews, resort developers, and the powerful foreign government that stood behind them: the United States of America.

Manu Pokui paced in front of his homeless "troops." A bandage barely covered a gash on his forehead, and blood had seeped through the gauze, giving him an almost heroic look. Although his movements were unusually fluid for a big man, Manu's face betrayed his anxiety.

A native cop stepped forward carrying a bullhorn. His black hair was graying at the temples, and his worn visage said that he, too, had fought these battles before. He raised the bullhorn to his lips. "You've had one month to vacate the beach. Your time is now up. Please evacuate peaceably."

Manu approached the cop and stopped a few feet away. He spread his feet and stood with his hands on his hips.

"This beach belongs to the Hawaiian people, not some *haole* corporation in California," he said. "We're not going anywhere."

The cop lowered his bullhorn. He looked at Manu with a mixture of curiosity and concern. He spoke in a soft voice, barely discernible above the roar of bulldozer engines. "What happened to your head, bruddah? You go see a doctor, yeah?"

"Why you doing this?" Manu asked. "Why you taking these people off the beach? Where they gonna go, huh? You know they got a right to be here."

"Look, bruddah, I'm just doing my job. I got a court order –"

"From an American court. They got no jurisdiction over us."

"We're all Americans."

"Look at your skin. We're not Americans; we're Hawaiians." Manu paused, gathering all the contempt in his voice he could muster. "Least you used to be."

"I got no choice, bruddah."

"You got a choice. You just made the wrong one. And I'm not your goddamn bruddah."

With a deep sigh, the cop stepped back. He turned and looked at the other cops behind him. He again sighed heavily, the weight of his decision evident in his slumping shoulders. He nodded.

The cops strapped gas masks over their faces and pulled down plastic visors. Brandishing their nightsticks, they began moving forward in unison. Behind them, the bulldozers revved up, their drivers also wearing gas masks. Smoke spurted from their stacks as they crept forward behind the advancing line of cops, like tanks forming the second line of attack.

Manu retreated until he was in the middle of the row of homeless. They all looked to him for his signal – to break and run, or to fight. As the gap between them and the police closed, many took baby steps backward, but Manu held his ground, forming the point of a wedge. He was aware of the sounds of his own deep breathing. His heart pounded inside his chest, and his fingers began to tingle. He sensed the men on either side of him shrinking back in the loose sand. Still he held his ground, his feet rooted by a combination of fear and principle, either of which could get him killed.

He locked gazes with a cop directly in front of him, a kid, really, no more than twenty-two or twenty-three-years-old. The kid's eyes reflected uncertainty, as if he couldn't quite figure out what he was doing there.

"Steady," Manu said to his companions. He struggled to keep his voice strong, his tone even. "Remember what we're doing."

The shuffling behind him stopped. They knew Manu was right. There would be no passive resistance here, no Gandhi-like civil disobedience. They were fighting for their homes, for their land, for their very existences. Courage renewed, the homeless moved forward again and regained the line with Manu, shoulder to shoulder. They held their ground as the cops continued to advance.

The melee began.

Nightsticks swung and fists flew as the two lines melded together, with Manu right in the thick of it. The kid swung a nightstick at him, but his heart didn't seem to be in it. Manu caught the stick in the palm of his hand, the stinging slap of wood on skin echoing. He gripped the end and yanked forward, pulling the kid toward him. Manu towered over him by nearly a foot. He looked down in the kid's face, his eyes now wide with fear.

With a flick of his powerful arm, Manu yanked the nightstick loose, grabbed it with both hands, and snapped it across his knee. The wood splintered in half like a matchstick. He grabbed the terrified cop by the shoulders, lifted him off the ground, and threw him into a group of blue-suited attackers. Like a bowling ball scattering pins in an alley, the cop tumbled them in a pile. In an instant, desperate Hawaiians pounced on top, fists jackhammering.

The initial surge of police had driven the Hawaiians on either side of Manu back toward the sea but, buoyed by his strength in the middle, the flanks regrouped and momentarily forced their way forward. Manu turned to his left to lend a hand, but a burly cop slammed him in the shoulder with his stick, then stuck out his foot and tripped him as he staggered for balance. A hole broke out to Manu's right, courtesy of well-placed nightsticks to the heads of an elderly Hawaiian and his grandson. Blood spurted beneath the impact of the wood; both men sagged to the ground.

A bulldozer instantly surged through the hole. Its driver, with his head down, aimed for the ramshackle neighborhood of tents and boxes. A second bulldozer followed and turned up-beach to the far end of homes. As the two dozers performed a pincer movement, the Hawaiians realized what was happening behind them. They broke and ran to protect their homes, trying to position themselves in front of the dozers. But the panic created even more gaps in the front line of defense. Other equipment quickly plowed through. Within minutes, there were more bulldozers behind the line than in front of it.

Manu had regained his balance but was locked in a wrestling match with the burly cop. They both fell to the sand, squeezing each other in mutual bear hugs. From the ground, Manu saw what was transpiring behind him. He released his grip around his opponent's shoulders, extended his arms, and clapped his hands together on the sides of the man's head. With a loud crack, the plastic helmet splintered. Manu extended his arms for a second clap. The cop immediately released Manu, put his hands over his ears, and rolled away.

Manu struggled to his feet and rushed toward the homes, but it was too late. The first bulldozer had gotten there ahead of him. It plowed a wide trench in the sand and crashed into a plywood lean-to. Its blade shredded the wood into kindling. At the other end, a dozer knocked down cardboard and canvas walls, and covered them with sand. Two more bulldozers lined up side-by-side and drove three homes into the surf.

Manu charged the nearest piece of equipment. With one leap, he climbed the side and grabbed the controls. The driver jerked his arm sideways; his elbow slammed Manu beneath his chin. Tears formed in Manu's eyes, blurring his vision. He released the control with his left hand and sent a roundhouse slamming into the driver's jaw. The man slumped sideways in the seat, his head lolled forward. Manu shoved him over the side and slid in behind the controls. With a quick turn, he shifted the dozer around and aimed it toward another one nearby.

The sound of an explosion echoed over the chaos, then another. Manu jumped and looked over his shoulder at two tear gas canisters flying through the air, silhouetted against the cloudless sky. When they hit sand, a dense white smoke instantly filled the air. Within seconds, the entire beach was so thick with gas that visibility was reduced to nothingness. The chemicals burned in the eyes of the Hawaiians. Their faces contorted in pain, and they rushed into the ocean in droves. They ducked their heads into the salt water and tried desperately to flush the stinging from their eyes. Cops waded in from behind, grabbing them and forcing them face down in the surf and cuffing them behind their backs. Those still on the beach raised their hands in surrender. Cops roughly threw them to the sand and clasped handcuffs on their wrists.

Manu, in a rage, trekked wildly about in the sand. He raised and lowered the dozer's massive blade and spun it in a circle. A construction worker grabbed hold of the rear of the machine and climbed aboard. With Manu blinded, the worker managed to grasp the key and shut off the engine.

As the bulldozer stilled, cops swarmed it. Manu thrashed desperately, his eyes squeezed tightly shut, burning and stinging, like an eyeless Samson fighting off the Philistines. He twirled in an ever-tightening circle, swinging his arms in all directions. Thick as tree trunks, they served him well for a while. He felt bone crush as his fist made contact with a helmet visor and broke through onto a face. When he pulled back, his hand stuck in the visor. He tried to extricate it but suddenly found himself yanked backward by hands on his shoulders. He kicked out with his feet, struggling to maintain his balance, but to no avail.

He fell from his perch and slammed back first into the sand. His wind escaped in a giant puff. A bevy of cops swarmed over him, nightsticks flying. The last thing he remembered was the feel of sunshine on his face mixed with the flow of his own blood.

CHAPTER EIGHT

After experiencing the sparseness of the Big Island, Honolulu seemed downright claustrophobic. Erin knew she was still in an island paradise, but with its freeway system, dense traffic, and concrete monstrosities of office buildings, hotels, and condominiums, Oahu's population center could have been any of a dozen mainland cities on either coast. What made Hawaii special was not its modern metropolis with streets crammed with tourists, vendors, and businessmen, but its green openness, its swaying palms and ocean breezes, and its laid-back atmosphere of aloha. Forget Honolulu, Erin thought, give me Hilo any day.

From the airport, Erin took a cab to Manoa Valley, fighting bumper-to-bumper gridlock on the H-1 freeway all the way. Not much aloha from the other drivers, who honked horns, drove aggressively, and flashed easily understandable hand signals. She might as well have been driving to downtown Dallas on Central Expressway but for the familiar outline of Diamond Head in the distance. The driver finally deposited her at the Paradise Island Apartments on Punahou Street, close to the University of Hawaii. She paid the fare then got out and studied the shabby building. It was set in a dense residential neighborhood in the shadow of the Punchbowl, whose crater held the National Memorial Cemetery of the Pacific, final resting place to over 21,000 service people. She wondered at the vagaries of zoning laws that could have produced this kind of haphazard development.

One of the first apartment complexes built after statehood was declared in 1959, Paradise Island was a squat two-story structure with an office in front and warped wooden doors lining both levels that extended east and west from the main staircase. Paint was peeling and it was in bad need of a new roof. At least it offered the usual quota of palm trees, as if to justify its use of the appellation "Paradise Island." Erin wondered why Charlie would have chosen such a low-rent base since he was on an expense account from the Senate. Surely that august body's members didn't impose similar restrictions on themselves when doing government business. She concluded the choice must have something to do with proximity to the University, where she knew he was doing much of his research, and not cost.

She entered the office, which was as aged and weather-beaten as the rest of the complex. A middle-aged white man with a bulbous nose and a bald head sat behind a metal desk, studying a ledger book. He wore an aloha shirt pulled tight by a bulging belly and oversized khaki shorts. An open filing drawer behind him almost touched the back of his head. Any sudden movement and he might give himself a concussion.

He apparently didn't hear her enter. When she cleared her throat, he looked up and peered at her over half-moon reading glasses. "Yes, ma'am, can I help you?"

"I hope so. My name is Erin Hanna and – "

"Charlie Cain's Erin?"

She was momentarily taken aback. "I take it he's mentioned me," she said.

The man stood and walked around the desk. He looked much taller when sitting, and she now realized how short his legs were in proportion to his upper body.

"Yes, ma'am. He talked about you all the time." He stuck out his hand. "My name is Robert Stines. I'm the manager."

She took his hand. "It's nice to meet you."

He folded his arms across his chest and sucked in his stomach. "Did he know you were coming?" Stines asked. "He's not here right now. In fact, he hasn't been here in about a week or two. He said he was going over to Hilo to follow up on some research he was doing. But I guess you know all about that."

"I went to Hilo to meet him, but nobody seems to know where he is," Erin said. "I thought I'd see if he came back here and just forgot to mention it."

"I haven't heard anything from him. I can take you to his apartment, though. We can check it out."

His use of the word *we* wasn't lost on her. She would have to find some way to get rid of him so she could search Charlie's apartment.

"Thanks. That would be great."

Stines grabbed a ring of keys from a bowl on the corner of his desk and dropped it into the cavernous pocket of shorts that rode low under his belly, hitched precariously on his hipbones. He pushed open the door and led Erin out into the bright sun. She pulled sunglasses from her purse and put them on, but Stines solved the problem by simply squinting. They walked down the front sidewalk, past rusting automobiles in the parking lot and shabby door fronts, to a second staircase at the end and started upward.

"Charlie tells me you're a famous lawyer in Dallas," Stines said.

"I've had a few high profile cases, but I don't think I'd call myself famous. Mostly I just teach these days."

"Yep, that's what he said. At the law school there, right?"

"That's right. SMU."

"Was Charlie one of your professors when you were in school?"

"No, I went to Texas Tech Law School, in Lubbock, but I met Charlie when I volunteered to help with the *pro bono* program that the SMU law students ran. Charlie was their faculty sponsor. We got to be pretty close after a while, and he got me the teaching job there."

"You know, I thought about going to law school."

"You did?"

"Yeah. But then my dad died, and I had to take over his hardware store. Next thing you know, I had gotten into apartment management, and this opportunity opened up over here, so I just hopped on a plane and never looked back. I think I woulda made a good lawyer, though."

"I'm sure you would," Erin lied.

When they reached the second floor, Stines pointed to the corner. "Just around there. So, you like teaching better than practicing?"

"They both have their moments."

Stines started fumbling in his pocket for the keys just as they cleared the corner, and he finally had success when he stopped in front of a faded green door midway on the backside of the building. "Right here."

He raised his hand to knock, but Erin grabbed his arm and pointed at the door lock. He had to slide his reading glasses up and bend over close to see what she pointed at: two fresh scratches on the lock and a slight splintering of wood on the door next to the jamb.

"Was it like that before?" Erin asked.

"No way. I would have noticed if it was."

"May I have the key, please?"

Stines singled out a key on the ring and started to insert it in the door lock. She took it from him before he made contact with the metal.

"Go call the police," she said. There was a note of urgency in her voice.

"What are you going to do?"

"Mr. Stines, please, just go call the police."

He took his glasses off and stuck them in his shirt pocket. "Ms. Hanna, what's going on here?"

"I don't know yet. But please, go call the police."

"Are you in any danger?" He hesitated. "Am I?"

"You'll be all right," she said. "I promise. But right now, I need you to call the police."

He nodded, then spun on his heel and walked as fast as his stubby legs would carry him. Erin waited until he turned the corner. Without trying the key, she pushed on the door with her foot; it slowly swung open. She saw that the interior of the jamb had been torn away, the deadbolt lock useless without it.

She pushed the door all the way open and stepped inside. The curtains were closed and the shades drawn, leaving the room in near darkness. She waited a moment for her eyesight to adjust. At first glance, nothing seemed out of place. The small living area with threadbare carpet was cheaply furnished with an eclectic mix of brown leather couch and plaid cloth chairs. It all looked like fire sale bargains. A stick-leg coffee table held a few magazines and a TV guide, and a two-drawer filing cabinet served as an end table. On the far wall, a television with an HD converter box sat on a wooden crate that doubled as an entertainment center. She checked the date on the TV guide. Three weeks old, but that didn't mean anything. Charlie never watched much television.

She crossed the living area, past a galley kitchen, to a short hallway. There were two doors, both closed, one in the middle of the hall and one at the end. She tried the door in the middle first; a bathroom. Nothing of any significance except a dried toothbrush and curled up tube of toothpaste. No shaving gear. Charlie hadn't been there recently.

She moved down the hall to the door at the end. She took a deep breath, steeling herself, then slowly pushed the door open. Inside was a room furnished with a double bed stripped to the mattress, one nightstand, and a chest-of-drawers that might all have come from the same fire sale as the den furniture. She crossed over to the closet, turned back, and surveyed the room, taking in every detail. No signs of life, nothing out of place.

She had just turned back to the closet and grabbed the

doorknob when the closet door suddenly rushed toward her, slamming into her face. The corner of the bed caught at the bend of her knees, and she toppled onto the floor on her back. As she fell, she caught a glimpse of a dark-haired person in jeans and a navy blue windbreaker dart around the door and into the hall. She saw nothing of the intruder's face, not even enough to recognize gender or race.

She struggled to her feet, momentarily dazed, and gasped for breath. She took a step.

Her knees buckled.

She caught herself on the mattress to keep from falling. She shook her head to clear away the fog and followed the intruder into the hallway. Footsteps sounded ahead of her, followed by the slam of a door. By the time she reached the living room, he was gone.

She staggered to the door, still woozy. She grabbed the door handle to support herself, opened it, and stepped out onto the landing. She looked both ways, but no one was in sight.

The roar of an engine and the squeal of tires drew her attention to the front of the building. Using the handrail for support, she retraced her steps to the corner stairway. As her eyes adjusted to the fog of near-unconsciousness, she saw an unmarked white panel van barrel out of the parking lot onto Punahou Street and speed off toward the mountains.

"Are you all right?" a man's voice asked.

She looked down to the first floor at the concerned face of Robert Stines. He stared up at her, mouth open.

"Did you see him?" she asked.

"See who?"

Erin watched the van disappear from view. "Never mind."

Her knees buckled again. The concrete floor raced toward her face.

*****

Erin leaned against the handrail, pressing a washcloth filled with ice to her blackened and swelling eye. The washcloth of ice was compliments of an overly solicitous Robert Stines, who danced around as if it were his personal duty to heal her eye before the sun set.

The police arrived less than ten minutes after the intruder made his escape but, unfortunately, had no luck tracking down the van since Erin had not gotten a license plate number. The crime scene technicians were now at work inside the apartment while Erin waited outside.

"Ms. Hanna?"

The voice from inside the apartment belonged to one of the two uniformed officers, both Anglo, who had answered the call from Stines. His nametag announced him as Officer Dudley.

Erin pushed off of the rail with her hip and stepped inside, glad to leave the manager outside.

"You're sure you didn't get a good look at him?" Dudley asked. He took a small notepad from his shirt pocket, ready to take notes.

"I couldn't even tell you for sure whether it was male or female. There was a lot of force behind that door, though. That tells me it was probably a man."

"We got strong women over here."

"Just trying to narrow your search parameters."

"You got any idea what the intruder was doing in the apartment?"

"Probably looking for Charlie's papers. His notes and his research."

Dudley looked at her as if she were speaking a foreign language. "You said something about that before, but I don't understand. What kind of papers?"

"Research he was doing on the sovereignty movement. Check with Detective Kanahele in Kona. He can fill you in. He's also got some prints you can check for a match."

"If we find any. The place looks clean."

Erin looked over his shoulder at a tech kneeling in front of the small filing cabinet-cum-end-table, dusting the top. "Check inside the drawers. See what turns up."

The tech looked at Dudley, who said to Erin, "I think we can handle this. We've done it once or twice before."

"Sorry. Force of habit."

When Dudley looked at his notepad, Erin caught the tech's eye, pointed at the cabinet, and mouthed the words, "Just do it."

The tech nodded and pulled open the top drawer. Empty. He opened the bottom drawer. Also empty.

Erin pulled the small key Harry had given her from her pocket. She rubbed her thumb over its edge. Robert Stines had said there were no storage lockers at the Paradise Island Apartments. And, no, Charlie never mentioned having a locker anywhere else.

Whomever she interrupted wasn't carrying anything. Did that

mean he or she was already too late?

Where in the hell were Charlie's notes?

CHAPTER NINE

Erin exited the jetway at the Big Island's Hilo International Airport sporting a black eye and a swollen lip. On the flight back, she felt as if every passenger had been watching her, maybe even pitying her as the victim of a bullying husband. "Look at her, the poor thing," she heard one woman say.

She followed the line of deplaning passengers, mostly tourists, up the ramp to the gate area. As they exited the door, they split in a Y formation, off in search of baggage claim. Detective Kanahele waited in the crook of the Y, his professional eye scanning each person as they passed. Then his gaze fell on Erin. She could swear she saw a look of concern flash on his face when he noticed her bruises, quickly replaced by pure police professionalism.

"Detective," she said, "to what do I owe the pleasure?"

"Doesn't look like you enjoyed your little trip to Honolulu very much."

"Not much aloha over there."

He laughed. "Lot of *haoles* say that."

She walked beside him through the gate area toward the main ticket counters. "Not very smart going into that apartment by yourself," Kanahele said. "You're lucky all you got was a black eye."

"Don't forget my fat lip."

"You could have been seriously hurt."

Erin grabbed his arm and stopped him. "Why, Detective, are you worried about me?"

That same smile she had seen the day before played at his lips. Laugh lines radiated from his eyes. He had a kind face, Erin thought. One she could get used to looking at.

He pulled away and continued walking. She hurried to catch up to him.

"It's just that I don't know who would tell me how to do my job if anything happened to you," he said.

"The Honolulu cops don't share your concerns."

The smile developed into a full-blown laugh. "No, I guess they don't. They said they nearly had to handcuff you to the railing to keep you from taking over the crime scene investigation. Got a few control issues, do we?"

"Maybe," she admitted. "Did they find anything?"

"Nothing usable."

When they reached the ticket counters, Kanahele took her arm and escorted her through a maze of sunburned mainlanders and a Japanese tour group to the exit door. His hand felt firm yet gentle. Erin felt a tingle of static electricity as he touched her, something she hadn't experienced in a couple of years.

Through the glass, Erin saw Kanahele's Jeep. Detective Montgomery leaned against the hood, wearing the same frown that graced his face the day before. Two police cruisers waited behind, uniformed officers inside.

"Am I going somewhere with you and Smiley?" Erin asked.

"I wouldn't piss him off if I were you."

"He was born pissed off."

"He just forgets to put happy pills in his cereal sometimes." He looked at Montgomery then back at Erin. "It looks like this is one of those days."

The automatic doors parted and they stepped outside. It was raining, more of a heavy mist, which seemed to be the standard weather in this city. Kanahele escorted Erin to the Jeep.

"I've got a rental car in the parking lot," she said.

"I'll bring you back to get it later."

Without acknowledging her, Montgomery got in the driver's side of the Jeep and cranked the engine. Kanahele opened the door for Erin, who crawled awkwardly into the back, then he got in the front. As Montgomery pulled away, Erin looked over her shoulder and saw that the cruisers followed.

"Do you mind if I ask where we're going?" Erin asked.

"No," Kanahele said.

"Well?" she said after a minute.

"Well, what?"

"Are you going to tell me where we're going?"

"Sure, now that you ask."

"As opposed to asking if you minded if I ask. I get it. You're a funny guy, Detective."

"I thought that, as a lawyer, you'd appreciate the preciseness of language."

He looked over his shoulder at her and smiled broadly. Smiles seemed to be a constant for him. She even caught a glimpse of Montgomery's smile in the rearview mirror. Messing with the *haole* woman seemed to amuse him.

"I'm sure you'll understand if none of this is very funny to me," she said.

Her tone chased the smile from Kanahele's face, but not from Montgomery's. On him, it settled into a smirk.

"You're right. I'm sorry," Kanahele said.

He shifted in his seat, eyes forward. His voice took on an official tone, and Erin mentally kicked herself for being such a hardass. She really couldn't blame them for resenting her intrusion. She'd probably feel the same way if an outsider suddenly showed up and told her how to handle one of her cases.

"We got forensics back from the Nissan at the City of Refuge, " he said. "The prints on the window and on the door handle belong to a man named Manu Pokui. He's well known to us. He lives here in Hilo, and we're on our way to execute a search warrant at his house. We thought you might want to go with us."

"I appreciate the courtesy."

"Well, it's more than that, really. We thought you'd help us know what to look for."

She snorted. "Ain't self-interest a bitch?"

"That's not all that's a bitch," Montgomery said under his breath. If he thought she hadn't heard him, he was mistaken.

"Who is this Manu Pokui?" Erin asked, addressing Kanahele.

"One of our local rabble-rousers," Montgomery said, unwilling to be excluded from the conversation, no matter how much he resented her presence. "He calls himself governor of the Nation of the Islands. That's just one of a half-dozen major sovereignty groups we've got over here."

"One of the ones that Charlie was investigating."

"Probably," Kanahele said.

The Jeep turned west on Highway 19 at Banyan Drive, toward downtown Hilo. They drove past the old Waiakea town clock, its hands still frozen at 1:05, the time it stopped when hit by the third, and largest, of the waves during the 1960 tsunami. Erin settled back into the seat and folded her arms over her chest. Fresh air flowed in from the open sides of the Jeep, rustling her hair and, remarkably, raising goose bumps on her bare arms even in the heat of a Hawaiian day.

As they continued between Hilo Bay and the wooden storefronts of downtown on Kamehameha Avenue, Erin was struck by the quaintness of this town that had known such tragedy over the years and the resilience of its people. She had read about the devastating tsunami in 1946, spawned by an underwater earthquake over 2,300 miles away in Alaska. That one killed ninety-six people in Hilo, alone. Afterwards the residents abandoned the waterfront to the sea. They converted the land between Kamehameha Avenue and the bay front – about two football fields wide – into a recreation and parking area that would, they hoped, serve as a buffer against other tsunamis. Unfortunately, they also rebuilt a number of homes and businesses in other low-lying areas, including Waiakea.

In 1960, an earthquake off the coast of Chile birthed another destructive tsunami that also devastated Hilo and stopped the clock they had just passed. After that, the oceanside buffer zone was extended and elevated. State and county buildings now stood atop the bluff that overlooked the buffer, because private citizens were afraid to rebuild in that area.

"Do the people in these sovereignty groups really think they're going to get Hawaii back?" Erin asked. "What's next? Give Texas back to Mexico, give the rest of the country back to the Indians?"

"We're not talking about Texas," Montgomery said. "And we're not talking about the rest of the country. We're talking about Hawaii being run by Hawaiians. What'd be wrong with that?"

"It's kinda like a dog chasing a car, isn't it? If he ever catches it, what's he gonna do with it?"

"If it's the dog's car to start with, it doesn't matter what he does with it," Kanahele said. "Just because it's stolen doesn't mean it's not his."

"You keep saying that Hawaii was stolen. What exactly do you mean by that?"

Kanahele and Montgomery exchanged looks. "Do you want to take that one?" Kanahele asked. Then, to Erin, "Joe's mama is a history teacher. He knows this stuff better than I do."

"I thought you said yesterday that you know your history."

"Joe knows it better."

"I have to know it," Montgomery said. "Otherwise she won't let me in the house."

Erin laughed, happy to see a hint of personality from Kanahele's partner.

"Just give me the condensed version," she said. "I don't need to pass a test on it."

"Okay. See, back in the old days, the Hawaiians were just

rocking along, minding their own business, doing a little farming, a little fishing, eating a little poi. Everything was copacetic. Everybody was happy. One of the reasons was because there was no private land ownership. The idea of 'private property' was pretty much non-existent. The *ali'i* – that means the chiefs – administered the land, but we believed that the gods, through the king, actually owned it. We believed the land was sacred."

"If you haven't already, you'll probably hear or see the phrase *ua mau ke ea o ka 'aina i ka pono* over here," Kanahele interrupted. "It means 'the life of the land is perpetuated in righteousness.'"

"Then the *haoles* started coming over here in droves and, got to give them credit for this, they knew a good thing when they saw it," Montgomery said. "Where we saw the *'aina* – the land – they saw real estate. The first thing they did was to talk Kamehameha the Third into leasing the land to foreigners. Then, once people got used to that idea, they opened the door to private ownership for foreigners by convincing him to divide up the land among the chiefs and the commoners, and then letting foreigners buy land from them. He kept a couple of million acres for himself that we called the Crown Lands. But that's when the real estate boom started.

"Before you knew it, *haoles* were scamming the chiefs and commoners, and pretty soon they owned most of the land and ran all of the plantations and industry. But they didn't like the fact that Hawaii was still a monarchy and they couldn't get their hands on the Crown Lands, which were the best in the islands. So a group of big shots got together and decided to get the United States to annex

Hawaii as a territory. In order to do that, they had to get rid of the monarchy first. By then, Queen Lili'uokalani was in power. She could see what was coming, so she decided to change the constitution to protect native Hawaiians. Well, the *haoles* couldn't have that. In 1893, they got the Americans to send in troops from the *USS Boston*, docked in Pearl Harbor, to back them up while they staged a two-day revolution. They took over the government, seized the remaining land, and threw Queen Lili in jail. Then they declared the Republic of Hawaii and, five years later, the U.S. annexed it as a territory.

"Now the *haoles* own everything – houses, resorts, plantations – and natives can't afford to buy land. They can barely feed themselves while *haoles* burn on our beaches, swim in our ocean, and treat our people like shit."

Kanahele looked over his shoulder at Erin. "I'd call that stealing, wouldn't you?"

"Do these sovereignty groups really want to undo over one hundred years of history?" she asked. "To go back to the Nineteenth Century of farming taro and fishing? To go back to poverty?"

"Man, look around you," Montgomery said. "They're already in poverty. Give a Hawaiian his land and his nets, and he'll be better off than he is changing sheets and cleaning toilets for tourists."

"Nobody wants to go back to the Stone Age," Kanahele said. "All we want is some say-so over our land and our lives, that's all. That's really not too much to ask for, is it?"

Erin held his eyes for a moment. It sounded reasonable, but

she was willing to bet it wasn't nearly as simple an issue as that. One thing was sure, though; it was an emotional issue for these people. She saw it in Kanahele's and Montgomery's faces and heard it in their voices. When emotions were raised high enough, they became converted into passion.

Passion was one of the classic motives for murder.

Kanaka Blues

CHAPTER TEN

After passing through downtown Hilo, the caravan turned uphill on Waianuenue Avenue, past Hilo High School, then turned again, this time into a residential neighborhood of cramped frame houses. Erin was struck by the richness of the small lawns, overflowing with every color of flora, which contrasted with the drabness of the homes. Montgomery slowed to a stop in front of a lime-green stucco house, its screen door hanging by one hinge. Hibiscus bushes bursting with blood-red blooms framed both sides of the door. The air was filled with the fragrance of plumeria, like a perfume perfectly applied, teasing the senses without making any overt promises.

"Are you sure this guy's not home?" Erin asked.

"He's indisposed at the moment," Montgomery said as he shut off the engine and got out, followed by Kanahele.

Erin scrambled out beside them. They waited for the other cars to arrive and their occupants to get out.

"What does 'indisposed' mean?"

"He assaulted a police officer – several of them, actually – during the latest eviction on the Kona Coast," Montgomery said.

"*Latest* eviction?"

"Like I said before," Kanahele said, "these people can't

afford housing, so they live where they can. For some of them, that means on the beaches. All beaches in Hawaii are public. These people don't hurt anybody, but they annoy the tourists, so we periodically have to run them off. But they always come back."

"Not this time," Montgomery said. "A big resort's going up there. That beach is destined to become another smorgasbord of oiled-up *haole* flesh."

"Where will the people go who lived there?"

"Do you really care?" Kanahele asked.

She met his gaze. No smile this time; he was dead serious about this. A man after her own heart. Damn straight, she cared. She had devoted a law practice to helping the same kinds of people back in Dallas.

The other cops assembled beside them, ready to serve the warrant. Kanahele took the lead. "Stay back," he said to Erin.

She nodded then promptly followed the pack of police officers to the front door.

Kanahele opened the swinging screen, which lost its tenuous grip on that last hinge and fell into the hibiscus. Kanahele banged on the wooden door with the side of his fist. The hollow wood swallowed up the sound.

"Police. Anybody home?"

He waited a moment and then, sure no one was inside, nodded at the officer behind him. The cop raised his leg and shot the heel of his boot against the door. The rotting frame splintered easily and the door flew inward. The cops entered, with Erin right behind them.

Erin was immediately struck by how cramped the house was

— couldn't have been more than 700 or 800 square feet, not much bigger than a small apartment. It was tidy, probably made easier to keep that way by virtue of being so sparsely furnished. A small love seat with a ripped fabric cover and a green bean bag chair pretty much took care of the living area. The efficiency kitchen was adjacent to a space that probably was intended as a dining area, but instead housed a small rattan desk and rolling chair. The desk was stacked with papers, all under guard of a Hawaiian flag attached to the wall by thumbtacks.

As the cops fanned through the house, Erin wandered over to the desk, hands behind her back so as to restrain herself from touching anything. The paper on the desk consisted mostly of fliers and newspapers protesting beach evictions of the homeless and touting The Nation of the Islands. A small framed picture lay face up on the corner of the desk. Erin leaned over for a closer look. It was a black-and-white pencil drawing of a fierce Hawaiian warrior, draped with robes, complete with feathered headdress, and carrying a spear.

"That's Kamehameha the First, also known as Kamehameha the Great."

Erin looked up and saw Kanahele watching her.

"How can you see it from there?"

"I've seen it before."

"Mean-looking sonuvagun," she said.

"That he was. He was the Hawaiian Kingdom's first great king. He united all the islands back in 1810. He was also there when they killed Captain Cook at Kealakekua Bay. Legend has it that they ate Cook."

"You buy that, Detective?"

"Nah. They weren't cannibals. But it sure sounds good. Makes him sound all fierce, you know?"

Erin looked at the flag on the wall. "Looks like a British flag."

"Close. In 1794, the British Captain Vancouver gave Kamehameha a British flag. The King liked it so much, he flew it wherever he lived. Then, in 1816, he designed a flag for Hawaii that incorporated the Union Jack in the corner but added the eight stripes to stand for the eight main islands."

"I thought there were six main islands. Oahu, Maui, Kauai, Hawaii, Molokai, and Lanai."

"You're forgetting Ni'ihau and Kaho'olawe."

She looked back at the flag, then at the picture of Kamehameha. "I'm impressed, Detective. You do know your history."

"History's all we got left." He flashed a smile. "And please, call me Tommy."

"If you'll call me Erin."

"We got a deal."

Kanahele-now-known-as-Tommy stood beside her and looked at the framed picture. "Manu says he's a descendant of Kamehameha."

"Is he?"

"Hell, they all say they are," Montgomery said from behind them. Erin hadn't heard him approach. "He might as well be, too."

Tommy shrugged, sadly it seemed to Erin. She still wasn't sure how to take him. He was obviously much deeper than she saw at first blush. Beneath his façade lurked someone far more interesting than most cops she knew. She also suspected there lurked some connection to Manu Pokui that she didn't know about.

"Tommy," Montgomery said, "take a look at something in the bedroom."

*****

To call it a bedroom was to vastly overstate the case. White walls that hadn't seen a new coat of paint in at least a decade confined a small square of cement floor space. It held an unmade pallet that served as a bed and a milk crate that served as a nightstand. In addition to a lamp, the crate supported a pair of wire frame glasses with a broken earpiece and some folded papers with red splotches on them.

Erin caught her breath. She had seen those glasses before.

Wearing latex gloves, Montgomery picked up the glasses and showed them to Tommy. "You ever know Manu to wear these?"

"Nope."

"May I see those, please," Erin said.

Montgomery extended his hand, holding the glasses palm up.

Erin started to grab them but Tommy stopped her. "Don't touch."

She looked closely, then pointed at the right lens. "See that chip?"

Tommy and Montgomery both looked where she pointed. Sure enough, a small chunk was missing from the lens near the bottom of the frame.

"I get wild with a racquetball racquet sometimes. Cost Charlie that chip and a couple of stitches."

"You saying these are Professor Cain's?" Tommy asked.

"No doubt about it."

Montgomery picked up the red-splotched papers from the milk crate and unfolded them. "Looks like blood." He held the page up for Erin to see. "That look like Professor Cain's handwriting?"

Written in pencil, with drops of red obscuring some of the words, Erin recognized Charlie's shaky scrawl immediately. "Yes. Not like him to write in pencil, though. He's a ballpoint pen guy."

Montgomery scanned the top page. "Here's your motive." He began to read aloud. "'I have also traced the genealogy of the self-proclaimed governor of the Nation of the Islands, Manu Pokui, and determined that his ancestry does not trace back to 1778 Hawaii.'"

"Damn it," Tommy snapped.

Erin looked at him sharply, puzzled by his reaction. "How is that motive?" she asked.

"Well, it means he ain't a native Hawaiian, for one thing," Montgomery said.

"How do you figure?"

"State law uses 1778 – the year Captain Cook first arrived – to define 'Hawaiian' and 'Native Hawaiian.' If you can trace your ancestry to people living in Hawaii in 1778 or before, you meet that definition. Otherwise – "

"I still don't see how that's motive," Erin said.

"Because everything revolves around that definition," Tommy said. He snapped on a pair of latex gloves and took the paper from Montgomery. He shook his head as he silently scanned what Montgomery had already read aloud, then looked at Erin. "Hawaii for Hawaiians, entitlements, everything. Even the benefits under the Hasegawa Bill will only extend to those who meet the definition. So if Manu's not Hawaiian, by that definition – "

"It'd kinda be like finding out Jesus Christ wasn't the Son of God," Montgomery said. "If you're running around calling yourself the self-anointed governor of the Nation of the Islands and it turns out you're not even Hawaiian, where does that leave you?"

Erin turned to Tommy. "You got more gloves?"

He pulled one off his right hand and gave it to Erin, who put it on. The latex, stretched by Tommy's hand, slipped loosely over hers. She took the page and studied it more closely.

"Like I said, it's not like Charlie to write in pencil. He always wrote everything in black ink. He even worked the *New York Times* crossword in black ink. He kept a box full of black pens in his office."

"But you said that's his handwriting."

"Yeah. Sure looks like it." She handed the page back to Tommy. "If this Manu guy did something to Charlie, why keep this stuff here? In fact, why keep it at all? It makes a whole lot more sense to get rid of both the glasses and those pages. Especially the pages. He'd want to make sure no one ever read those words."

"Maybe that's why he disappeared the professor," Montgomery said.

"Disappearing the professor . . ." Her voice trailed off. She fought back tears, not wanting to cry in front of all these men. She dropped her head, but out of the corner of her eye, she saw a look of concern on Tommy's face. She realized what it was she liked about him: He had the kind of eyes that allowed you to see into his heart, not the cold eyes that kept emotion sealed inside.

She cleared her throat and continued. "Disappearing the professor, as you so eloquently put it, doesn't do him any good if he leaves the disappeared professor's words around for you to find. Those words are more threat to him than the professor is."

Tommy perked up. "You're starting to sound like a defense lawyer. Don't stop now."

She looked back at Montgomery. "And you say this is motive? But motive for what? We don't even know where Charlie is or what happened to him."

Erin's eyes fell back on the red splotches on the page in Tommy's hand. She didn't have to say what they were all thinking: *But we have a pretty good idea.*

CHAPTER ELEVEN

The giant dwarfed the plastic chair on which he sat at a wooden table. His hands were cuffed together and his jail overalls barely fit, way too short at his wrists and ankles, and straining to confine his massive arms. As Erin watched through the one-way mirror at the Hilo police station, she was reminded of *The Incredible Hulk* when the star transformed into a monster and burst out of his clothes. She thought Manu Pokui was about one flex of a bicep away from adding indecent exposure to his charge sheet.

Most striking about him, though, were the bruises and contusions that covered his face, with both eyes blacker than her own. A bloody bandage barely clung to his forehead. He sat stoically, obviously aware that he was being watched, yet totally unconcerned. He was a man thoroughly comfortable in his battered skin.

"What happened to him?" Erin asked.

"Resisted arrest," Tommy said. "It took a small army to bring him in."

"Do you think all that was necessary?"

Montgomery scowled, but Tommy just shook his head. "There's not a mark on him that he didn't bring on himself. Except maybe whatever's under that bandage on his head. That was there before. We're going to match it up with the blood on the Nissan and on the papers we found at his house."

"How do you know he brought the others on himself? Were you there?"

"You just can't stop being a defense lawyer, can you?" Montgomery snapped. "He's not your client. And remember, he may have done something to your Charlie Cain."

Erin nodded. Montgomery was right. Sometimes it was hard for her to turn off the lawyer part of her brain. If ever there was a time to turn it off, it was now. Time to start thinking like a cop. Charlie's life might depend on it.

"The uniforms know they answer to me if they hurt him," Tommy said. As he spoke, he kept his eyes locked on Manu through the mirror. But Erin heard something in his voice that convinced her that her earlier suspicions were correct: There was some deeper connection between them than just cop and outlaw.

"Phone records show he made a call to the Seasurf Hotel the night Professor Cain disappeared," Tommy said. "Right about the time the desk clerk says he put a call through."

"You're sure it was this guy?"

"All we know is that it came from his home phone. We'll get the desk clerk in here for a voice line-up, but that's about the best we can do unless he admits it."

"I wouldn't want to stake my case on a voice line-up based on a phone call," Erin said. She thought back to her own "Whozit?" call.

"Yeah, you lawyers would love that, wouldn't you?" Montgomery said.

Erin turned on him, her face passive, but her voice tight. "What is your problem, Detective?"

Montgomery raised his hands in a fake show of surrender. "No problems, *counselor*."

Erin turned back to Tommy, relegating Montgomery to invisibility. "Does he have a lawyer?"

"Said he doesn't need one," Montgomery said, regaining visibility before Tommy could answer. He snorted. "Says we don't have any jurisdiction over him because he's a citizen of the sovereign Nation of the Islands. Of course, his sovereign ass is still sitting in our non-jurisdictional jail."

"What happens now?" Erin asked.

"The same thing that usually happens with these guys," Tommy said – wistfully, Erin thought. "The judge will appoint him a lawyer, Manu'll ignore the lawyer, and he'll draw some jail time and a fine. He'll serve a few months and then he'll get out and start all over again." He paused, then added, "Hard-headed sonuvabitch. Always was."

Erin watched Manu for a moment. There was something almost regal about the way he held himself as he sat at the table. Even battered and bruised, handcuffed, and dressed in a clownishly undersized jumpsuit, he held his shoulders back and his head high with nobility, yet mixed with an aura of melancholy that struck a chord with Erin. She didn't know this man, but she knew men like him. Men on the streets of Dallas, disenfranchised by fortune, bad judgment, or personal weakness, yet even the hard life of homelessness couldn't quite snuff out those sparks of the proud souls buried inside, yearning to get out.

For reasons she couldn't explain, she didn't believe that this man had harmed Charlie. But he might be the key to finding out what happened to him.

"Has he said anything about Charlie?" she asked.

"We haven't talked to him about that yet," Tommy said. "He still thinks this is all about the eviction over on Kona."

"Can I talk to him?"

"You've got to be kidding me," Montgomery almost exploded.

"You'll be right here," she said. "You can hear everything I say."

"Ever since you got here, you've been acting like you're running the show. I understand you want to find out what happened to your friend, but goddamnit, you're not in charge. We are."

"No problems, huh?" she said.

"You don't tell us how to run our investigation."

"That's why I asked nicely."

"Besides, he hasn't asked for a lawyer," Tommy said. "You're not licensed in Hawaii, are you?"

"I won't be talking to him as a lawyer. He doesn't have a history with me like he obviously does with you. And – " she cut a look at Montgomery, who was shaking his head, " – I'm not the police. But I am a friend of Charlie's, and maybe that'll mean something to him."

Tommy looked at Montgomery, who accelerated the shaking of his head. After what seemed like an eternity, he said, "Five minutes."

Montgomery turned and stormed from the room, muttering

under his breath.

Tommy's voice softened. "Don't make me sorry."

Then he opened the door to the interrogation room for Erin.

*****

The big man eyed her suspiciously as she entered and sat across from him. She locked eyes with his, as if trying to look into his soul. But he had his filters on, blocking any depth. He wore a scowl on his face the way Montgomery did, though Manu's was a mask of protection, not a mask of hostility. This was a man who had been hurt before, who guarded his emotions as if his very life depended on it. She wouldn't know his heart by merely looking into his eyes. Her skin color, alone, made him wary.

"Mr. Pokui, my name is Erin Hanna. I'm a lawyer." She spoke with all the confidence she could muster. She thought she saw a flicker of recognition when she said her name.

"I didn't ask for a lawyer."

"I didn't say I was *your* lawyer. I said I was *a* lawyer." She softened her tone. "I'm also a friend of Charlie Cain's. I'm trying to find him."

Manu's scowl flickered for a second, as if he was about to drop his guard. But just as quickly, it hardened again.

"What do you mean you're trying to find him?"

She detected genuine puzzlement in his tone, but with a hint of knowledge mixed in. Her task was to separate the two.

"He's disappeared. I think something bad happened to him."

"And you think I did something to him?"

"I don't know," she said. Her voice quivered slightly, and she wondered if he noticed.

"I would never hurt Mister Charlie," he said in a softer tone.

"So you know who he is."

"He came to Tutu's once when I was there."

Erin's puzzled glance implied a question, one he answered without further prompting. "Tutu is my mother. He said he was working for the U.S. Congress and he wanted to talk to me, so he came to her house."

"Did you agree to talk?"

"That *haole* government's not my government. Nothing good comes from it. I had no reason to talk, so I left."

"Did you know he might be making recommendations to Congress about the Hasegawa Bill?"

For the first time, emotion crept into his voice, bordering on passion. Motive, perhaps?

"We don't need any law to tell us what we already know. That we are a free and independent people, and we're entitled to nothing less than sovereignty and our land back, not some half-assed government program. We don't need handouts from the likes of the United States doling out what's already rightfully ours."

"But you knew that's why he was here, right?"

"That's what he said. He could have been lying for all I know. That's what you *haoles* do."

"If you didn't have anything to talk to him about, then why did you ask him to meet you at the City of Refuge?"

The question startled Manu, surprise obvious on his face. He leaned back in his chair and put his hands in his lap. The chain of the cuffs rattled as they slid off the table. "You got it backwards, sistah. *He* wanted to meet *me* there, not the other way around."

"But you did call him at his hotel last night, didn't you?"

A smirk twisted up his lips. "You're still backwards. He called me." But realization that he might have been set up started to sink in, wiping the smirk away. He leaned forward again. His eyes drifted upward as if he was deep in thought. After a moment of silence, he added, "At least somebody who said he was Professor Cain did. He said he wanted to meet me at the City of Refuge."

"Did you think it was odd that he wanted to meet you there when you were both in Hilo?"

Another pause as Manu digested the question. "I didn't really think about it then. I just figured maybe he was over there doing research or something. Now it makes me wonder if he just wanted to get us alone."

"Did you meet with Charlie at the City?"

"I never saw him there."

"So you *were* there?"

Erin saw plainly that these realizations were only now piling on Manu: If something happened to Charlie, Manu had just admitted to going to meet him. He clammed up.

"Mr. Pokui, Charlie's my friend. I just want to find him." Her voice quivered again. "Do you know where he is?"

Kanaka Blues

CHAPTER TWELVE

A twin-hulled catamaran anchored in the arc created by Molokini Island, a comma-shaped extension of an ancient volcanic cinder cone that lurked below the water's surface. The northern rim of the cone was below sea level, the southern above, creating an almost perfect cove. About two-and-a-half miles off the Wailea coast of Maui, the crater basin was home to a plethora of colorful sea life, making it one of the most popular tourist attractions for snorkelers.

Most of the excursion group had already donned their masks and snorkels and were floating on the surface in a pack close to the boat, as if afraid to venture too far away. On board the catamaran, two overweight housewives from Tulsa baked on towels on the deck, clad in two-piece swimsuits that testified to their poor judgment in choosing swimwear. A balding man with a paunch, husband to one of the grotesquely pink sunbathers, strapped on his snorkel and headed to the side of the boat away from the bulk of the tourists. He spent most of his days at work around crowds in office buildings and airports. Surely out here in the middle of the ocean, he could find some space just to get away by himself.

With his mask securely in place, he climbed down the ladder and into the ocean. He was surprised at how cold the water was.

He expected something more akin to the bathtub-like warmth of the Mexican Caribbean, his usual vacation spot, but the Pacific refused to cooperate. He gasped briefly for breath, then kicked out from the catamaran, face down. Instantly he was transported to a world beyond his wildest fantasy. He had read that nearly 250 species of fish lived here, and it seemed as if all 250 had sent representatives to greet him in a kaleidoscopic mix of yellows, reds, blues, and greens. He kicked with his flippers and glided across the surface, fascinated by what he saw. With the sun on his back and the marine life menagerie below him, all tensions of offices, bosses, and traffic melted away with each surge.

He reached the northern rim of the cone, which sloped down to unknown depths. Treading water, he raised his head and looked the other direction where the southern rim rose upward, creating a solid wall that extended above the water line. He put his face back down. With his sights set on the submerged rim, he took a deep breath and kicked downward. He extended his hands in front of him and reached for the rock-hard surface. It felt rough to his hands, like sandpaper.

Then something caught his eye on a pile of lava rocks to his right. It looked at first like an eel but, on closer inspection, proved to be a rope, wrapped around the base of a rock. He kicked over, grabbed the rope, and began to unwind it, doing his part to preserve this delicate ecosystem. After a few pulls, the rope snagged. He shifted into an upright position and set his flippered feet, as if digging in his heels. He leaned back and gave a quick tug on the rope. It resisted for a brief moment, then it suddenly gave way.

A man's body, tied to the other end of the rope, floated up out of the coral, just inches from his face.

His eyes widened in horror. He let out all his breath in one *whoosh* and desperately kicked upward. A tightness grasped his chest as he struggled for air, the pain unbearable. His fingers and toes tingled. It seemed as if he'd never reach the surface.

At last he broke free, gasping for breath. Two feet away, the body popped up, then settled on its front and floated.

From the direction of the catamaran, he heard his wife scream.

Kanaka Blues

CHAPTER THIRTEEN

Erin seemed to have reached an uneasy truce with Manu, and their exchange settled into a rhythm that resembled a conversation more than an interrogation. He no longer acted as if she was out to trick him, but instead he appeared to buy into the notion that she really was just trying to find out what happened to her friend. He still hadn't completely opened up to her, though. After all, she was a *haole* – whatever that meant; the word grated on Erin whenever he used it, much the way certain racial epithets likely impacted other ethnic groups – and a *haole* lawyer at that.

"Tell me a little about the Nation of the Islands," she said.

Manu tensed. "Why? Are you working for the government, too?"

"Look, Mr. Pokui, I don't have a dog in that fight. I'm trying to understand what it's all about so I can figure out what Charlie was doing. That might help me find him."

"You sounded like him just then, when you talked about the dog in the fight. He talks like that."

"Yeah, I guess he does."

Manu scooted his chair back and stood, then paced on his side of the table. "It's simple, really. We want our land back."

"I keep hearing that. But do you want all the islands back? So you can run out all the tourists and set up on your own little kingdom?"

"It worked for hundreds of years before you *haoles* came along."

"I keep hearing that word, *haole*. What does it mean?"

Manu stopped pacing and sat down. He leaned back in his chair and smiled. He had no intention of answering and seemed to enjoy her discomfort at his use of the term.

"This is the Twenty-first Century," Erin said. "Are you prepared to lead your people back into the Stone Age?"

No answer. Just a smirk.

"And are they really your people?" she asked.

The smirk disappeared, replaced by a look that, for the first time, struck fear into Erin's heart.

Thankfully, the door to the interrogation room opened, and Tommy stuck his head inside.

"Ms. Hanna, may I have a word with you?"

Still feeling the laser glare from Manu, she left the interrogation room and rejoined Tommy and Montgomery. She knew by the looks on both their faces that they didn't have good news for her.

Tommy's next words chilled her to the bone.

"They've found a body on Maui."

*****

Erin felt numb as Tommy and Montgomery escorted her down the hallway to the front entrance. Tommy said the body was found submerged off the coast of Maui. The last body she identified had also been submerged in salt water, and she certainly didn't want a repeat of that, looking at the bloated, rotting corpse of someone she loved and saying, "Yes, that's him." But it looked like that was exactly where she was headed.

Through the glass doors, Erin saw that a large crowd of Hawaiians gathered in the rain outside the station, many clad in native garb, holding signs and placards. Some signs contained Hawaiian slogans, unintelligible to Erin, but the common theme seemed to be: FREE MANU. The group broke into a cacophony of jeers and catcalls as soon as Tommy pushed open the doors and led Erin into the mist. He pushed his way through the throng of bodies, using his elbows and shoulders, like a pulling guard opening a hole for a running back. Erin ducked her head and followed in his wake, with Montgomery bringing up the rear.

They jumped in the Jeep parked curbside, and Montgomery peeled off for the heliport. Within minutes, a police helicopter lifted off. Erin sat behind the pilot and Tommy, while Montgomery returned to the station. As they rose straight up, the rain fell harder, coating the windshield with water. Her mind dulled by the prospects of where she was going, Erin didn't remember getting in the helicopter and now realized she was sitting in the same spot she had occupied on her last flight. Without conscious thought, she unbuckled her seat belt, slid across the bench seat, and rebuckled on the other side. The side where Chris had sat.

The helicopter banked and whirled off to the west. Erin pressed her cheek against the Plexiglas and stared down as they rushed over Hilo. Then the lush greenery of the island's windward side faded to rock and hardened lava as they flew above the Saddle Road. To the south, Erin could just make out Kilauea volcano, sputtering and smoking. A cloud of steam rose where the lava flow emptied into the Pacific. For just a brief second, it was as if Chris were sitting beside her. She reached her hand for his but felt only air.

CHAPTER FOURTEEN

Two uniformed officers led a handcuffed Manu down the same hallway that Erin had traversed just minutes earlier, then paused in front of an elevator. One of the officers pushed the up button and they waited.

Outside, one of the protestors, a teen-aged boy in ragged jeans and a T-shirt, spotted him through the glass doors. "There's Manu."

Almost as if someone had yelled "Fire!" in a crowded theater, the throng of protestors surged as one against the building. They exploded through the doors in a lava flow of humanity. The officers escorting Manu had no chance, quickly overwhelmed by sheer numbers and native rage. In just seconds, more police arrived, and the scene soon resembled that on the Kona beach just a day earlier, with fists, nightsticks, and protest signs swinging. The hallway filled with shouts and sounds of the scuffle.

As the elevator doors opened, the officer nearest Manu fell and disappeared beneath a mass of feet and legs. Manu grabbed him and dragged him into the elevator, out of harm's way. The officer looked into Manu's face. The words "thank you" formed on his lips. Manu nodded, then grabbed the handcuff keys from the officer's belt, hit the "close" button on the wall, and stepped out into the fray as the doors shut.

He pressed against the wall while the melee continued and removed the handcuffs. Free of his chains, he squatted, as if withdrawing into the mass of humanity in the hallway. Four protestors surrounded him, concealing him with their bodies. The struggle continued down the hallway behind them, the battle now joined by every cop in the building, while the football huddle that surrounded Manu eased its way toward the front door and outside. A rusted Mitsubishi minivan waited curbside, its engine idling. Eddie Laenui, a twenty-seven-year-old surfer and *pakalolo* farmer, sat behind the wheel. His eyes widened when he saw Manu dash his way, followed by the four who had shielded him. He put the minivan in drive, waited until Manu and his cohorts jumped inside, then screeched away.

"Hey, bruddah," Manu said. He flashed ivory teeth and waggled his hand in a *shaka* sign – the Hawaiian "hang loose" gesture with thumb and pinky finger extended from a fist.

"I didn't think they could do it," Eddie said. "I been sitting out here figuring we just wasting our time."

"We got lucky," Manu said. "Now let's get the hell out of here."

Eddie glanced in his rearview mirror, made eye contact with a chunky man in the back seat. "Let 'em know we coming."

The man nodded, pulled out his cell phone, and dialed.

*****

The police helicopter landed at the Kahului airport on Maui, where a squad car waited to take Erin and Tommy to Maui Memorial Medical Center in nearby Wailuku. Erin shivered as she entered the morgue, in the basement of the hospital. Sparsely furnished with metal tables and trays that held a variety of medical instruments, its temperature was considerably lower than the eighty-five degrees outside. Everything about it evoked memories of that last identification she had made two years earlier at Hilo Medical Center. Just as then, a lone stretcher held a human body, covered with a sheet. A native Hawaiian doctor stood beside it. Erin guessed he was the coroner.

She hesitated, reluctant to look at the corpse for fear it was Charlie. If it was someone else, she could cling to the faint hope that he was still alive. After a few deep breaths, she strode over to the stretcher, followed closely by Tommy. She locked eyes with the coroner, who stared back and nodded almost imperceptibly. She held his stare until she reached the head of the stretcher. Tommy moved to her side, close enough that she felt his warmth.

She glanced at him, then back at the doctor. She took another deep breath, nodded, and closed her eyes. The doctor gripped the sheet with both hands and pulled it back to just below the body's neck.

Erin slowly opened her eyes.

The elderly man's face was battered, one eye puffy and swollen. The other eye was not swollen, but was badly discolored. The lower lip was distended grotesquely, split from top to bottom in the center. His left cheek was caved in. The whole face rainbowed in various shades of discoloration, ranging from black to blue to green. The darkened skin was also broken in various places, those wounds ranging from cuts to lacerations.

Despite the damage, Erin recognized him instantly. Her voice caught as she said, "That's Charlie."

Tommy nodded. "Looks like someone wanted something from him."

"Why do you say that?"

"This wasn't just a beating. This was a systematic beating."

"Torture?"

"Yeah."

Then she dissolved into tears. Tommy put his arms around her, and she buried her face in his chest.

CHAPTER FIFTEEN

A muddy road, pitted with water-filled potholes the size of bomb craters, snaked its way through dense jungle along the windward coast of the Big Island. Palm trees reached skyward, surrounded at their bases by every foliage known to these islands, their branches thick with leaves extending into the road, narrowing it like cholesterol narrows arteries. This area was sparsely populated with a largely native citizenry, many who thrived as *pakalolo*, or marijuana, farmers. They guarded their crops with shotguns and shoot-first attitudes. Not even the local police ventured in here without a damn good reason.

On the *makai*, or ocean, side of the road, six brown-skinned men gripped a thick rope. They braced their legs against the slippery mud as if engaged in a tug-of-war. But this tug-of-war was not with a competing team of men. Instead, the rope elevated upward at a steep angle to a point fifty feet above the ground, where it was tied off just beneath a cluster of coconuts. At the base, sawdust and wood chips testified that this particular tree was completely sawed through. The trunk swiveled on its precarious base as wind tossed the top about. The Hawaiians dug their feet in with each new twist, hoping they had enough strength to hold on until the appointed time.

99

Behind the group of six, a longhaired woman held a cell phone to her ear. She folded the phone and tucked it into her shorts pocket.

"They're coming," she said.

*****

The minivan sped through the outlaw town of Pahoa. Plank boardwalks lined quaint wooden storefronts, giving it the feel of the old west. A few residents – probably *pakalolo* farmers or maybe even federal fugitives, as such was the reputation of the town – stood transfixed as the parade of chase vehicles barreled past. A few cheers went up from a dreadlocked man and his dreadlocked son, who pumped their fists in the air.

Beyond Pahoa, the pavement swept past numerous turn-offs to mud roads that pierced the rain forest. With one eye peeled to the rearview mirror, Eddie slammed on the brakes, fishtailed right, then turned sharply left onto one of those roads and disappeared into the lushness. Branches slapped at the windshield and dug their fingernails into the side of the van. Mud splotched the window with each bounce of a pothole. Manu grabbed the door handle and held tight.

Behind them, the police cars executed the same fishtailing maneuver and turn before following into the jungle. Wipers slapped away gobs of mud that assaulted them from the spinning tires of the minivan. The lead car eased up a bit to avoid the thickness of mud but stayed in sight of the rooster-tailing flow up ahead.

Eddie took his eye off the mirror and looked for the landmark. When he spotted the rusting hulk of an ancient Volkswagen on the side of the road, overgrown with foliage, he raised his hand. The man with the cell phone in the back seat nodded, then keyed in the number on speed dial.

*****

The tug-of-war team held its ground, keeping the palm tree upright. They heard the roar of engines approaching, the rattle of metal as vehicles lumbered across the uneven road. The woman grabbed the chirping phone from her pocket, held it briefly to her ear, then turned it off.

"Now."

All six men let go at the same time. The tree remained vertical for a few seconds, as if perfectly balanced on its sawed stump. The lead man put the sole of his foot against the trunk and pushed. Almost imperceptibly at first, then with increasing speed, the tree started its descent.

*****

The driver of the lead police car leaned forward, then squinted through the mud-spattered windshield. The mud was too thick, merely smearing with each pass of the wipers. He rolled down his window and stuck his head out, only to have mud decorate his face from his own spinning tires. He pulled his head back in just as his partner screamed, "*Damn.*"

When he looked where his partner pointed, the driver could barely make out movement, then he recognized it for what it was – a tree hurtling downward onto the road like a security gate. Indecision froze his leg for a moment: accelerate or brake? Then a message made its way through from his brain.

He jammed both heels on the brake pedal at once, almost standing up in his seat. The vehicle slid forward, back end sliding right, as all four wheels locked and stuttered, locked and stuttered. Behind them, the other cars mimicked his lead, slipping and sliding on the muddy road.

The driver and his partner both ducked for the floorboard at the same time as the tree slammed into the angle where the windshield slanted upward from the hood. The car stopped in mid-skid, pinned by hundreds of pounds of wood. The first trailing car spun sideways, then slammed into the lead. A chain reaction brought the entire chase to a muddy halt. A quarter of a mile down the road, the minivan disappeared from sight.

CHAPTER SIXTEEN

Erin sat silently on the edge of the bed in her small hotel room. Her suitcase was packed and waiting beside the door. Outside, it was raining again, as it seemed it had been ever since she arrived in Hilo. She wondered, after all that had happened, if she were destined to be alone. Was love, for her, merely a precursor to sorrow? What had she done to anger God that he favored her with such sadness?

A light knocking at the door roused her from her melancholy. When she opened the door, Harry, the desk clerk, stood outside, hands clasped below his ample belly.

"Miss Erin, Detective Kanahele is here to take you to the airport."

"Okay, I'm ready to go."

He grabbed her suitcase and lifted it, then turned for her to follow. They walked silently down the passageway, Harry shuffling and flip-flopping in the lead. A tourist group had gathered in the lobby, waiting to file onto a red and yellow bus that blocked the porte-cochere. Just in front of the bus, Tommy stood by his Jeep.

"Miss Erin, I know I said it before, but I'm so sorry," Harry said. "We all really liked Mr. Charlie. He treated us good, and he was nice to everyone."

"That's the way he was."

"Yes, ma'am."

Tommy hustled over and took Erin's suitcase. He carried it to the Jeep as Erin turned to face Harry. She extended her hand. He took it, swallowing it in his giant paw.

"Thank you for your kindness," she said.

"I talked to the owner of the hotel. He said that if you ever want to come back to Hilo, you can stay here free-of-charge. He said to consider this your home on the Big Island."

"Thank you, Harry."

They looked at each other awkwardly for a moment. Then he wrapped his arms around her in a bear hug.

"I know it may not seem like it now, but you'll always find aloha here, Miss Erin."

*****

Neither Erin nor Tommy spoke on the short drive to the airport. Tommy pulled the Jeep curbside in front of the departure gates and turned off the engine. He walked briskly around to Erin's door and helped her out, then grabbed her suitcase from the back seat and escorted her to the ticket counter. After checking her in, he walked with her toward the boarding gates. At the security checkpoint, he spoke for the first time.

"You gonna be all right?"

"Not for a while. But I've been down this road before."

He looked at her quizzically, but she said nothing in response.

"We're gonna find who did this," he said. "And if you can think of anything that might help us, give me a call. You got my card, right?"

"Yeah. But I can't imagine I know anything that'll help."

"Maybe in his papers back in Texas. He might have some notes or something."

"I'll see what I can find. Just don't count on anything."

"I never do," he said. He held her eyes with his for a moment, and she sensed that he wanted to say something, but he looked away, toward the security gate.

"You better get going," he said. "Don't want to miss your flight."

She nodded, then turned and walked away.

*****

Erin changed planes in Honolulu for an American Airlines wide-body with a non-stop flight to Dallas-Fort Worth. She made her way down the narrow aisle toward a window seat on the right side over the wing. Halfway there, she glanced out a window and saw a cart carrying a wooden coffin pull up beside the plane.

She froze.

"Miss, is everything all right?"

The woman's voice shook her from her trance. She realized that she was holding up the line of boarding passengers. A flight attendant looked at her with concern.

"Are you all right?" the attendant asked again.

"I'm sorry. Yes, everything's fine."

She hurried on down the aisle and took her seat. She pressed her face to the window and watched as three men loaded Charlie into the belly of the plane.

CHAPTER SEVENTEEN

Waipio Valley on the Big Island was known as the Valley of the Kings. Located at the end of the Hamakua Coast on the northeast side of the island, it vee'd inward to lush green mountains that guarded it. Once a population center, tsunamis and disease had thinned its residents to less than one hundred who lived off the land and the ocean. Many of Hawaii's great kings were buried there, and many Hawaiians believed that their *mana*, or spiritual power, protected the valley and those who sought refuge there.

A tiny thatched hut sat in a clearing below Hi'ilawe Falls at the Valley's corner. An ancient Hawaiian woman, her back bent from years of hard labor, carried a basket of seared ahi and poi to the open doorway. With the deliberation of her age, she stooped and set the basket on the ground then retreated to the trees surrounding the clearing.

After she vanished from sight, Manu emerged from the jungle on the other side. He sat in the dirt with his back against the hut and ate from the basket. As he did, he kept his eyes alert, his ears finely tuned. It was one thing to be arrested for an act of civil disobedience; it was yet another to be suspected in the disappearance and possible murder of a *haole* professor from the mainland.

He had just finished the last of the ahi when he heard a rustling in the jungle. He bolted forward, every sense on high alert, every muscle in his brawny body on standby. The rustling continued, drawing closer. He stood slowly and raised his hands to waist level, palms out, ready to strike or grab. Directly across from him, he saw leaves move. He bounced on the balls of his feet, flexed his knees.

A Hawaiian warrior, fully clothed in Hawaiian tapa cloak and helmet with red-and-yellow feathered headdress, stepped into the clearing. He was a big man, easily Manu's equal in stature and weight. Manu recognized him immediately.

"*Me ke aloha pumehana, Manu,*" the great warrior King Kamehameha said. *Warm aloha, Manu.*

Manu bowed his head in supplication. He spoke in a subdued voice, reverence and awe filling his tone. "What do I do now, oh Great One? All I have worked for is in jeopardy. I have tried to help my people – your people – but now I am a fugitive from the American police. I am forced to hide like a dog. Now I fear for my people."

"Do you fear for your people, or do you fear for yourself?" Kamehameha asked.

"I can do my people no good while hiding. Yet, if I don't, and I am accused of a crime I didn't commit, I can also do my people no good. Not from an American prison. So tell me, oh Great One – what do I do?"

Kamehameha crossed the clearing and walked up to Manu. He put his hand on Manu's shoulder. Manu raised his head and looked into the king's eyes.

"Protect the weak from the strong," the king said. "*Malama pono, Manu.*" *Preserve that which is good.*

He removed his hand and stepped back. With a nod, he turned and walked toward the jungle. He faded from view before he reached the far edge of the clearing.

Manu stared at the trees. Had Kamehameha really been there, or was it his imagination? He couldn't be sure. As he turned to enter his tiny hut, Kamehameha's last words rang in his ears: "*Malama pono, Manu.*" *Preserve that which is good.*

CHAPTER EIGHTEEN

On the day of Charlie's funeral, the skies cleared at dawn in a glorious sunrise that gave way to a crystal clear spring day of bright sunshine and comfortable eighty-degree temperatures. A steady breeze blew from the north, complementing the greening of Dallas after the passage of winter. Erin would have preferred a Hollywood-style, dark, rainy day to match her spirits. The clouds that seemed to have taken permanent residence inside her heart clashed with the brightness of this day.

After the interment at the cemetery, Erin went to the law school at SMU where a buffet had been set up for Charlie's friends and colleagues in the student courtroom. A group of suited professors had preceded her there. She noted a sharpened silence when she entered, as if they had been talking about her and stifled their tongues when they saw her. She made her way to the buffet table, not really hungry, but she knew she needed to eat to keep up her strength. She had last eaten nearly twenty-four hours ago, and she was feeling the effects.

She heard a few muted condolences and felt hands pat her back and shoulders as she numbly went through the line, keeping her head down. She filled a plate with fruit and vegetables, along with a miniature egg roll. At the end of the line, she finally looked up into the face of a man with thick gray hair, wearing a blue pinstripe suit. His face was craggy and rough, but his smile was tender.

Decades earlier, Albert Lawrence, the senior senator from Texas, had been one of Charlie's students at SMU law school. After a brief career in the U.S. Attorney's office for the Northern District of Texas, he went into politics, first as a state senator then as a United States Senator, a position he had now held for three terms. He was also the man who sent Charlie to Hawaii in the first place.

"How are you holding up?" Lawrence asked.

"You never get used to it. No matter how many people you love die."

"I can't tell you how sorry I am."

She dropped her head and stared at her plate.

"You want a cup of coffee to go with that?" he asked.

"No, thanks."

"He was doing something important, you know."

"I really don't care what he was doing or how important it was. All I care about is that he's gone."

"It mattered to him, though. He believed in what he was doing. Just like I knew he would."

"Yeah, he was always a sucker for a good cause."

"That he was."

An awkward silence fell over them as the sound of silverware and idle chatter made Erin's nerves stand on end.

"Someone needs to finish what he started," Lawrence said

abruptly.

Erin met his gaze with a mixture of confusion and anger in her eyes.

"But not me."

"Just hear me out, Erin. I know he talked to you about it. And you know the way his mind worked better than anybody else. You could take his notes – "

"Whoever killed him stole his notes," she snapped.

As soon as her temper flashed, it was over. She took a deep breath and waited for the heat in her cheeks to dissipate. When she felt she could talk again without raising her voice, she said, "I'm sorry, Senator. It's just that I'm not the right person for this. You need to find someone else."

She abruptly put her plate down and walked away.

*****

Erin sat at her desk and stared at the law school courtyard beyond her window. Students came and went in twos and threes, carting books and backpacks, talking and laughing. Most of them probably hadn't known Charlie, who retired a couple of years earlier, but that didn't seem to justify their cheeriness on the day he was put into the ground. She pulled at an unruly lock of hair, twisted it in her fingers, then put it in her mouth and chewed on it. Was it her fault Charlie died? Would he be alive if she had answered his calls and warned him? But warned him of what? She had no way of knowing what was going to happen, nor did he. Still, it seemed wrong that he had needed her and she hadn't been there for him.

She shook her head and tried to put the irrational thought out of her mind. She was back in Texas now, and the investigation was in the hands of the Hawaiian police. If they needed her, Detective Kanahele had her phone number. Nothing for her to do but throw herself back into her work. There were classes to teach, papers to grade, and final exams to prepare.

She looked at the stack of envelopes on the edge of her desk. And mail to open.

She grabbed the stack, leaned back in her chair, and thumbed through it quickly, looking at return addresses. Mostly junk mail, letters from legal publishing companies, announcements of Continuing Legal Education programs – and one with a return address from: CHARLIE, HILO, HAWAII. Just like Charlie, she thought; he never was much for e-mail.

Fingers trembling, she ripped the envelope open and pulled out a letter that was handwritten in black ink on yellow legal paper. It was dated the day before he disappeared. She set the page on her desk and leaned over it.

Dear Erin:

If this letter catches you by surprise, it means I never had a chance to tell you this over the phone. It may also mean things have gone horribly wrong. I'll let you draw your own conclusions.

I'm just about finished with my investigation and am ready to make my report to the Senate. The ramifications are enormous. If they approve the bill pending in Congress, it could mean that the United States will give back to the Hawaiian people about two million acres of land that it took after the overthrow of the Queen in 1893. It could also mean that the United States will have to compensate the Hawaiian people for having taken the land in the first place. If you know anything about the value of real estate in Hawaii, then you know what that means. Sugar and pineapple plantations aren't the only things on the land that may be affected. Dozens of hotels, resorts, and golf courses are now built on land that once belonged to the Kingdom of Hawaii. How do you compensate for that?

There's also the question of political power. If a new and sovereign nation is created within the state's borders, even if it's only a nation-within-a-nation like the U.S. has done with Native Americans, a lot of people will be jockeying for leadership roles. With the United States Supreme Court's decision in Rice v. Cayetano, the Bureau for Native Hawaiians will be looking for new authority. The bill may give them that opportunity.

And then there's the sovereignty movement, itself. Within the movement, the different factions have been grappling for years for leadership of a new sovereign nation. Whichever way Congress decides, it'll make a lot of people unhappy. Now I'm afraid I've bitten off more than I can chew. I need your brain on this one. But if you get this letter and haven't heard from me, that means it may be too late. Start with Professor Tanaka at the University of Hawaii Law School. He'll show you where my locker is. Inside you'll find what you need to get started.

Finish it for me, Erin.

Love, Charlie.

Kanaka Blues

CHAPTER NINETEEN

No vestiges remained of the homeless city that held up construction on the beach where Manu was arrested. The sun was barely up, its rays just reaching the Kona coast from behind Mauna Kea, but bulldozers already moved freely about, pushing sand and lava rock to make way for the resort's new foundation. Two workers in jeans, denim work shirts, and hardhats stood next to a Dodge pick-up truck, architectural drawings spread across the hood. A third man – the construction foreman – stood nearby, cell phone to his ear. The other two waited expectantly for the results of his call. All three men had the darkened skin of native Hawaiians.

"We'd have to move the outer wall about ten or twelve feet to do that," the man on the cell phone said. "I can't just make that kind of change without the architect signing off. We'd have to – "

An ear-splitting explosion suddenly erupted behind him.

He spun and looked over his shoulder as a bulldozer rose five feet, then slammed down on its edge and tipped over. Its Japanese driver spilled onto the sharp-edged *a'a* lava rock. Shockwaves from the explosion blew hardhats off all three men by the truck and peppered them with bullet-sized chunks of lava. They hit the ground and covered their heads with their arms, like a precision team. The blueline caught air and swirled away inland.

The foreman raised his head when the dust settled. "What the hell was that?"

The three men staggered to their feet, eyes on the bulldozer on its side. Its driver crept toward them on his hands and knees. A trickle of blood flowed from his left ear and across his cheek.

"Somebody call an ambulance," the foreman screamed.

He scrambled for his driver, who keeled over and lay still. He cradled the man's head in his lap. The man's eyes fluttered and opened. His eyes were crossed, fighting for focus.

"Hey, bruddah," the foreman said. "Stay with me, brah."

A second explosion fractured the morning, sending another spray of lava shrapnel inland. The foreman ducked and covered the injured man with his upper body. Rock and sand pelted the top of his head and his back.

A third explosion followed, then a fourth and a fifth in rapid succession southward along the beach. Construction workers abandoned their equipment and dove for cover, but there was none. No one knew where the next charge might be harbored or where the next blast might occur. A sixth explosion hit, taking a vacant dozer skyward then over onto its side. Confused shouts filled the air as the workers got to their feet and ran inland, as far from the beach as they could get.

Behind them, lava rock and sand fell like rain.

*****

With a row of craters lining the beach and encroaching onto

the rock-hard lava field, the stretch of sand on the Kona coast looked like Omaha Beach on D-Day. Wrecked bulldozers lay strewn on their sides, one completely upside down. Stakes had been driven in the sand and police tape roped off the entire area. Dozens of cops explored the damage. Explosives experts had been sent over from the Navy and now examined the craters and remnants of whatever had been used to make the bombs.

About twenty feet from the police tape, the press gathered. Mini-cams rolled and cameras shuttered. Across the way, a group of about thirty Hawaiians gathered, carrying the same kinds of protest signs they had carried at the big brawl a few days earlier. They chanted, clapped, and sang native songs, praising the bomber, whoever he might be.

"Any excuse for a party," Detective Joe Montgomery said to his partner as they crossed the lava field toward the beach, where a uniformed cop waited. His badge identified him as M. Howell.

Tommy Kanahele nodded. "Any injuries?"

"A lot of shit-laden britches, but nothing seriously hurt other than pride," Officer Howell said. "Some cuts and bruises, but that's about it."

"I heard one of the dozer operators had to be taken to the hospital," Montgomery said.

"Yeah, they were pretty worried about him at first. It looked like he was bleeding from his ears – ain't nothing good about that – but it turned out it was a gash on his scalp that was running down the front of his ear."

Tommy and Montgomery stood with their hands on their hips, as if mimicking each other. Both men wore sunglasses, giving them a casual men-in-black look.

"They've never been violent like this before," Tommy said after Howell left to join the other cops on the beach.

"Who?"

"Who do you think?"

Montgomery took off his sunglasses and looked at his partner. "You think this is one of the sovereignty groups?"

"If it's not, someone sure wants us to think so."

"You think Manu had something to do with this?"

"I doubt it," Tommy said. "This had to have been in the works before he got away." He shook his head. "Besides, this isn't his style."

A commotion behind them drew their attention. It was the clamor of reporters shouting questions at two men, one in charcoal-colored slacks and an aloha shirt, a hardhat atop his head, the other a gray-haired man wearing a blue blazer, white shirt with khaki slacks, and silk tie. Both men were in their mid-to-late fifties. The man with the hardhat seemed agitated. His voice rose and his arms gestured as he spoke to the press. The other man seemed more in control, standing silently by.

"Who's that?" Montgomery asked.

"GQ over there is Ted Hotchkiss. That means the other guy is probably the developer."

"How do you know that?"

"Don't you watch the news or read the papers?"

"Sports and weather, brah; sports and weather."

"Oh, yeah, I forgot. You're a regular Renaissance Man."

"What the hell does that mean?"

"Never mind." Tommy folded his arms across his chest and watched as the reporters called their questions and scribbled down the hardhat's answers. "Ted Hotchkiss is the grease on the wheels of progress. If you define that as hotels, condos, and resorts, that is. Some people call him a lobbyist, some a consultant. All I know is, he spreads money around and, just like that, zoning ordinances get changed, building permits issued, deed restrictions disappear. Whatever it takes to turn sand into income-producing property, Hotchkiss is the man."

Hotchkiss spotted Tommy and Montgomery staring at him. He returned their stare, smiled almost imperceptibly, and nodded. He walked toward them, picking his way carefully across the lava so as not to scuff his Bruno Maglis.

He extended his hand and turned up the smile wattage as he neared. "Are you the detectives in charge?"

Tommy shook his hand. "I'm Kanahele, this is Montgomery."

"Ted Hotchkiss."

"So what can we do for you, Mr. Hotchkiss?" Tommy asked.

"Well, as you can see, my friend over there is quite unhappy."

"Yeah, we noticed that."

"I don't want this to put him behind schedule, but now he's got a lot of equipment he has to replace."

"That's not our problem," Tommy said.

"I understand you had the man in custody who did this, and he got away from you."

"First of all, we don't know who did this. And secondly, this is a police matter, not a political matter."

Hotchkiss gazed seaward and chuckled, but there was no

mirth in his laugh. "Everything is political, detective."

"Mr. Hotchkiss, what do you want?"

"I want you to catch this man before this can happen again."

"We're doing our best."

"That's all I wanted to know. Good day, detectives."

He picked his way back to the hardhat, who had finished talking to the reporters and now waited for Hotchkiss, a forlorn look on his face.

"Good day, asshole," Montgomery said.

"What do you think that was all about?"

"I don't know, but I don't like it."

"Neither do I."

CHAPTER TWENTY

Eddie Laenui sat on a bunk with his back against the cell wall and stared at the ceiling. Even with the open bars across from him, it seemed as if he were confined in a coffin. A band tightened across his chest, squeezing the breath from him. Sweat trickled down his brow and his hands tingled, starting at his fingertips and radiating up to his wrists.

They couldn't possibly know he had driven the getaway car for Manu. He was confident no one had seen him at the wheel. But he knew that story about assaulting a police officer at the eviction on the beach was bogus, just a made-up excuse to get him behind bars. If that was what this was all about, they would have arrested him at the beach. But they didn't. All they wanted was Manu. And all Eddie was, was bait.

He heard footsteps approach on the concrete floor. Keys jangled as a guard moved into view. He inserted a key in the lock and turned it. Eddie bolted to his feet and waited for the door to open. He bounced on his toes and shook his hands, trying to get the blood flowing again. His breathing eased at the mere prospect of exiting the cell.

"The detectives want to see you, Eddie."

"About time, bruddah. I got to get out of here."

The guard opened the gate and escorted Eddie to the same interrogation room where Erin had talked with Manu. Detectives Kanahele and Montgomery waited inside, Kanahele sitting at the table, Montgomery leaning against the far wall.

Eddie stepped inside and stood there for a moment.

"Have a seat, Eddie," Kanahele said. He pushed back the chair across from him with his foot.

Eddie slipped into the seat and leaned forward on his elbows. The two detectives just stared at him – the "cop stare" – while Eddie's focus darted back and forth between them. Kanahele finally broke the silence.

"You want out of here?"

"Who I gotta kill?" Eddie laughed, but neither cop joined him.

"You think this is a joke?" Montgomery said. "You think you can just laugh this all away?"

"I damn sure don't think it's funny. You got no right to lock me up."

"This is no longer just about evictions on the beach, Eddie, or throwing a punch at a cop. It's gotten a lot more serious than that."

Eddie tried to read their faces but failed. "What's this all about?"

"Civil disobedience is one thing, but killing people is another," Montgomery said. "And you helped him escape. That makes you an accessory after the fact."

"I don't know what you're talking about. Who's killing people?"

"I think you know."

"No, I don't." A note of panic slipped into his voice. He looked at Kanahele.

"What's he talking about, brah?"

Kanahele looked at Montgomery. "Give us a minute."

Montgomery nodded and left the room.

Kanahele stood and walked around the table. He put his hands on the edge and loomed over Eddie.

"It's just you and me now, bruddah," the detective said. "I've known you since you were a boy. Me and your brother played a little football together, played a little baseball. I don't want to see you get hurt."

He straightened up and returned to his seat. "I also know what you got growing in your field down in Puna. A little *pakalolo*, huh?"

Eddie shifted his eyes to the table.

"That's good that you won't look at me," Kanahele said. "You're ashamed. But I also know that's how you put food on the table for your kids. That's why I never said anything before. But I need your help now, bruddah. And believe it or not, Manu needs your help, too. I need to find him before he gets in any more trouble."

Kanahele rapped his knuckles on the table for emphasis, then turned his back on Eddie and headed for the door.

Just before he reached it, Eddie said, "What I gotta do?"

Kanaka Blues

CHAPTER TWENTY-ONE

It seemed like déjà vu as Erin sat in a taxi cutting across Honolulu toward the University of Hawaii, which was just up the street from the Paradise Island apartments. At Senator Lawrence's suggestion, her first stop had been Senator Hasegawa's office, where a bright young staffer named Coby Howell greeted her like a puppy dog and offered his assistance in her research. For starters, she got directions to the law school. At the administration office, she was directed to the law library where, she was told, "You can always find Professor Tanaka when he's not in class."

She pushed through the double doors to the library like a gunslinger entering a saloon, nearly bumping into a distinguished-looking gentleman with gray hair and a tailored suit.

"I'm so sorry," she said.

"Not a problem" the man said. "Nothing like being anxious to get among the stacks."

She smiled, embarrassed – probably the dean, she thought – and walked to the front desk. To Erin, it looked like every other law library she had ever been in, with its familiar tomes of bookshelves stacked perilously close to each other. A young woman in white shorts and a T-shirt, probably a student, looked up from a volume of *Federal Reporter* as Erin approached.

"Can I help you?" the woman asked.

"I was told I could find Professor Tanaka here."

The woman smiled, as if Erin had shared an inside joke. She pointed over Erin's shoulder to a smallish Japanese man standing at a shelf near the far wall. On a table beside him, open books were stacked at least a foot tall across half the surface. He set an open book on top of the nearest stack. Standing on tiptoes, he reached for yet another volume.

As Erin approached, she thought how much he resembled Mr. Moto from the old black-and-white movies, with a Charlie Chan mustache and beard and thick glasses. He wore gray slacks, sandals with black socks, and a white, short-sleeve dress shirt with a narrow tie. She was also struck by how small he was, surely no more than five feet tall. Her shadow fell across him, and he looked up into her face, squinting behind the lenses of his spectacles.

He smiled. "You must be Erin," he said. Despite his appearance, he spoke perfect English with no trace of an accent.

Erin stopped, astonished. "How'd you know that?"

"We Japanese are a mystical people." He paused dramatically then added, "Besides, Charlie showed me your picture. He said you were the daughter he never had. When I heard about what happened to him, I knew you'd come calling."

"I'm only here to find out why he was killed. I'll leave the rest to the politicians."

"Don't you think that's better left to the police?"

"Probably." She paused. "Will you help me?"

Tanaka shook his head and laughed. "He was right about you."

"Does that mean you will?"

"You have the key?"

Erin pulled it from her jeans pocket and showed it to him.

"All right, then," he said, "let's go."

They walked silently until they had exited the library and gone down the steps to a courtyard in the center of the campus. A few students passed, dressed casually in shorts and T-shirts, and lugging heavy law books. Most of them were either Hawaiian or Japanese, with very few white faces in their midst.

"Do y'all have a policy against white students here?" Erin asked.

"We take all comers."

"Doesn't look like it."

"How many black students do you have at your school?"

"I don't know. About ten percent, I guess."

"Well, that's about what we got of *haoles* here. They are Hawaii's minority, you know."

"Point taken. I do note that you have white staff or faculty, though. I nearly ran over one of your professors on the way in."

Tanaka laughed. "I'm sure they're accustomed to eager students anxious to get into the library."

"Yeah, aren't we all?"

Tanaka pointed between two buildings to the main library on the campus. They shifted their route and headed toward it.

"Did you get Charlie back to Texas?" Tanaka asked.

"Buried him two days ago."

"He loved Texas. He always said, 'Never ask a man if he's from Texas. If he is, he'll tell you; if he's not, no reason to embarrass him.'"

Erin laughed. She'd heard Charlie say that at least two dozen times.

"He thought the world of you," Tanaka said. "He said you were the best damn lawyer he had ever seen."

"I think he was exaggerating."

"Hyperbole wasn't his style." His tone turned serious. "He was afraid something like this was going to happen."

"I know. But I don't understand it. I know there's a lot at stake, but I'm not sure I understand why it's such a big issue in the first place."

"You and all the other *haoles*."

"I keep hearing that word. What on earth does *haole* mean?"

"When Captain Cook and his boys first came to these islands, the natives had never seen people with such pale skin. I don't think suntanning was all the rage for the early Brits. The Hawaiians couldn't believe people with such pale skin and frail bodies were actually alive. They looked like the walking dead. The Hawaiian prefix *ha* means breath, or breath of life, and the suffix *ole* means an absence of. So the Hawaiian word *ha'ole* literally means without the breath of life."

Tanaka led her up the steps to the university's main library, which was three times the size of the law library, and through the front doors. Again, Erin was struck by the dearth of white faces, which even she was now starting to think of as *haole*. Tanaka weaved his way through students and bookshelves to a locker room at the rear of the first floor. Rows of metal lockers filled two walls, about six feet high. He tapped on one of the metal doors, near the bottom in the middle of the side wall.

"That's Charlie's."

Erin inserted the key. She held it tightly for a few seconds, her nerves tingling, then turned it. *Click.*

She opened the door to find the small space completely crammed with papers. Here at last were Charlie's notes.

"Looks like we got our work cut out for us," Tanaka said.

"We?"

"You don't think I'd let you have all this fun by yourself, do you? I can at least help with the paperwork."

"Then we might as well get started."

She grabbed a handful and headed to a nearby table.

Kanaka Blues

CHAPTER TWENTY-TWO

The Kilauea Caldera at Hawaii Volcanoes National Park must be what hell looked like: a huge hole dug into the ground, venting ghosts of sulfur gas, with millions of tons of fiery lava lurking just beneath. On occasion over the years it had spewed its contents hundreds of feet into the air, which then snaked their way as rivers of molten rock toward the ocean, destroying everything in their path in spontaneous puffs of smoke and flame. Located on the eastern slope of Mauna Loa, the park drew thousands of tourists on a daily basis. They came by the busload to walk in the cold and rain around the rim of the crater, snap pictures of dancing vapors above gas vents, and eat fried chicken at the Volcano House buffet.

In spite of a constant drizzle of cold rain that day, tourists of every nationality roved the park, carrying umbrellas and wearing slickers and windbreakers. There was lots of chatter as they ambled about the park, excitedly pointed out the sights, and posed for pictures with the crater in the background. In their midst, though, were a few tourists who seemed more interested in scoping out the crowds than enjoying the sights. Though they were dressed like the others, they seemed far more alert than merely wide-eyed. They had ear buds that didn't match any music players currently on the market and telltale bulges of handguns under aloha shirts and windbreakers.

A tourist helicopter circled the perimeter of the caldera, along Crater Rim Road. Blue with yellow stripes, the four-seater Sigorsky didn't seem out of place from the outside, but inside was a different story. Its pilot, Walter Takai, a grim-faced Japanese-Hawaiian with a Fu Manchu beard and mustache, wore a handgun in a holster on his hip, and its passenger, Tommy Kanahele, held binoculars to his eyes, scanning the crowds below. His focus was on Eddie Laenui, walking amongst the masses.

Eddie wore a gray sweatshirt and khaki painter pants, his ponytail escaping from beneath a battered baseball cap. He glanced about as he walked along a path through thick green foliage that threatened to overwhelm the concrete walkway. He followed a sign that directed him to THURSTON LAVA TUBE, a 450-foot long tunnel formed long ago by flowing lava. At the end of the path, crowds congregated at the entrance to the tube, then disappeared inside.

Eddie separated himself from the pack, wandered over to a metal bench, and sat in the rain. Arms over the back of the bench, he tried to act casual, but nervous energy betrayed his tension. Near the entrance, a white man in a rain slicker, with a fanny pack around his waist, studied a park brochure, keeping it dry under a black umbrella.

"He's by the entrance," the man said.

Tommy's voice came back in his ear. "Keep him in sight."

The man nodded. He looked up and saw the helicopter pass by overhead. Behind him, Montgomery and a blonde-haired woman, both dressed in tourist garb, ambled toward the mouth of the lava tube, holding hands. Montgomery broke off and posed by a thicket of bird of paradise. He smiled while the woman snapped a photograph. All the while, he kept his gaze on Eddie, who sat on the bench behind his picture-taking companion.

"See anything?" Montgomery said, his voice low.

"Negative," Tommy's voice came back. "Just be patient."

"My prayer last night," Montgomery said. "'Lord, give me patience and give it to me right now.'"

The helicopter made another pass over the entrance. Tommy kept his binoculars glued to Eddie Laenui while hordes continued to flow into the tube.

"Joe, anything?"

"Negative," came back Montgomery's reply in his ear.

"Keep your eyes peeled. We're going down to the bottom and make a pass."

He dropped his binoculars and nodded at the pilot. The chopper made a big sweep then headed toward the exit.

*****

The well-lit interior of the tube slanted downward at a roughly twenty-five-degree angle. Its pathway was slick with water that leaked from the sides. Excited tourists flowed into what seemed like a cave, with rock walls and ceiling. Sound echoed as lowered voices bounced around, the acoustics downright spooky.

Deep within the bowels of the tunnel, a big hand reached for a fusebox and opened its door. With one flick of a finger, everything was suddenly plunged into pitch darkness.

*****

Eddie bolted from his seat on the bench when he heard the screams from inside the tube. The undercover cop with the brochure dropped it and reached for his gun. Montgomery abandoned his posing for pictures and looked toward the opening.

"What the hell's going on?" Tommy asked.

Montgomery peered into the tube but could barely make out the shadows as he heard excited voices and sounds of running feet. The shadows transformed into human shapes as frightened tourists fled. Others, though, excited by the prospect of adventure, continued to flow inside.

Then Montgomery saw it – one very large shadow still inside the tube, moving slowly, looming over the others. Eddie saw the shadow at the same time. He nodded almost imperceptibly, then raised his eyebrows. As Manu came clearly into view, Eddie blinked twice, rapidly.

Manu's antennae went up. Eddie was telling him something. He stopped, trying to figure out what the message was.

The cop who had dropped his brochure ambled toward the opening. Montgomery took the hand of his picture-taking partner, and they resumed their tourist couple front. Just before they entered, Montgomery nodded at the cop across the way.

Manu recognized Joe Montgomery immediately. He glanced the other way and saw another man nod at Montgomery, then take a sharp angle toward the tube. He looked back at Eddie, who blinked and wiggled his eyebrows furiously. A clump of tourists cut in front of the couple and entered. Manu turned and planted himself at the head of the clump, back into the darkened tube.

Kanaka Blues

CHAPTER TWENTY-THREE

Erin and Professor Tanaka sat at an isolated table near the library locker room, surrounded on three sides by parallel stacks of bookshelves to their north and south and the outer wall to their west. They had scattered Charlie's notes across the table, the task of recreating his investigation made nearly impossible by his cryptic handwritten scrawls.

Erin looked up from the page she had been deciphering for the past fifteen minutes. "This is hopeless. I don't think I can do it."

Tanaka smiled at her, his eyes owlish behind the thick lenses of his glasses. "Charlie would say that, for a Texan, 'can't do, won't do.'"

"Easy for him to say. He's the guy who can't write a legible sentence."

"Tell me what it is you hope to accomplish, Miss Hanna."

"I don't know for sure. My official job is to complete Charlie's research and report back to the Senate on the pros and cons of recognizing Hawaiian sovereignty. I need to tell them who the players are and what the issues are. Unofficially, I guess what I really hope is that I'll find something in here that will tell me who would have felt threatened enough to kill Charlie."

"I see nothing here that threatens anyone or any group." Tanaka gestured at the pages strewn across the table. "All this does is tell us what we already know. Who the sovereignty groups are and what their stake is in the whole affair." He ruffled through some pages. "There's background here on sovereignty leaders and the trustees at the Bureau for Native Hawaiians, but nothing alarming that I can see."

"Then we're missing something." Erin found a document that she had set aside earlier and showed it to Tanaka. On it, Charlie had written names and drawn lines with corresponding dates.

"Take this, for instance. It's a genealogical chart. There are a bunch of them here. Why would he be interested in genealogy? And here in the margin, 'Western Pacific.' What does that mean? It doesn't fit with the chart."

Tanaka looked closer, almost in a trance. He stood and circled the table, then positioned himself behind her so he could read over her shoulder. "He's tracing lineage back to 1778. That's the date – "

"When Captain Cook arrived. I know. And I know that's the magic date for defining 'native Hawaiian,' but why would he care if he's just reporting on groups and issues?"

"Because it might disenfranchise some very prominent people and sovereignty leaders. It could undermine their right to any official position in a federally recognized nation."

"I suppose. But what does 'Western Pacific' mean?"

"I have no idea."

She pushed the page aside and rubbed her eyes. She felt a headache coming on.

"Are you all right?" Tanaka asked, a touch of genuine concern in his voice. "Perhaps we should stop and have something to eat. Clear our heads a bit. I'll take you over to the International Marketplace to a great spot I know."

"Good idea."

"Let me put these in Charlie's locker first. We don't want anyone disturbing them. You can wait outside if you like. Get some fresh air."

"Thanks, Professor."

*****

Inside the Thurston Lava Tube, the crowds had gotten thick again. The panic was over and tourists thronged inside, as if eager to share the adventure in the dark. A group of teenagers entered, laughing and giggling, showing the bravado that comes from the ignorance of youth.

Manu looked toward the entrance but was unable to make out faces or even distinct shapes. He knew the police were back there, but he didn't know where or how many. He lowered himself into a half crouch. The beat of his heart quickened. He couldn't believe Eddie betrayed him. Manu had thought it odd when Eddie got a message to him that they needed to meet, but he never dreamed this would be the result.

The gaggle of giggling teenagers overtook the group he walked with, so he shifted over and joined them. The cops had seen him assume the lead of a pack of adults; they wouldn't expect the switch.

He rounded a slight bend and saw light ahead. The exit. Once he reached the outside, he would no longer be able to hide himself in a pack. He flexed the muscles in his legs, going all the way up on his toes with each step. Getting ready to run. But then he saw them at the exit: tourists who seemed to be idly hanging around but who also seemed to have an inordinate interest in eyeballing the people coming out.

Manu felt hemmed in, with a welcoming committee waiting at the end of the path and other cops dogging his footsteps from the rear. No escape in sight. He kept walking, drawing closer to daylight, his mind twisting, seeking an escape route.

Then he saw it. A slight recess in the wall to his right. Not much, noticeable only because of a deepening of the darkness. He eased his way to the side of the gaggle of teens, then stepped silently into the depression. He pressed himself flat against the wall, willing himself to become invisible, and held his breath.

After a few seconds, he saw shadows he felt sure were cops. They walked three abreast, fanned out across the breadth of the path. They moved slowly, deliberately. If he squinted, he could see their heads shift back and forth, seeking him.

He pulled back as deeply into the indentation as possible. One of the shadows drew closer, just a few yards away now, on a path that would bring it within inches. He made out a bit more about this shadow – long hair. He even smelled a faint scent of perfume. Light, airy, very feminine, but not overpowering. A clean smell.

He took a deep breath and held it.

Now she was almost directly in front of him. If he reached

out, he could touch her shoulder without fully straightening his arm. His breath was starting to slip. He needed air, yet he dared not exhale and bring in another merciful lungful.

Then she was even with him.

He blew air out slowly between his lips, hoping the slight hissing sound was drowned out by the sounds of footsteps and laughing voices echoing in the tunnel. Just as he drew in another breath, she stopped, barely past where he stood, and spoke in a whisper, addressing her comrades.

"He's not up there," she said. "As big as he is, we'd see him by now."

Manu looked toward the exit, and he had to agree with her. The exiting tourists were clearly visible, and the waiting cops ensured that he had not yet left the tunnel.

"If he's not ahead, then where is he?" he heard a male voice say.

The cop turned her shoulders, swiveled her head. And stared face-to-face with him.

Even in the dark, Manu saw her eyes widen as they met his. She opened her mouth to speak, but before she could utter a sound, he lashed out a stiff-arm. The heel of his hand slammed into her solar plexus. She inhaled sharply, fighting for breath as she staggered backward across the path, then hit the ground hard.

Manu burst out of the indentation and sprinted up the slick pathway.

The other cops heard her fall. As they rushed to her aid, she spoke calmly and firmly into her microphone. "He's coming out the top. Watch the top."

*****

When Manu emerged from the tube, all he heard was the loud blast of helicopter blades, their unmistakable *whoomp whoomp whoomp* pulsating the rain-saturated air. He raced along the concrete path for about twenty-five yards. Just then, the helicopter roared into sight, no more than fifty feet over his head. He looked up into the face of Detective Tommy Kanahele, who stared straight down at him. He also pointed a gun directly at Manu's head.

They locked eyes and something unspoken passed between them. Manu ducked his head and plunged into a crowd of tourists heading for the entrance. They were unaware of the drama that played out in front of them but were vaguely aware that there was something out of place with the tourist helicopter hovering so low. Their ignorance was short-lived as a cluster of cops emerged at full speed and raced toward them.

Manu swung his arms in a swimming motion, scattering tourists in his wake. They bounced off the pursuing police officers like bowling pins. He suddenly veered at a sharp angle, directly into thick vegetation of underbrush and yellow-orange montbretia flowers, then disappeared beneath a canopy of fern and ohia trees.

*****

After eating at a tiny Chinese restaurant that lived up to Tanaka's billing, Erin and the professor strolled along a sidewalk fronting Waikiki Beach, eating Hawaiian shave ice. Traffic barely flowed on Kalakaua Avenue beside them, thick with exhaust fumes and bumper-to-bumper cars. The beach itself was equally as thick with people, a series of beach towel islands as far as Erin could see. Beyond the white sand, surfers sat astride their boards and waited for the perfect wave. The sun was high and powerful in a cloudless sky, baking its worshippers below. Diamond Head loomed ahead, standing guard over the southern entrance to the city.

"Thanks for lunch," Erin said. She bit into a spoonful of coconut shave ice, savoring the flavor on her tongue and the coolness on her throat.

"My pleasure. It's not often I get to take tall *haole* girls out to eat." He paused, then added, "Of course, almost all *haole* girls look tall standing next to me."

She laughed. That was probably true, but her nearly six feet made her look like a giant next to him. "Are you from Hawaii?" she asked.

"Born in Tokyo, but I went to the University of Hawaii for college, then law school. I've been here ever since."

They reached a bronze statue of a surfer with his board, looking seaward.

"Who's this?" Erin asked.

"Duke Kahanamoku. He's known as the father of modern surfing. He also won many swimming medals in the Olympics back in the 1920s. After that, he went to Hollywood for a while and made a few movies, then he returned and became sheriff of Honolulu."

Tanaka pointed at the surfers on the water. "Every one of those kids dreams of being the next Duke. They hope there's something bigger for them than just working in hotels and restaurants for the rest of their lives, waiting hand and foot on people who come over here to visit and then leave their messes behind."

They watched the surfers for a few moments, silently eating their shave ice.

"Let's get back to what we were talking about at lunch," Erin said. "Do you have any feel for how Charlie was leaning on this thing?"

"Nothing concrete. He liked to think out loud, but that usually meant giving both sides of an argument. If I had to guess, though, I'd say he was opposed to federal recognition of sovereignty."

"What makes you say that?"

"He talked about how the Apology Bill and other legislation specifically denied Hawaiians the right to seek reparations for any wrongdoing that happened over a century ago. He said that recognizing sovereignty and giving land to the natives was akin to reparations. We also talked about other aspects, like the fact that the state of Hawaii's economy is driven by tourism. Take away land that might be subject to development and you restrict economic growth, and that hurts everybody. He may have been an idealist, but he was also a very practical man."

Erin digested that for a moment. Charlie had been, indeed, a practical man, but she had never known him to let practicalities override his idealism. He was also a man who believed in the law, and his thought that giving land back to native Hawaiians would be too much like reparations, which were expressly prohibited by law, made sense to her.

It was his strong belief in the law that led her back to something else she and Tanaka had discussed at lunch. "I have to admit, you lost me when you were talking about the Bureau for Native Hawaiians," she said. "Run that by me again, a little more slowly this time."

"Sure. It's a lot like the Bureau for Indian Affairs that deals with Native Americans. You familiar with that?"

"Not really, so just start from square one."

"Okay." Tanaka finished his shave ice, tossed the container in a trash can, then put on what Erin could only interpret as his "professor face" – brow furrowed, eyes squinted in concentration.

"The Bureau for Native Hawaiians was set up to generically make life better for the native peoples. Here's how it's supposed to work: When the Hawaiian monarchy was overthrown, the land that belonged to the crown and the government lands – about one point eight million acres – ended up in the hands of the leaders of the Republic of Hawaii. When the United States annexed Hawaii as a territory in 1898, those lands were ceded to the U.S. government, but when Hawaii was admitted as a state in 1959, most of them were then given to the state."

"What do you mean 'most of them'?"

"The federal government kept about four-hundred-fifty-thousand acres for its own use. The rest was given to the state, to be held in public trust. In the late seventies, the BNH was set up to make sure a portion of that land was used for the betterment of conditions of the native Hawaiians. It was to be funded by twenty percent of the revenue from the ceded lands, administered by a nine-member board of trustees. They were supposed to look out for things like economic development, research and grants, housing, education, and the like."

"How much is in the fund that BNH oversees?"

Tanaka closed his eyes, as if deep in thought. "Probably about four or five hundred million dollars, give or take. Add the actual value of the land, itself, and this is a billion dollar plus enterprise."

"Who are the trustees?"

"They're elected. Four are at-large, then one each from Oahu, Maui, the Big Island, Molokai/Lanai, and Kauai/Ni'ihau. You saw the name Joseph Keala in Charlie's notes. He's the chairman of the Bureau."

"And you have to be a native Hawaiian to vote for trustees or run for trustee, right?"

"Well, that's not so clear anymore. That used to be the law, but the U.S. Supreme Court's decision in *Rice v. Cayetano* puts that all in doubt."

"Charlie mentioned the *Rice* case in his letter. I should have read it before now, but I didn't. I guess that makes me guilty of something I get on my students about: coming to class unprepared."

"Ah, yes, the law student's nightmare. Getting called on in class when you haven't read the case."

Erin finished her shave ice and disposed of the trash, then they resumed their stroll along the sidewalk bordering the beach.

"Give me the *Rice* holding in a nutshell."

"*Rice* said that to limit voting for BNH trustees to native Hawaiians who traced their ancestry back to 1778 – the year Hawaii's isolation ended with the arrival of Captain Cook – was tantamount to using a race-based voting qualification. And a race-based voting qualification – "

"Violates the Fifteenth Amendment to the United States Constitution. 'The right of the citizens of the United States to vote shall not be denied or abridged by the United States or by any state on account of race, color, or previous condition of servitude.'"

"You know your Constitution. Even though the Fifteenth Amendment was specifically designed to protect freed slaves, and was never intended to include something like this, it says what it says."

"So, if I follow this through to its logical conclusion, if the election is unconstitutional, then the trustees who were elected have no legitimate claim to their seats. That means they lose their control over the trust funds."

"That was Charlie's argument," Tanaka said. "You also have to consider whether this is just the first step to finding that you also can't limit the assets of the trust to just native Hawaiians. Next thing you know, *haoles* will be voting for trustees, *haoles* will be getting elected as trustees and dispensing funds to other *haoles*, and the Hawaiians will be getting screwed all over again."

"So if the Hasegawa Bill doesn't get passed, native Hawaiians on the BNH come out the loser."

"You can ask Keala about that. And if it's passed, and the United States actually recognizes Hawaiian sovereignty, it's no longer a Fifteenth Amendment issue for the natives. BNH is sitting pretty. You can ask Keala about that, too."

"And you think Charlie was leaning against recognition."

"That's my interpretation of what he said, but it's just a guess."

CHAPTER TWENTY-FOUR

Manu emerged from the jungle at the edge of the huge crater. He braked hard to keep from flipping over a rail that hit him at mid-thigh. Had he failed, he would have taken a two-hundred-foot drop straight down, with nothing to break his fall but his head. He gasped for breath; his lungs felt as if they might burst. A nasty cramp stabbed at his right calf. He stepped back, extended his leg, and placed his heel on top of the rail, like a hurdler stretching before a race. He massaged the knotted muscle. His powerful fingers dug deep, trying to pry out the knifeblade of pain.

He heard the sounds of police thrashing in the trees, drawing nearer. He also heard the sounds of the helicopter. The treetops behind him rustled viciously, troubled by the chopper's whirling blade. Suddenly it broke into view above the foliage. He saw Kanahele point, then the pilot dipped the craft directly for him.

Manu took a deep breath, dropped his head, and sprinted along the perimeter of the crater. He knew exactly where he was and where he was headed as he passed a sign with an arrow pointing the same direction, announcing that the Kilauea Iki Trail lay ahead. He heard shouts as police broke into the clear behind him and followed, guided by the helicopter.

At the trailhead, Manu started on a sharp descent. His top-heavy torso threatened to pitch him head over heels, so he grabbed the handrail as he struggled for balance. Overhead, a second police helicopter joined the chase. It dipped into the crater, attempting to stay level with Manu as he descended into the depths, while the first chopper went into a hovering pattern above.

The trail became a series of switchbacks the farther down it went. The second helicopter continued to stay level with him, while the pursuers on foot reached the head of the trail and began their descent. Manu ran at a steady pace. His hand barely touched the handrail, just enough to maintain an even keel. There was no panic on his face, only determination. The deeper he got, the thicker the air became as steam flowed at high pressure from vents in the crater's surface. Sweat beaded on his forehead, rolled down his jaw and nose, then dropped. The acrid sulfur smell filled his lungs, but still he kept on, rapidly becoming obscured in steam as thick as fog on a New England seacoast.

*****

Walter Takai's face reflected his disbelief. "Once he gets to the crater floor, he can run around in that soup all he wants, but he's got nowhere to go. Why run himself into a dead end?"

"Probably because he knows where there's an infeeder tube," Tommy said.

"A what?"

"This damn mountain is honeycombed with lava tubes. If he knows where one of those is, he could end up anywhere. Hell, some of them go all the way to the ocean."

They watched as the other chopper dipped into the fog of steam and disappeared from sight.

Takai toggled his radio. "H-two, H-two, come in."

A brief moment of static was followed by the other pilot's voice. "I'm here. Just looking for a place to land to cut him off. The steam vents are too close together, though, and the visibility sucks. I can't tell where the floor is."

"There he is," Tommy said, pointing.

Manu emerged from a cloud of steam along the edge of the caldera and headed diagonally across the crater floor. Both helicopters spun and followed. The pursuers on foot also disappeared into the steam, but they had seen Manu across the way. Guided by a vague awareness of the geometry of the crater, they fought their way through the whiteness and finally broke out about a hundred yards behind their prey.

The chopper bore down on Manu, dipping low. Manu had to duck to avoid the skids below its belly.

"Don't hit him," Tommy said. "We've got prying eyes."

Takai looked out the side window, amazed at the ring of tourists encircling the perimeter of the crater, watching the chase.

"Swing around and come at him from the front," Tommy said. "Sandwich him."

Takai executed a nifty maneuver, rising, spinning, and dropping, that brought him on a path head-on into Manu. Behind Manu, the other pilot dropped to the same elevation. Now they had him. Tommy saw from the expression on Manu's face that he had run out of options. Yet he continued running, straight ahead, as if playing chicken.

"Ease closer," Tommy said.

Takai complied while his counterpart on the other side accelerated, closing the gap with Manu. Still, Manu sprinted. Tommy noticed sweat pouring down the side of his face, his bronze complexion reddening in the heat and stifling air of noxious fumes. They locked eyes.

And then he saw it – a smile. It took a second to register, but Tommy suddenly screamed, "*Pull up. Pull up.*"

Manu planted his left foot and broke ninety degrees to the right, a move that would have made any NFL receiver proud. For the first time, the pilots in both helicopters took their eyes off their prey and realized they were on course for a head-on collision. Maybe thirty feet apart and closing fast.

Takai yanked back hard on the stick, ascending almost straight up. His counterpart banked hard right, his tail rotor just clearing Takai's rising chopper. Behind him, the foot-pursuers dove to the ground and covered their heads, in anticipation of flying debris. Tommy's head pressed back against his seat as the chopper fought for elevation, then leveled off.

"Looks like you were right," Takai said. He pointed toward the crater wall, Manu's obvious goal. "There."

Through the thick steam, Tommy could barely see a lava tube in the wall.

"Cut him off before he gets there," Tommy said.

"Can't do it. We're too high."

The other chopper swung around again after banking hard right. It dipped slightly, then accelerated toward the sprinting Manu. His broad back made a perfect target through the wisps of steam. The cops on foot were up and running again, but they had no hope of catching Manu before he reached the tube. Tommy watched as Manu narrowed his distance from the opening while the chasing helicopter narrowed its distance from Manu. All bets were off; it was a horserace.

Tommy heard the rumble before he heard the explosion, but not much before. Suddenly the ground erupted upward in a thin but explosive torrent of rock, sparks, and fire. A bright orange river of fiery lava spewed forth, rocketing hundreds of feet into the air, shooting past just beyond his helicopter. Takai yanked back hard on the stick and circled to spin out of reach of the lava.

Rocks and dirt exploded skyward with the lava, then spread in a shotgun blast. Huge chunks slammed into the underside of the chasing chopper, forcing it upward. It twirled higher in large, arcing circles, driven by chunks of rock almost a quarter its size. Then it disappeared from view in an envelope of molten lava.

The foot cops put on the brakes. They tumbled into each other as they tried not to slide into the river of fire spewing skyward. In an almost precision-like move, they spun and ran in the opposite direction.

Somehow Manu kept his feet, notwithstanding the rocking earth beneath him. He stumbled toward the tube entrance. Just as he reached it, he turned to look at the chaos behind him. Then he ducked into the tube.

*****

Professor Tanaka dropped Erin off in front of the State

Capitol Building, with its flat roof above columned concrete that gave it the appearance of a jewelry box.

"I'll find a place to park, and then come meet you," he said.

As Tanaka drove away, a royal blue Mercedes pulled to the curb where he had been. It nearly clipped Erin's knee with its front bumper. She jumped out of the way, onto the sidewalk, then ascended the stairs two at a time. Once inside, she passed through the security checkpoint, its metal detector busily scanning visitors. Following directions from a security guard, she walked up the stairs to the third floor, turned left, and continued down the hallway to its end. There she faced a door that bore gold embossed letters announcing it as the home of the Bureau for Native Hawaiians.

She opened the door and stepped into an office she had seen countless times before: government-issue *faux* wood desks and bookshelves, metal filing cabinets, and harried employees. Beyond that, a short hallway branched off to other offices, presumably those of the individual trustees.

A graying Hawaiian woman sat at the front desk. She looked up from a stack of documents that held a tenuous grip on her attention.

"May I help you?" she asked.

"I'm looking for Joseph Keala."

"Do you have an appointment?"

"No, but I hoped to steal a few minutes of his time."

A door slammed in the hallway behind the woman. A nice-looking Hawaiian man with a neatly-trimmed beard that barely lined his jaw walked briskly toward them, a black leather briefcase in one hand and a folded newspaper in the other. He wore an aloha shirt, tidily tucked into an expensive-looking pair of dark blue slacks, and bolted past them without so much as a glance.

"Mr. Keala," the Hawaiian woman said, "this lady would like to speak to you."

Joseph Keala stopped, turned, and appraised Erin with a critical eye. She took him for forty years of age, the first hints of gray in his black hair giving him a distinguished look. His entire appearance seemed calculated to convey style and power simultaneously. She knew him instantly to be a consummate politician.

"Do I know you?" he asked.

"No, but I'm a friend of Professor Charles Cain. I hoped I could talk to you for a minute."

"I'm running late for a meeting, so you'll have to walk with me. We can talk on the way."

He opened the door and held it for her. She led the way out, and then he fell in beside her. The soles of his shoes clicked on the linoleum floor. He moved with an almost military precision, more of a march than a gait. Even with her long legs, Erin struggled to keep abreast of him.

"First, let me say how sorry I was to hear about Professor Cain," he said. "I didn't know him well, but he seemed like a very nice man. He was a gentleman in every sense of the word."

"Thank you."

"I'm sorry, I didn't catch your name."

"I'm Erin Hanna. I was a colleague of Professor Cain at SMU Law School."

"Let me guess – you're taking over his investigation," Keala said as they began their descent on the stairwell.

"I wouldn't say I'm taking it over. I'm just trying to find out a little more about what he was doing. I figure it might help us to know why he was killed."

"Don't you think that's better left to the police?"

"That's what people keep asking."

"Aren't you afraid that whoever killed Professor Cain might not like someone else poking around into what he was doing? Assuming, of course, that's why he was killed."

"I think we have to assume that's why he was killed," she said. She couldn't decide whether Keala asked the question as a veiled threat or whether he was just throwing it on the table for discussion. Either way, it was a legitimate question.

They reached the ground floor and headed for the front. Again, Keala opened the door and followed her out. As they descended the stairs outside, she noticed that the blue Mercedes still sat at the curb. Its driver saw them coming and got out, walked around to the curbside, and opened the back door. Obviously this was Keala's car.

"Are you working for the Senate Committee?" he asked.

"I'm mostly just doing this for myself – and for Charlie."

"So why me?"

"Your name was in his notes. You are the trustee from Oahu, right? In fact, you're the chairman of the Bureau."

"What is it you want to know from me?"

"I want to know where the Bureau for Native Hawaiians fits into all this."

"By 'this,' you mean sovereignty."

"Yes. And the Hasegawa Bill. Doesn't the Bureau stand to lose a lot, if not everything, if it fails? Under the *Rice* case, there could be a new election for BNH trustees, and it would open the door for non-Hawaiians."

"Our current members would be eligible to run in any new election. We got lucky once; maybe we'll get lucky again."

"Are you really willing to rely on luck? After all, non-Hawaiians could vote."

"What choice do I have? And if it doesn't work out, I've got a law degree to fall back on. It's not like I'd go hungry. I've worked hard for native rights, even gave up my law practice for a government salary so I could help my people. But I've also helped all Hawaiians, not just natives. I think they know that, and I think they'd vote for me again. Besides, you don't know that non-natives would be eligible or permitted to vote, do you?"

"Given what the Supreme Court said in the *Rice* case, why isn't an administrative entity that's limited to native Hawaiians unconstitutional?"

They reached the Mercedes. Keala tossed his briefcase and newspaper into the back seat, then turned to face Erin. His shoulders rose and fell in a big sigh.

"Have you actually read *Rice*?" he asked.

"I have." As of about fifteen minutes ago, on-line at the Honolulu Public Library.

"The Commerce Clause of the United States Constitution carves out exceptions for Indian tribes. Native Americans. They have their own sovereignty, their own governments, their own laws and elected officials. I see no reason why Hawaiians can't fit under that same umbrella even if the Hasegawa Bill fails."

"So you're saying that native Hawaiians are an Indian tribe?"

"Essentially," he said.

"Even though Hawaiians were never organized as a tribe and even though non-Hawaiians were permitted to be citizens of the Kingdom of Hawaii. If the monarchy didn't require native status for citizenship, why should the United States? And don't you first need federal recognition of Hawaiian sovereignty in order to fit the Native American analogy?"

"I see you know the arguments well."

"I knew a professor who once said that no matter how thin you sliced the bologna, there's still two sides to it."

Keala chuckled. "Look, all I'm saying is that history gives us the right to a little latitude here. After all, it was the United States that stole our lands in the first place. We didn't ask to be under its Constitution. Now, if you'll excuse me."

He turned to get into the car.

"Charlie didn't buy into this Indian tribe theory, did he?" Erin asked. "He was leaning against Hasegawa and against restricting BNH to native-Hawaiians, wasn't he?"

Keala stopped, one foot in, one foot out. He thought for a moment, as if unsure how to answer the question. Erin watched him carefully, looking for telltale signs, but he offered none.

"How would I know what Professor Cain thought?" he said at last.

*****

The lava tube was ample at its opening, but soon narrowed. Within a few steps, Manu found himself slowing his pace, handicapped not only by the quivering of the earth, but also by his broad shoulders brushing against outcroppings of rock on both sides. Shortly after that, he found himself ducking his head for fear of bashing it on the lower ceiling.

He had been here before and knew exactly where it came out. What made his trip along its path different this time was that he had never before been in it after an eruption. Not only did the floor quake, but the walls and ceiling shook and rumbled. A loose rock broke free and fell in front of him. The path soon dipped downward at a forty-five degree angle, as if leading to the fiery depths.

The tightening tube intersected with a much larger tube, about half the size of the Thurston Lava Tube. Manu stopped in the middle of the intersection for a moment to get his bearings. What should have been an instinctual turn became jumbled in his mind as the world around him fell apart. The new tube angled downward from left to right. He started to turn right just as he heard a low rumbling, hissing sound behind him. He looked back into the darkness of the small tube and saw an orange glow emanating from its depths. Looking left, upward in the larger tube, he saw the same orange glow approaching. He turned downhill and sprinted.

After scarcely a quarter of a mile, the tube narrowed until it was barely large enough to contain Manu, who ran in a hunched, stumbling gait. At least the earth's trembling had ceased, but he still lurched from side to side. His head occasionally scraped the roof, and blood mingled with sweat. It coated his cheeks and brow, filled his eyes, and blinded him. He wiped the mixture from his eyes and peered ahead into the eery orange-glow lighting that illuminated no more than five feet of visibility at a stretch.

He felt as if his chest would burst. He had run out of healthy oxygen and now breathed gas fumes and cinders. The lining of his nose ached, dry as a desert. His head pounded and swirled. The muscles in his legs threatened to quit with every step and leave him in a quivering heap for his fiery pursuer.

He had long since given up hope of escape. He could stay ahead of the lava for now, but for how much longer? Had he really come in here just to die alone and never be discovered, his molten body mixing with the magma and pouring into the ocean? What of his people then? What good would he have accomplished? Maybe the smart thing, the easy thing, was to quit. To stop running, turn around, and face his fate like a warrior. But each time he hesitated in his step, each time he eased his pace, new resolve kicked in. No, warriors didn't surrender; warriors fought.

Then he saw something ahead that gave him hope. Light. Not the orange tint of fire, but white light, like a spotlight from overhead. He knew immediately its source: a vent to the outside world.

He doubled his resolve, gutted it up, and kicked into overdrive.

The tube widened a bit, and the ceiling lifted, sloping upward. He saw a narrow opening in the rock, maybe eight or ten feet high. He took a large last step, then pushed off hard with his right leg, calling on every reserve of strength his muscles had to offer. He sprang into the air. His fingers hit the edge of the vent and scrabbled for purchase. He squeezed down hard, suspended like a basketball player clinging to the rim of the basket. Below him, the flow rushed past. It hissed and bubbled under his feet, venting gases upward that sought escape through the opening.

He hung there for a few seconds, gathering his wits about him. He inched his fingers forward, one knuckle at a time, seeking a better grip, looking for a full-fledged handhold. But his fingers cramped and his forearms seized up, unable to complete their mission. His right hand slipped loose, then his left.

Suddenly he jerked to a stop, still suspended above the flow. He looked up, astonished to see a hand grasp his wrist. A bronze hand, a powerful hand. Holding him.

He raised his line of sight –

And found himself staring into the face of the great warrior Kamehameha.

The king's hand pulled Manu upward, until Manu regained his grasp on the edge of the vent. As his savior pulled, Manu helped himself, now with a good grip, then out up to his elbows. He closed his eyes, gritted his teeth, swung his leg up and, with a final grunt of effort, lifted himself out of the tube onto solid earth.

He stood and opened his eyes. But Kamehameha was nowhere to be seen.

He swayed unsteadily, his head spinning and almost breezy. Had he been imagining things? Was it all a figment of his imagination, simply his own resolve rescuing him? He had spoken to Kamehameha once before, hadn't he? Or had he?

He became vaguely aware of a familiar sound encroaching on

his consciousness. He listened for a moment. As he breathed deeply the fresh air, with its life-giving oxygen, his senses returned. He looked uphill, where he saw a swarm of police officers covering the mountainside, heads down, guided by a hovering chopper. He immediately dropped on his belly and pressed himself as flat as he could. Hugging the ground, confident he was unseen, he began to crawl away.

Then he saw it, on his outstretched arm as he grabbed rock and pulled himself forward: the imprint of a hand around his wrist.

CHAPTER TWENTY-FIVE

Erin and Professor Tanaka stood with a throng of parade-watchers as hundreds of Hawaiians, dressed in colorful native garb, marched toward Iolani Palace. The stone façade of the Palace, built in American Florentine style with Corinthian columns, stood to their backs as the marchers advanced down South King Street. Off to the right side, a gilded bronze statue of King Kamehameha loomed, right arm raised in a gesture of aloha and left hand clutching a spear as a symbol of peace. Dozens of red and white plumeria leis, nearly twenty feet long, were draped around his neck.

A cheer went up from the crowd as the parade reached the statue. Many of the marchers carried Hawaiian flags and banners that proclaimed such slogans as SOVEREIGNTY NOW, HAWAII FOR HAWAIIANS, and KINGDOM OF HAWAII. The banner that led the parade bore the words UA MAU KE EA O KA AINA I KA PONO, and underneath, its English translation: THE LIFE OF THE LAND IS PRESERVED IN RIGHTEOUSNESS. Tommy and his partner had told Erin that she would see that sooner or later.

A dais with a podium and microphone had been set up on the left in front of the palace, and the leaders of the parade started making their way there. At the forefront walked a petite Hawaiian woman, no more than five feet tall with a slight build, but with flowing black hair that emerged from a blood-red crown of plumeria blossoms. Even from where they stood, Erin could see fire in her eyes and fierceness in her countenance.

"That her?" she asked.

"Yep. Heilani Gaskill, leader of the Sovereign Kingdom of Hawaii. Number one competition to Manu Pokui and his Nation of the Islands. That's why I think you should talk to her. You need to see the whole picture. And she's one badass mama."

"I can see that by looking at her. What's her story?"

"It would be easy to write her off as a nut, but she's got some intellectual heft behind her."

"What does that mean?"

Tanaka laughed and stroked his beard between his thumb and index finger. "It means she's smart. She's got her PhD in philosophy from Stanford, and she teaches Hawaiian Studies at the University."

"Is she a native Hawaiian?"

"Born in Hilo. Her mother was a native, but her father was a *haole* from New Mexico. He came over as a visiting professor at the university's Hilo branch, and that's where they met."

"You said her mother 'was' a native and her father 'was' a *haole*. Are they both dead?"

"Her mother died of leukemia. She couldn't get the treatments she needed because of insurance disputes. Heilani blames *haole* insurance companies for her death and the government for protecting them. After her mother died, her father couldn't deal with it. He pretty much drank himself to death. He ended up dying in a one-car drunk driving accident. That happened while she was at Stanford. When she got back to Hawaii, she went on the warpath and has been there ever since."

The program was about to start, so Erin and Tanaka eased their way forward. A chant started with the marchers that crescendoed as it made its way to the parade-watchers. The rally leaders, including Heilani Gaskill, stood on the dais and led the chant. Although she couldn't understand a single word, Erin did recognize the emotion in the voices speaking them: rage.

*****

After the rally, while Professor Tanaka spoke to friends, Erin approached Heilani Gaskill with more than a little trepidation. Although Erin stood almost a foot taller, this tiny woman intimidated her. She had watched, mesmerized, as Heilani stood at the microphone and rallied the troops with what could only be described as hate speech.

"We are not Americans; we are Hawaiians," she had said, her voice rising to a furious crescendo. Her features hardened, the venom spewing from her mouth. "We were here long before the first American ever set foot on our shores. And we will be here long after the last one is gone."

The crowd went nuts, cheering each word, hanging on each nuance. Erin was amazed at the anger in Heilani's voice and at the visceral reaction she elicited from the crowd.

"It is only by force of arms that the United States stole our land. It was only on the backs of our people that the United States built its resort paradise. Never forget what they have done to us. Rise up. Rise up, Hawaiian people, and drive the Americans from our land."

The crowd had erupted at those closing words. Erin found herself more than a little nervous. She even sensed Tanaka edging a few steps away, as if he didn't want to get caught in the crossfire.

Now, as Erin neared Heilani, the message still echoed in her ears. The woman stood with a small group of supporters, her stern visage equally as fierce in an unguarded moment as when she was in the limelight.

"Ms. Gaskill?" Erin said.

Heilani turned from her group, eyes lasering right through Erin.

"Ms. Gaskill, my name is Erin Hanna. I'm a friend of Charlie Cain's."

Heilani's face softened. Something that might have passed for a smile tugged at her lips.

"He was a friend to everybody," Heilani said. "Even to a rabble-rousing siren like me."

At least she has some self-awareness, Erin thought. "May I talk to you for a few minutes?"

Heilani turned to her supporters. "I'll be back soon."

She fell in at Erin's side as they strolled the grassy grounds of Iolani Palace. "So you're a friend of Charlie's," she said. "How well did you know him?"

"He was my mentor when I first started teaching at the law school. And then he became like a second father to me. More like my only father since I lost mine when I was young."

"I know what it means to lose your father," Heilani said wistfully. "And now you've lost two fathers."

"That's what it feels like."

"Charlie was very kind to me when he didn't have to be. I certainly didn't give him any reason for kindness, but I think he thought I was all bark and no bite."

"Your bark scares the hell out of me."

Heilani laughed, the sound like a rippling stream. More of a giggle, like that of a small child.

"Leadership is part passion, part showmanship," Heilani said. "It's all about lighting fires under people."

"As long as those fires aren't on fuses."

Their wanderings stopped once more in the front of the Palace. The ground around it was soft and thick with a snowfall of multicolored blossoms from the hundreds of flower leis earlier.

"Did you know that this is the only royal palace anywhere in the United States?"

Erin nodded but kept silent. Since it seemed to be one of Heilani's talking points, she decided it was better to listen.

"That's because only Hawaii was once a royal kingdom," Heilani said. "Although I suppose you Texans think you still are."

A brief flash of a smile told Erin not to read anything into the barb. Maybe somewhere deep inside this smurf a sense of humor was struggling to get out.

"When the United States decided it wanted her, it sent troops ashore to ensure that the so-called revolution led by the American sugar interests succeeded. It's an old story. When the U.S. wants something, it simply takes it. Troops came here to arrest our queen

– Queen Lili'uokalani – and this palace became her prison."

She looked up at the distant statue. "I suspect Kamehameha wept that day."

Heilani led Erin up the front steps to the palace's lanai. They stood for a moment and gazed out at the throng that had, minutes before, been chanting and cheering for a call to revolution against the United States. Erin didn't miss the irony in standing in a place where a previous revolution had displaced that throng's rightful heritage.

The flame returned to Heilani's eyes, the steel to her voice. "What can I do for you, Miss Hanna?"

"Right now you can just help me understand all the sides to this thing."

"You mean our right to sovereignty over our land."

"I mean whatever the hell got Charlie killed." Erin's own voice took on some bite. She didn't want to get into a pissing contest with Heilani, but she wasn't going to be her whipping-girl, either.

Heilani turned away and leaned on the rail. She looked at the remnants of the parade and rally. A few people still mingled, carrying their signs, as if they had nowhere else to go. And maybe they didn't.

"You want to know where I stand on the Hasegawa Bill," Heilani said.

"Are you for it or against it?"

Heilani remained silent for a beat, as if thinking. Erin knew it was an act. This woman already had her mind made up, and there was nothing for her to think about.

Then, in a voice dripping with sarcasm, Heilani said, "Let's see, if we accept the bill, that means we acknowledge that the United States has authority over us. It means we give up our claims to full sovereignty and accept whatever the United States has to offer – a façade of sovereignty and a puppet government answerable to the Department of the Interior and the State of Hawaii."

She paused for maximum dramatic effect. "You're a smart woman, Ms. Hanna. You tell me: Am I for it or against it?"

"I understand Mr. Keala is backing the bill."

"Wouldn't you be if it was the only way you could keep your hands in the money?"

"Sounds like you don't think much of him."

"He and his fellow trustees are more interested in staying in power than in helping the people they were put into office to help."

She walked to the end of the lanai and started down the steps. "What I want, what my people want, is to turn this palace back over to the people to whom it belongs, not just keep it as a curiosity or a museum. Keala doesn't care about that."

Erin rushed to catch up to her. "What about Manu Pokui?"

Heilani hesitated on a step and looked at Erin. "I understand the police think he killed Charlie Cain."

"I think they may be wrong."

She continued walking. "Imagine that, the police wrong about something."

"So what do you think about Manu Pokui?" Erin repeated.

"I think he's well-meaning but misguided. And now I understand he's escaped from the police, which makes him a fugitive from the very authority he proclaims doesn't exist. I think there's some irony in that, don't you?"

"This bill seems like your best hope of getting the ceded lands back and maybe keeping them out of the hands of resort developers."

"Not ceded; stolen."

"Either way, it could get them back for you. Why make it so hard on yourselves?"

They stopped at the foot of the steps, where Professor Tanaka waited for Erin. Heilani looked up at Erin. There was no doubting the fervor in her voice or the belief behind her next words.

"We stand on principle, Ms. Hanna, not convenience. Nobody said it was going to be easy. Your Charlie Cain understood that, and that's probably what got him killed."

CHAPTER TWENTY-SIX

With Professor Tanaka's help, Erin boxed up Charlie's papers and flew them to Hilo with her. She picked up a rental car and drove straight to the hotel. Harry the desk clerk was studying a newspaper from his perch behind the front desk with the pages spread open before him. He didn't hear her approach and looked up with a start at the sound of her voice.

"I hear you've got rooms for rent," she said.

He smiled broadly. "Aloha, Miss Erin. I didn't know you'd be back so soon."

"Got a little unfinished business."

He became somber. "Did you get Mister Charlie laid to rest?"

"I did. Thank you for sending the flowers, by the way. He would have loved that lei of plumeria."

Harry got off of his stool, turned, and grabbed a key. "We got a room all ready for you."

"If you didn't know I was coming, how do you have a room ready for me?

"'Cause we always got a room ready for you."

He smiled again, a big cuddly bear. He shuffled around the desk, flip-flops flapping on his heels. Erin felt a sense of comfort at the sound.

"Let me get your bags." He picked up her suitcase as he called to someone through the open office door. "Esther, cover the desk, yeah?"

"I've got a box of documents in my car. Can you get those for me, too?"

"We get you into your room first, then I'll go get them."

As they walked, Harry chattered about Manu Pokui's escape, the weather – rainy, what else? – and the inane goings-on of some of the tourist groups staying at the hotel. It was as if he were afraid of silence and chose, instead, to keep the air filled with his voice. Erin had seen this before, and she knew it for what it was. When she was a girl, they called it puppy love; when she grew older, it was called a crush. Whatever you called it as an adult, it was obvious that he was smitten with her.

Harry led her to the same room she had occupied before and set her suitcase on one of the double beds. She gave him her car keys and described the car. He returned a few minutes later carrying two cardboard boxes. They had been dead weight for Erin but seemed dwarfed in Harry's arms in front of his massive chest. He stacked them on the floor in a corner then returned her car keys.

"Anything else I can do for you, Miss Erin?" he asked.

"I think I'm gonna freshen up a bit, then grab a bite to eat. Will you keep me company?"

He struggled to keep the smile off for fear it would split his face. "It would be my pleasure."

*****

An elderly Hawaiian woman opened the oven and checked on the baking sweetbread. Already the aroma filled the tiny two-bedroom house in the Big Island town of Laupahoehoe where she lived with Alex, her husband of fifty-nine years, and their nine-year-old grandson, David. She heard the television in the other room where Alex watched some silly sitcom with David, who had finished his homework earlier. She longed for a better life for her grandson than living in a wooden house that was rotting in the ocean air and spending day after day fishing like Alex had done almost every day of his life. He would be up and out on the water again tomorrow, retirement just a word they read about in fantasies. But life for David would be different. College, maybe even law school. That would make her and Alex proud, if they lived long enough to see it.

She pushed a strand of gray hair from her face as she bent to check on her bread. The same arthritis that twisted her fingers and swelled her ankles made even that simple task a chore. At eighty-one years of age, it was anybody's guess when the day would come that she stooped over and never straightened again.

Using hot pads, she pulled the pans of sweetbread from the oven and set them on the counter. She was just about to dump the first loaf onto a cutting board when she heard the squeal of the screen door behind her, followed by the creak of a foot on protesting floorboards. She spun around quickly; her mouth dropped open in shock.

CHAPTER TWENTY-SEVEN

Erin hugged the coastline as she drove north out of Hilo on Highway 19. Although it was only a quarter 'til nine, the sun was already high above the Pacific on her right, which shimmered in its light. On her left, the island sloped upward, lush greenery marking this side of Mauna Kea. She saw the snow-capped peak of the mountain emerging from a mass of gray clouds.

She slowed as she entered the city limits of Laupahoehoe, a town on the Hamakua Coast that experienced great tragedy during the tsunami of 1946. Its school had been built on low-lying Laupahoehoe Point, near the seawall. When the tsunami struck that April Fool's Monday morning, it took with it cottages that housed the teachers, the school building, the playing field's grandstand, and twenty-five lives, including sixteen schoolchildren and five of their teachers. The school was rebuilt on the upslope of Mauna Kea, leaving Laupahoehoe Point a greenbelt and memorial to the lost lives.

As Erin turned uphill, her car almost immediately lurched to a thirty-degree angle, climbing fast. Following directions Harry had given her to the address she had found in Charlie's notes, she turned off again, this time on a gravel road that pierced a very poor neighborhood of crumbling frame homes and shacks. In contrast to the structures, the yards bloomed with the greens, reds, and yellows of Hawaii's rich plant life that flourished naturally without help from human hands.

There were no house numbers at the far end of the first block, so she pulled to the side of the road in front of a house where a group of children of both sexes, ranging in ages from four or five to about ten, played. Erin rolled down her passenger window and called out.

"Hi, there."

The kids stopped their playing and stared at her. They probably didn't get many *haoles* in their neighborhood. Even Erin was beginning to think of herself as one of those white interlopers.

"Can y'all help me?" she asked.

A few of the younger kids giggled, a tittering sound that swept the group. A tall girl, who seemed to be the oldest, approached the car. She was slender with black hair to her waist. Her features were clear and fresh. Erin knew she would be a beauty when she grew up. The other kids followed a few feet behind, acknowledging her as their leader.

"Don't y'all have school this morning?"

More giggles, louder this time. Erin looked at the kids behind the lead girl, unsure what she was missing.

"They not laughing at you," the girl said. "They laughing at how you talk."

"You mean because I said 'y'all'?"

The giggles came again.

"Yeah, I guess that does sound kind of funny, doesn't it?" Erin said. She affected an exaggerated drawl, much to their delight.

"Well, I'm from Texas, y'all, and that's how we talk there. How are y'all doing?"

Each "y'all" drew another fit of giggles, crescendoing to a full-blown laugh. Even the tall girl joined in.

"Y'all, y'all, y'all," Erin said, then joined in their laughter.

The tall girl leaned over and rested her elbows on the open window. "We don't go to school 'til nine-thirty," she said.

"Must be nice. What's your name?"

"Elika."

Erin stuck out her hand. "Elika, my name is Erin. I'm pleased to meet you."

Elika shook hands uncertainly. "Are you lost?"

"I'm afraid I might be. I'm looking for Kela Pokui's house, but I don't see any house numbers."

"Tutu Kela lives in the last house, at the end of the block."

"I've heard that word 'tutu' before? What does it mean?"

"It means grandmother."

"Is she your grandmother?"

"No, but she's like a grandmother to all us *keiki*. It's like one big *ohana* here."

Erin made a face, lost in a foreign language.

"*Keiki* means children; *ohana* means family," Elika said.

"And y'all think I talk funny."

The giggles returned. Erin stuck her tongue out at a small boy who stood just behind Elika, clinging to her waist. He erupted in a fit of laughter that brought the house down.

After thanking Elika, Erin drove on, watching in her rearview mirror as the kids went back to their games. At the end of the block, she stopped in front of a tidy house with a screened-in porch. As she got out, she took no notice of a black, older-model Buick Century that drove past and turned onto a dirt path at the end of the gravel road. She grabbed a small briefcase from the rear seat, then got out and went to the front porch. There was no doorbell so she knocked as loudly as she could on the frame of the ragged screen. The wood sounded hollow beneath her knuckles. As she waited, she admired the beautiful flowers in the tiny yard, everything from bird of paradise to a hedge of red, orange, and white hibiscus that swept around the front of the house to the side.

She heard a faint voice from inside. "I'm coming."

After a few seconds, the door opened, and Erin found herself looking down at a wizened old woman wearing a green apron over a red muumuu.

"Aloha," Erin said. "Mrs. Pokui?"

The woman regarded Erin suspiciously, her brow furrowed. Probably not too many *haoles* arrived at her doorstep. At least not for any good purpose.

"May I help you?" the woman asked.

"Are you Kela Pokui?"

"Why you want to know?"

"My name is Erin Hanna. I'm a friend of Charlie Cain's."

And just like they had all across the islands, those again seemed to be the magic words. All suspicion was swept away as Kela opened the screen door.

"*E como mai,*" she said. "Please come in, Miss Erin. Mister Charlie talked about you. He said you and he were *ohana.*"

Family. The word filled Erin's heart with warmth as she

stepped across the threshold into a world gone by. Though small, the house was spotless, lovingly filled with knick-knacks and Hawaiian mementoes. The floor was polished hardwood, testifying to long hours spent by someone, probably Kela, on her knees, sanding and buffing. The furniture was rattan, the walls tatami, or straw. The only evidence of modernity was a small television in one corner, sitting on a low table with stick legs. In the other corner was a bookcase, one shelf of which was filled with photographs, mostly black-and-white, of the Hawaii of yesteryear.

"Would you like some coffee?" Kela asked. "I just made it fresh. It's Kona."

"I'd like that. Just sugar, please."

After Kela went into the kitchen, Erin walked to the bookcase and studied the photographs. Pictures of workers in the cane fields, fishing boats in Hilo Bay, schoolchildren at a frame schoolhouse on a point near the ocean. Above the doorway to the structure were the words Laupahoehoe School. Erin wondered if any of these children were among those swept out to sea by the tsunami of 1946.

She picked up a framed photograph of a young boy. In color, it looked like a school picture.

"That's my grandson, David," Kela said as she re-entered. "He's nine now. He lives with Alex and me."

She extended a cup and saucer to Erin, who set the photo down and took the coffee.

"Thank you, Mrs. Pokui."

"You call me Tutu."

Tutu sat in a koa wood rocker. She gestured at the rattan

couch, its cushions, with patterns of anthuriums in red against a green background, threadbare at best. Erin sat, and then took a sip of the dark black coffee. She inhaled its aroma, drawn back to better days, sitting on the lanai at the Kona Coast Cottages, feeling a faint sea breeze brush her face, cup of Kona coffee in one hand, Chris's hand in her other.

"Thank you, Tutu." She put the cup and saucer down on the coffee table. "Is David Manu's son?" she asked.

"You know Manu?"

"I met him once. We didn't talk long."

"After his mama died, Manu brought him here. He said he couldn't take care of him alone. I think, also, that he reminded Manu too much of Abbie."

"How did she die?"

Tutu Kela looked as if she had retreated somewhere deep into her mind, considering the question, the answer, or merely searching a bad memory. Erin watched closely as she closed her eyes and leaned her head back. A shadow crossed her countenance. It looked to Erin as if she shivered, then she shook her head and opened her eyes.

"I was sorry to hear about Mister Charlie," she said. "He was very kind to me."

"He was kind to everyone."

"Yes, he was a man of aloha. The world is a poorer place without him, but heaven is richer for him."

Erin felt a pang inside. She fought it down, as she had trained herself to do in public.

"Thank you," she said. "That's a nice thing to say."

"He came here to see me."

"He did?"

"Yes. At first, it was to talk about his work, but later it was just to talk. He and Alex – my husband – got along well. And he would always bring something for David. A sweet, a toy, something. He spread aloha."

Tutu Kela looked at Erin for a moment, her eyes boring right into Erin's. Then she smiled, warmth radiating from it.

"He used to sit right there on the couch, on the other end from where you're sitting. He would drink my Kona coffee and talk story. He talked about you."

"Me?"

"Yes. He always talked about you. You made his face light up."

Erin looked at the other end of the couch. She imagined Charlie sitting there, smiling and laughing with Tutu Kela and Alex, sipping Kona coffee. Then his image faded and Erin once again stared at an empty couch.

"When he talked about his work, what did he talk about?" Erin asked.

"He wanted to talk to Manu, not to Alex and me, but Manu wouldn't talk to him. He showed me some papers."

The words piqued Erin's interest. "What kind of papers?"

"Just some old papers. Some history papers. I never quite understood what they meant."

"Can you describe them for me?"

"Oh, I can do better than that. I can show them to you. I'll be right back."

Tutu Kela struggled from the rocker and shuffled into the rear of the house.

*****

The black Buick Century had turned around on the dirt path at the end of the gravel road and now sat under a royal Poinciana tree, facing Kela Pokui's house. A heavyset Hawaiian man with close-cropped black hair and a mustache sat behind the wheel. He wore wraparound sunglasses and a straw Panama hat, his eyes lasered to the front door of the house.

The "William Tell Overture" drew his attention to his cell phone on the passenger seat beside him. He answered.

"Yeah?"

"She still there?"

"Yeah. She went inside a few minutes ago."

"She got anything with her?"

"She was carrying a briefcase."

A pause. "I'm sending help. Don't do anything until they get there."

"Wait a minute." The Hawaiian man watched a Jeep crest the hill then stop behind Erin Hanna's car. "Not now," he said. "We got company."

"Get out of there."

The Hawaiian man hung up and cranked the engine.

CHAPTER TWENTY-EIGHT

Tutu Kela returned with a sheaf of papers that she handed to Erin. "Maybe you can make something of these."

Erin set them on the coffee table next to her coffee, then leaned over and studied the top page, which appeared to be a genealogical chart. Some of the names were filled in, but others remained blank. At the top was one name that stood out: MANU POKUI.

"Did he say what he was doing with this?" Erin asked.

"No, but he asked a lot of questions about our *ohana*. Who begat who and who begat who and who begat who. He wrote down a lot of notes, then went away and came back later with this. He told me he was still looking to fill in the blanks."

Erin glanced at the end of the couch and again imagined Charlie, glasses perched on the end of his nose, furiously scribbling notes on a legal pad. Then he faded from her imagination.

Tutu Kela took a bundle of letters from the pocket in her apron and handed it to Erin. The envelopes were yellowed with age, the paper fragile. A pink string tied in a knot held them together.

"He was also interested in these," Tutu said. "He said they

might help him with the begatting. But he never took them with him. He said they belonged here with me and that he would come here to study them. He was supposed to come one day, but he never did. That's when I found out he had been killed."

She sniffed back a tear. Erin felt the need to comfort her, even though it was she who had suffered the real loss, not Kela Pokui.

A knock at the front door startled Erin. She jumped, nearly dropping the bundle on her coffee cup.

"Excuse me," Tutu said. She shuffled to the door and opened it.

Erin saw grim-faced detectives Kanahele and Montgomery standing on the porch. Surely they weren't looking for her. They didn't even know she was back in the islands.

Despite their grim faces, Tutu Kela seemed delighted to see them. "Tommy Kanahele, you get in this house."

His face involuntarily transformed into a smile. Whatever his message, Erin could see he was truly glad to see Tutu. He leaned down and hugged her, squeezing hard.

"Aloha, Tutu," he said. "We need to talk to you about Manu."

She stepped back, grabbed his hand, and pulled him inside. "Come in, come in. You, too, Joey."

Erin saw a look of shock wash over Montgomery's face when he saw her but thought she saw a pleased look on Tommy's.

"Ms. Hanna, you do get around," Tommy said.

Tutu looked back and forth between them. "Oh, you know each other?"

"We've met, yes," Erin said.

"Sit, Tommy, Joey – sit," Tutu said.

Tutu went back to her rocker. Tommy took a seat at the far end of the couch but Montgomery remained standing. Erin saw their faces go back to the look of grimness they wore on their arrival.

Tutu saw it as well. "You said you wanted to talk about Manu, Tommy. What is it?"

"Tutu, can I get a glass of water?" Montgomery asked.

"Sure, Joey. I get it for you."

"No, that's okay. I got it."

He went into the kitchen, but Erin knew it wasn't for water. It was to snoop around.

"I think I'll get a refill on my coffee," Erin said, standing. "Can I get you some, Detective Kanahele?"

"Oh, I'm being a poor host," Tutu said. She struggled to the edge of her rocker.

"You stay there, Tutu," Erin said. "Talk to the detective and I'll help myself."

Erin went into the kitchen without bothering to take Tommy's order. Sure enough, she found Montgomery checking things out in the kitchen. He had opened the back door and was squatting at the threshold, scrutinizing the floor.

"Find any water down there, Detective?"

He looked back over his shoulder. She detected a smile on his face. "Hand in the cookie jar, huh?"

"You're a cop. You can't help it."

He motioned Erin over. As she got closer, he pointed at a large footprint on the threshold, outlined in what looked like soot, and small particles of black crystal.

"That tells me he's still alive," Montgomery said, "and he was here last night."

"I assume you're talking about Manu. And I didn't think there was any question about his being alive."

"That's right, you weren't there."

"Weren't where?"

"I assume you heard about the eruption at Kilauea yesterday."

"Everybody did. It was all there was on the radio and TV."

"We had Manu cornered in the crater. When that thing blew, it nearly took out one of our choppers. The last time anyone saw Manu, he ran into a tube with a river of lava hot on his heels. I had pretty much written him off as dead until I saw this."

It took a moment for the words to sink in. "So you're up here to make the notification to family."

"Not really. Tommy didn't buy it. He kept saying if anyone could get out of there alive, it's Manu. And that he would come here. Looks like he was right."

"So now what?"

"Now we ask her where he is."

Montgomery went back into the living room with Erin close behind. Tommy looked up as they entered. "I was just telling Tutu we needed to talk to her about Manu," Tommy said. "She said she hasn't talked to him in days."

Montgomery looked at Tutu. "That right?"

"That's right," she said.

"Looks to me like he might have been here last night,"

Montgomery said. "A little charred, maybe, but alive and well."

Tutu wouldn't have made a good poker player. Her face was tantamount to an admission that Montgomery was right. The other face that was of interest to Erin was Tommy's. It reflected relief – huge relief.

"Where is Alex?" Tommy asked.

"He and David go fishing."

"David's not in school today? Is this some kind of special holiday or something?"

"I think it's some kind of teacher holiday. I don't know."

But Erin knew that this was no holiday. The kids up the street were going to school today. She could see that Tommy knew that, too.

Tommy nodded at Montgomery, who left through the front door. Erin watched him through the window as he went to the Jeep and spoke into the radio microphone.

"Tutu, I really need to find Manu," Tommy said. "I don't want him to get hurt."

"He won't get hurt if you leave him alone," she said. "He's a good boy. You know that."

"I can't leave him alone, Tutu."

Tutu looked at Erin, then back at Tommy. "You still think he killed Mister Charlie? Is that it? Tommy, you've known Manu your whole life. You know he wouldn't kill anyone."

"Do I?"

There was some unspoken message passing between them, but Erin couldn't figure out what it was.

"I don't want to see Manu get hurt, Tutu," Tommy said. "Not

like last time. If you see him, you tell him to come talk to me." He kissed her on the cheek. "Okay? You tell him."

Then he nodded at Erin. "Miss Hanna."

After Tommy left, Tutu looked at Erin. Her lip quivered as she said, "Tommy's a good boy, too. He won't hurt Manu. Will he?"

"Of course not." Erin looked out the window and saw Tommy and Montgomery getting into their Jeep. "Listen, Tutu, I've got to go. But I'd like to come back and talk to you again. Would that be all right?"

"Oh, yes, I'd like that very much."

Erin grabbed the sheaf of papers and the bundle of letters. "May I take these with me? I promise to bring them back."

"Sure, sure. You take them."

Erin put them in her briefcase and headed for the door. Tutu Kela hugged her, as if she'd known her her whole life.

"You come back soon. We'll talk story, and I'll tell you about the begatting."

"I will."

Then Erin hustled out the door, but the Jeep was already gone.

CHAPTER TWENTY-NINE

David Pokui stood on the dock and waited while his grandfather checked out the motor on the ancient wooden boat. It took several tries but the engine finally roared to life. David untied the rope from a cleat at the end of the dock, then clambered over the side and into the hull. He hitched up his sagging shorts, then crossed his arms over his frail chest. David had curly black hair that neatly framed his oval face, but his most prominent feature was his eyes, so brown they were almost black. As a baby, he could bore a stare right through his parents, mesmerizing them. Even today, it was almost impossible for people to look away from those eyes.

"Do you need me to do anything else, Grandfather?" David asked.

Alex Pokui smiled. His hair gray, his brown skin leathered, and his frame bent and wiry, he looked like a man who had spent many a hard year in the sun, yet he never seemed to lose his smile. He pointed at the lunch sack and thermos on the deck by the cabin. "Take that and go inside. The water looks a little rough out there."

"Okay."

David picked up the sack and thermos and disappeared through the small doorway. Alex scanned the horizon both ways along the coast as he shifted the boat into gear, then pulled the throttle all the way back.

The boat cabin was barely large enough to classify as a cabin. Its ceiling was too low even for the stooped Alex to stand upright, which explained why Manu sat on the floor, his back to the front wall. He smiled when his son handed him the food.

"*Mahalo*," Manu said. He opened the sack and took out a slab of bread, held it to his nose, and inhaled deeply. "Ahh, your grandmother's sweetbread is the best on the island."

"She made it last night."

"I know. I smelled it a mile away."

He tore off a hunk and devoured it. David leaned against the far wall and watched his father eat. Manu opened the thermos and poured a cup of Kona coffee into the lid. As he screwed the cork back on, he realized David was staring at him.

"What is it, *keiki*?"

"Tutu says you talk to Kamehameha," David said. "She says he tells you what to do."

"That's *pupule, keiki*. Kamehameha's been dead for a long time. Over a hundred years. You know that."

"She said she hears you. At night."

Manu swallowed the bread and took a sip of coffee. He squinted at his son. "Maybe Tutu's just dreaming. She's an old woman, and old women dream."

David nodded, but said nothing.

"What do you think?" Manu asked.

David looked at him for a long moment. The only sounds were the chug of the boat's engine and the waves sloshing against the hull.

Finally David nodded again. "I think maybe you do. I think maybe you talk to him."

*****

Alex steered the boat northwest along the Hamakua Coast, toward Waipio. It was his normal fishing route and shouldn't have aroused anyone's suspicion. Yet when he looked back, he saw a powerboat bearing down on him. He grabbed his binoculars from a hook and looked through them.

He stamped his foot twice, then shifted the throttle to neutral and cut the engine. There was no point in running. His boat barely made a ripple in the water, much less had a chance to outrun a police boat with its twin engines. He sat on the captain's bench and waited.

"What is it, Papa?" Manu's muffled voice reached him from the interior of the cabin.

"Police."

Manu stepped into the cabin doorway. Alex handed him the binoculars and pointed at the approaching boat. Manu held them to his eyes and confirmed what his father said. He handed them back and slipped around to the other side of the cabin, putting it between him and the police. He grabbed an anchor tied to a sturdy hemp rope and lowered it overboard. As the sounds of the police boat drew nearer, he grasped the side of the boat and lifted himself over. He slid into the water while holding onto the anchor rope. He heard the police boat ease into idle and knew it had reached his father's vessel. He sank deeper and leaned his head back until only his eyes and nose remained above water.

*****

Two policemen, one *haole* and one Hawaiian, stood in the bow of their boat as it eased up next to Alex's. A third officer remained at the helm. The Hawaiian cop, a big man with a bodybuilder's physique, tossed a foam rubber fender over the side to buffer the two boats as they bumped against each other. David stood by his grandfather's side as they waited for the interrogation that was sure to come.

"Aloha, grandfather," the Hawaiian said.

"Aloha." There was no friendliness in Alex's tone, just suspicion. For once, his smile was gone.

"How's fishing?"

"We not there yet. You know that. We headed up Waipio."

The Hawaiian nodded. "I hear the fishing's real good up there. You catch plenty, yeah?"

"You not here to talk about the fishing," Alex said. He put his fists on his hips, arms akimbo. "Why you bothering me?"

"You want to get straight to it, eh? Okay, you know Manu Pokui?"

"You know he's my boy. That's why you here."

"You know where he is, grandfather?"

"Haven't seen him since he was arrested," Alex said. "Now you know what I know, so you go now."

The *haole* policeman threw his leg over the side of Alex's

boat and came aboard. David shrank back behind his grandfather, eyes wide.

"You mind if I look around?" the *haole* asked.

"I mind, but it don't stop you."

The *haole* stuck his head inside the cabin. Nothing of interest in there but an open thermos and a lunch sack. A half-eaten slab of sweetbread sat on top of the flattened sack, a half-drunk thermos lid of coffee beside it.

"Early lunch or late breakfast?" the cop asked.

"What you talking about?" Alex replied.

"I think you know."

"I got hungry," David said, stepping back in front of Alex.

"You drink coffee, too, *keiki*?"

"The coffee's mine," Alex said.

The cop nodded, but he clearly wasn't buying it. "If we take that sweetbread to the lab, whose DNA we gonna find on it?"

"Don't be surprised if you find DNA that matches Manu," Alex said. "David is his son."

"You know about DNA, grandfather?"

"I watch TV. I saw the O.J. trial."

The cop snooped around the deck, then brushed past Alex and David to the far side of the cabin. His eyes fell on the rope over the side.

"What have we got here?"

"Anchor," Alex said.

"Why you anchored here? I thought you said you were going up to Waipio to fish."

"I anchored when I saw you coming."

The cop grabbed the rope and gave it a tug. Then he started pulling it up, hand over hand.

*****

Manu pressed up against the bottom of the boat, his hand tightly gripping the anchor rope. He heard the muffled sounds of footsteps above, then he felt a tug on the rope. He let go and watched it move upward. He'd been under for about a minute now, almost the limit of his ability to hold his breath. He dug deep, called on the same reserves that had energized him in the lava tube. He wasn't about to survive that only to fall into police hands now. And he wasn't about to see his father arrested for harboring a fugitive.

The anchor broke the surface of the water at the boat's bow. The cop pulled it completely out of the ocean to make sure nothing else was attached. Sure enough, just an anchor.

He let go and it splashed back into the water.

He crossed the deck of Alex's boat quickly. "He's not here," he said to his partner as he climbed back aboard the police craft.

"You see your son," the Hawaiian cop said, "you tell him to turn himself in."

"Manu quit listening to me a long time ago," Alex said. "He makes his own mind."

The police boat's engine whined in reverse, then roared into gear as the driver held a sweeping arc and headed back toward the south.

*****

Everything appeared fuzzy to Manu. Not just the usual fuzziness of being underwater, but the fuzziness of being out of oxygen. His head spun, his chest burned, his arms and legs tingled. He faintly heard the splash of the anchor and saw a blur as it sank past. He stretched for the rope that danced just out of his reach. He missed, tried again, but his depth perception was totally out of whack. He heard the buzz in the water as the police boat moved away. He knew it was safe now, he was free to surface and breathe again, but his body betrayed him as he tried to carry out that simple task.

He pushed away from the bottom of the boat and felt for the rope. Then a hand dipped underwater, grabbed his wrist, and pulled him out from under the boat. Manu looked up. Rays of sunlight streamed into the clear blue water and, in the midst of those rays, he saw a man above the surface. He blinked, shook his head, and looked again. A faint, ephemeral Kamehameha seemed to float over him, his hand gripping Manu's. Guiding him to the rope.

At last, Manu's fingers touched hemp. He grasped it and pulled, working his way upward, hand over hand. When he broke the surface, he felt as if his lungs would burst. He gasped as he surged out of the water, mouth open, and sucked in a huge lungful of oxygen. The pressure in his chest eased and the lightheadedness departed. He settled back into the water, kicking with his feet to stay afloat. He looked around but, as when he had emerged from the lava tube, no Kamehameha.

He held his hand in front of his face and studied his wrist. No handprint this time.

Then he felt hands grabbing him again, pulling at his arms and shoulders. He clutched the rope with both hands and tugged upward as Alex and David helped him into the boat. He sprawled on the deck, still struggling to breathe normally. As the sweet oxygen refreshed his bloodstream and cleared his head, he looked into the concerned face of his son.

He smiled. "Aloha, David."

"I saw him, Papa," David said. "I saw him."

CHAPTER THIRTY

Erin sat on the lanai of her room at the Seasurf, overlooking Reed's Bay, and beyond, Hilo Bay. A strong ocean breeze mussed her hair and rattled the papers she studied – the ones Tutu Kela had given her. On the floor beside her sat a stack of Hawaiian history books that detailed the advent of *haoles*, the decimation of the native Hawaiian population, and ultimately the overthrow of the Hawaiian monarchy. She also had a file of Charlie's notes on the plastic-top table in front of her chair.

She found Tutu Kela's letters to be of particular interest, giving her a picture into Hawaii's past. The people she read about lived simple lives as recently as half a century earlier, without the modern conveniences now available to even the poorest residents of the islands. Their days were spent working the land and fishing the sea, doing whatever was necessary to put food on their tables, and their evenings were spent gathering with family to sing and "talk story." They were poor, but they were happy. Maybe going back to the past wasn't such a bad idea.

A knock on the door pulled her away from her reading. She tucked the letters under a book to keep them from blowing away and went inside to answer it. She stood by the door, hand on the chain latch, and asked, "Who is it?"

A man's voice answered. "Detective Kanahele sent me."

Not a voice she recognized, but she knew the man who had sent him. She unlatched the chain and turned the deadbolt.

The door suddenly slammed into her face, driving her backward across the room. Just as in Charlie's apartment in Honolulu, the corner of the bed caught her at the bend of her knees. She sprawled backward on the floor. Blood trickled from a vertical crease on her forehead.

The large Hawaiian man who had sat behind the wheel of a Buick near Tutu Kela's house stepped inside, closed the door, and locked it. He held a .38 in his hand, pointed at Erin's head as she lay motionless on the floor. He scanned the room, his attention diverted by the open sliding door to the lanai and the papers on the table. He headed that way, holding the gun at his side.

Erin stirred, looked up, and saw the gunman looking at Charlie's notes. She shook her head to chase the cobwebs. Her skull ached and blood trickled into her eyes. Moving slowly, so as not to attract his peripheral vision, she wiped the blood away, then rolled over and got to her knees.

He must have seen the movement because he turned his head to look at her. Their eyes met as she slowly rose to her feet.

Then she surprised the hell out of him.

She charged.

CHAPTER THIRTY-ONE

"Here ya go," Harry said as he handed a room key to a new guest. The man took it, grabbed his luggage, and left. Harry turned to put the registration slip in a file box as another man approached.

"Howzit, bruddah," Harry said, his back still turned.

"Howzit," Tommy Kanahele replied.

Harry spun around and looked into the face of the man he had come to think of as his rival for the attention of Miss Erin, even though he knew she had no interest in him and never would.

"You checking in?" Harry asked.

Tommy smiled. "You know I'm not."

"Just wanted to make sure. Gotta keep law enforcement happy."

"I'm here to see Miss Hanna. You got her room number?"

"Can't give out room numbers, bruddah. You know that." Harry smiled a non-smile, his lips pulled back to expose clenched teeth.

Tommy smiled back, perhaps realizing for the first time that his interest in Erin was no longer a secret. "That's okay, brah, you can call her and tell her I'm here."

"She expecting you?"

"No, but – "

A gunshot shattered the standoff. Both men jumped at the unmistakable sound.

Tommy pulled his gun. "Where's her room?" Tommy asked.

"Dis way." Harry scrambled around the counter faster than he'd ever moved before, leaving Tommy in his wake.

*****

Erin saw the shot coming before the man pulled the trigger. Instinctively she dove to the floor, and the bullet whizzed by above her head. She scrambled back to her feet and continued her charge. The man froze for an instant, disbelief plastered on his face that she was attacking him, not once but twice.

Erin thrust her arms out, fists clenched. They slammed into his solar plexus just as he ripped off another wild shot. He stumbled backward, gasping for breath. He kicked over the stack of history texts, and his ankle hit the plastic-top table. The table flipped onto its side, scattering the papers that had rested on it and tangling his feet. He waved his arms in a failed effort to maintain his balance. His gun hand banged against the top of the railing. His fingers involuntarily released their grip; the .38 hit the floor and skittered to the edge of the lanai.

The gunman plummeted to the ground on his back. He rolled quickly, scrambled forward, and reached for the gun. Erin picked up the overturned table and slammed it on the back of his head. He sprawled facedown on the lanai floor. She held the table by one leg and swung it again, arcing over her head then downward. He grunted and went still.

Erin scanned the lanai for the papers. She saw that one of Tutu's letters had wrapped itself around the railing. Both ends flapped in the breeze, threatening to sail off toward the Bay. She dropped the table and grabbed it just in time.

Suddenly, hands yanked her from behind. She hadn't heard him regain his feet, but now he hooked his arm under her chin and clamped it on her throat. She lifted her left leg, placed the bottom of her foot against the railing, and pushed off, propelling both of them backwards into the room. His heels caught on the track for the sliding glass door, and he pitched onto his back, pulling Erin down on top, his arm still hooked around her neck.

She squirmed, struggling to break free from his grasp. Oxygen was quickly becoming in short supply, and she felt her consciousness slipping away. She wedged her thumb and index finger under the thumb of his clenched fist and yanked back. It was a tug-of-war for a moment. She wormed her hand in further and levered his thumb until it almost touched his wrist.

He yelled in her ear and let go of her neck. She sat up, gasping for breath while he fought his way out from under her. On his hands and knees, he scampered across the floor and onto the lanai. In one smooth move, he snatched up the gun and rolled onto his back. He sat up and aimed at Erin.

There was too much distance between them for another frontal assault. Her senses were still too dulled to allow her any quick movements. She closed her eyes in resignation.

The deadbolt suddenly ripped out the jamb and tore the night chain from its weld, the door splintering inward. Tommy stepped inside, gun leveled.

The gunman raised his aim from Erin to Tommy.

Tommy squeezed the trigger a split second before the gunman. The bullet drove into the man's chest and knocked him against the railing. His hand flew higher as he fired. His bullet slammed into the door frame above Tommy's head. Wood splinters showered into his hair.

Erin screamed and fell flat on her back.

Tommy dropped to one knee and ripped off two more shots. Both hit dead center in his target's torso. The man slumped to his side; the gun fell from his hand.

Erin struggled to her feet and raced to Tommy. He held her to his chest with one arm, his gun hand still leveled toward the dead man.

Harry stepped into the room behind them. "Damn."

CHAPTER THIRTY-TWO

Under Detective Joe Montgomery's supervision, a couple of cops zipped up the dead man in a body bag. Tommy watched as the body was carted out.

"It's a good shoot, Tommy," Montgomery said.

"Yeah."

Montgomery looked at Erin. She sat on the end of the bed while a paramedic painted the gash on her forehead with an antibiotic, then taped on a gauze bandage. Harry hovered nearby, hopping from foot to foot and keeping up a constant nervous patter with her.

"She all right?" Montgomery asked.

"She's tough," Tommy said.

"What was the guy after?"

"She thinks maybe the professor's papers. If he'd simply been after her, he'd have come in blasting or just grabbed her and run. But she said he seemed awfully interested in the papers."

"Why don't you follow up with her? I'll write it up back at the station."

"Thanks."

"And like I said, don't worry; it's a good shoot."

Tommy approached Erin, who was getting the finishing

medical touches.

"I don't think you'll need stitches," the paramedic said, "but I'd keep an eye on it. Change that bandage every few hours and keep the cut clean."

"Thank you."

He packed up his kit, nodded at Tommy, and left.

Erin looked at Tommy then at Harry. "Thanks, Harry. I'll be all right. I just need to talk to the detective for a bit."

"You sure? Anything I can get you?"

She took his hand and patted it. "Really, I'm fine."

Without looking at Tommy, he shuffled off.

Tommy sat on the bed beside her. "So," he said.

"So."

"You keep leading with your face."

"Yeah, I hate when that happens."

He touched the bandage gingerly. She winced.

"That hurt?" he asked, jerking his hand back.

"No." She laughed. "Just wanted to see what you'd do."

He smiled. "You always this funny when people try to kill you?"

"It's a gift." She felt the bandage herself before folding her hands in her lap. "What are you doing here, anyway?"

He looked down, as if afraid to make eye contact. "Well, we really didn't get a chance to talk this morning. I was glad to see you back in Hawaii."

"Unfinished business."

"Yeah. I was, uh, just wondering what you were doing at Tutu Kela's."

"I knew that Charlie had talked to her, so I wanted to find out what about."

"And you never saw this guy before?"

"No."

"How do you suppose he knew you were here?"

"I don't know. I talked to some people on Oahu, but they didn't know where I was staying. For all they knew, I was staying in Honolulu."

"Who'd you talk to?"

"Joseph Keala, at the BNH. Heilani Gaskill with the Sovereign Kingdom. And Professor Tanaka at the University of Hawaii. You know them?"

"I know who Keala is. And Gaskill. Doesn't make sense either of them would have anything to do with this. Who's Tanaka?"

"He was working with Charlie."

"Could somebody have followed you from Tutu's?"

"I suppose. I didn't notice."

She paused, studying him carefully. He met her eyes then looked away. If she didn't know better, she'd think he was embarrassed.

"You could have called if all you really wanted to know was why I was at Tutu Kela's," she said. "Why are you really here?"

"I just live on the north side of Hilo, so it's no big deal."

"Which doesn't answer my question."

He looked over his shoulder as the last of the cops left. Funny how he didn't seem so brave now that bullets weren't flying and no one was trying to kill him.

"I was just wondering if I . . . maybe I could take you to dinner."

She put on the most serious face she could muster. "You mean a professional consultation? You know, cop to lawyer, to talk about the case?"

She could see that he wasn't sure how to respond. "I thought maybe that we could just, you know, talk," he said. "Like regular people."

She broke into a smile, and his tension eased instantly. "Well, we're nothing if not regular people, Detective. I'd love to go to dinner with you."

CHAPTER THIRTY-THREE

The new room Harry moved Erin to didn't have blood on the floor or splinters in the doorjamb, but her hands still trembled as she paced anxiously around the bed. Had Tommy not arrived when he did, she likely wouldn't have been moving at all. That thought, alone, was enough to keep her pacing. The man who attacked her carried no I.D., nor was there any unaccounted-for vehicle in the parking lot. Tommy figured he had parked elsewhere and walked to the hotel, but no one remembered seeing him enter.

After the body was removed, Erin went for a walk along Banyan Drive, ending up at Hilo Bay. She sat on a bench and gazed at Mauna Kea across the water, with its snow-and-observatory-capped summit. She tried to empty her mind of any thoughts, just clear her head and relax.

Whoever killed Charlie obviously knew that she had taken up his mantle, and that made her a threat as well. But threat to whom and of what? Charlie must have discovered something, but she had no idea what or where. Unless the killer was simply trying to head her off *before* she found whatever it was, there was one other possibility behind the attack. She had earlier assumed that there must have been some incriminating document in Charlie's possession that was stolen. The events of earlier today, though, convinced her there was still something floating around out there that they didn't have their hands on. The question, though, was whether *she* did. Based on what she had seen thus far, she concluded that either she had it and simply didn't understand its significance, or she hadn't found it yet.

To get her mind off the attack, she switched tracks to her upcoming dinner with Tommy. It wasn't a date, exactly, just dinner, but she still felt as if she were about to betray Chris. Though he had been gone for two years, she had not dated since the accident. Maybe now it was time. Her social life couldn't, and shouldn't, remain forever frozen in limbo. And maybe Tommy was the guy to start with. They lived on different sides of the ocean, thousands of miles apart, so there was not much chance of a long-term relationship developing. Without that possibility – or threat – it would be more like dipping her toe in than jumping off the board into the deep end.

A couple rollerblading behind her shook her from her reverie. She glanced at her watch, shocked to see that it was nearly seven-thirty. She had been sitting there for over an hour, oblivious to the passage of time. Now she would likely be late to meet Tommy, or worse, she might run into him in the lobby before she had a chance to get ready. She bolted to her feet and quickly retraced her steps to the hotel. A light mist had started, she couldn't remember when, and was accelerating into actual rainfall. Not only would she have to hurry to dress, she'd have to deal with her hair.

She entered the lobby at precisely 7:29. No Tommy yet, but Harry looked up as she hurried across the floor.

"When he gets here, tell him I'm just about ready," she told him.

"You don't look about ready." His tone was friendly, but she read the expression on his face clearly enough.

Back in her room, she opened her suitcase and looked for something to wear. She had packed the usual wardrobe she wore in Texas, which consisted mostly of jeans and T-shirts. There was nothing suitable for dining with a gentleman caller, as her mother would have called him. She selected her best pair of jeans, which meant partly faded instead of completely faded, and a green aloha shirt she had bought on her honeymoon. She splashed water on her face, brushed her teeth, and held a blow dryer to her hair for a few minutes.

She looked at herself in the mirror. That was the best she could do under the circumstances. She grabbed her purse and left the room.

*****

Tommy stood at the counter talking to Harry when she came down the stairs. He wore a blue golf shirt, sharply-creased khaki slacks, and deck shoes, and looked very preppy. Erin thought he would fit in well at SMU dressed that way.

Tommy saw Harry look over his shoulder, and he turned to face her. "Hey, how you feeling?"

"Not bad for a girl who got shot at today."

"I'd say not bad, period," Harry said. Almost immediately, he blushed, noticeable by a darkening of his bronze skin.

"I thought we'd walk to one of the hotels on Banyan,"

Tommy said. "That sound okay?"

"Is it still raining?"

"It stopped about the time I got here."

"Then let's go."

She waved good-bye to Harry, then fell in beside Tommy as they exited the hotel. They walked silently at first, taking in the salt air. Out on Hilo Bay, a cruise ship steamed in. A handful of other people walked Banyan Drive ahead of them.

"So how are you really doing?" he asked, breaking the silence.

She thought about the question, toyed with a snappy comeback, then settled for honesty. "Let's just say I'm glad you got there when you did."

"Yeah. You and me, both."

He nodded and took her arm in his hand. Nothing dramatic, just took hold, as if simply to let her know he was close by and would take care of her. To Erin's surprise, she found the gesture comforting. She also felt a spark of electricity at his touch. She drifted toward him.

*****

At the Hilo Hawaiian Hotel, they went downstairs to the hotel's restaurant, where they were shown to a two-top table next to a wall of plate glass windows looking toward the Bay. Tommy held Erin's chair as she sat. As he walked to his side of the table, Erin saw the reason for the sharp creases in his khaki slacks: The price tag and size label were still sewn to the waistband, just noticeable above and below his thin belt. Apparently he worried about what to wear, too, and had gone shopping after the shooting.

Erin unfolded her linen napkin and placed it in her lap, looking down to hide her smile. Then she looked up. "This is nice. I feel underdressed."

"There's no such thing as underdressed in Hawaii."

"Are you overdressed?"

He smiled. "Probably. But, hey, it's not often I get to hit the tourist spots with a beautiful *haole* girl."

Unlike the darkening of Harry's bronze skin, Tommy's blush was bright red, noticeable even in the faint light of the restaurant.

"Thank you," Erin said.

A native waitress appeared, gave them menus, and took their drink orders. After she left, Erin scanned her menu. "What do you suggest?"

"Never eaten here before, but if they got *ahi*, I'd say go for it. That's yellowfin tuna."

Erin had fallen in love with *ahi* on her honeymoon so she decided to go with his recommendation. By the time their meals arrived, a Hawaiian trio was set up to entertain. Three heavyset Polynesian men, who dwarfed their ukuleles, sang in falsetto voices that one would never associate with men of their girth. The mood was light, and the dark cloud that had descended on Erin lifted, if only for the evening.

"You said you lived in Hilo, but I thought you were stationed on the Kona Coast," Erin said. "Isn't that a bit of a commute?"

"Joe and I both live in Hilo and carpool together. The tourist development over there has pretty well priced us out of the Kona housing market. Especially on a cop's salary."

"Why did you become a cop?" Erin asked.

"When I was a kid, I always wanted to be McGarrett of Five-O. Then I wanted to be Magnum. Still do, but I figured I'd starve as a P.I. At least being a cop pays a salary. Not much, but it puts a roof over my head and food in my fridge."

"Do you like it?"

"Most of the time. I feel like I do some good for people. That matters to me."

"That's the same reason I became a lawyer. I wanted to do good for people."

"But you don't practice anymore, right? I mean, you teach now."

"I still practice some. I run the *pro bono* clinic at the law school, and I take on cases I'm passionate about. When I was in active practice, I mostly represented folks who couldn't afford to pay much, so I was never going to get rich. I also took a lot of court appointments."

"Criminal appointments?"

"Yeah, some. Sorry."

He laughed. "Don't apologize. Everybody's entitled to representation. That's what makes the system work."

"But it doesn't always work."

"You got that right."

After the dishes were cleared, and coffee and apple pie a'la mode brought, Erin said, "This morning, at Tutu Kela's, what did you mean when you said 'not like last time'?"

"Refresh my memory."

"You told her you didn't want to see Manu get hurt. 'Not like last time,' is what you said."

"It's a long story." He sipped his coffee, and a look that could only be described as anguish crossed his face. "It's a sad story."

"Well, isn't that what you Hawaiians like to do? Talk story?"

He held his cup in both hands and swirled it around. The surface of the brown liquid rippled in concentric circles. He appeared to be debating whether to tell her. Erin waited, aware that it must be painful for him.

He took another sip, then cleared his throat.

"It happened about four years ago. Manu's wife, Abbie, used to work as a housekeeper at one of the smaller hotels over in Kona. This particular hotel is where a bunch of *haole* construction workers from the mainland stayed while they worked on a big resort up at Waikoloa. For some reason, the construction company didn't think the Hawaiian workers were good enough, so it imported its own crews.

"Anyway . . ."

Kanaka Blues

CHAPTER THIRTY-FOUR

Abbie Pokui, a petite twenty-six-year-old, stopped her cart outside the door to a room in the interior hallway of an aging hotel. She had been working there since she was fourteen just to help her family of seven make ends meet. Now wife to Manu Pokui and mother to five-year-old David, the pittance she was paid barely bought groceries and clothes for them. The years of labor had already taken their toll and, though still a very pretty woman, she could easily have passed for her late thirties. She worked hard and was proud of the work she did, determined to clean every room, every day, the best they had ever been cleaned.

She knocked on the door of Room 301 and called, "Housekeeping."

No one answered.

She used her master key to open the door and stepped inside. Almost immediately she stopped short at the mess and the odor. The covers on the bed were pulled completely loose and left tangled in a wad in the center of the mattress. The sheets hung off the far side, between the bed and the wall. Dirty clothes were strewn across the floor, and the trash can overflowed with fast food sacks and beer cans. Mud was tracked across the threadbare carpet, and food remnants on the nightstand attracted a convention of insects.

She opened the bathroom door and discovered the source of the odor. In addition to piles of wet towels on the floor, the toilet had backed up, brown murky water to the brim, filled with human waste. The guest had apparently tried to clean up some of the mess on the floor with towels, then had given up and left the lion's share of the work to the maid.

She sighed and closed the door. She'd save that for last.

She turned on the radio on the nightstand, found a station that played Hawaiian music, then set about her clean-up. She started by picking up the sheets on the far side of the bed, but they wouldn't give when she tugged on them. She figured they must be tangled around the bed rail or the leg. She leaned over the edge of the bed to see. With her back turned, she didn't see the beer-bellied *haole* construction worker who entered.

A big man, well over six feet tall and topping the scales at 276 pounds, Sam Marcus was the guest in Room 301. He had forgotten his wallet in the nightstand and came back during his lunch break to retrieve it. He could have gotten one of his co-workers to spring for lunch, but it was the condom package in the bill section that brought him back. Every Friday evening after work, he and the boys gathered at one of the local watering holes, and you never knew what you might find there.

The first thing he saw when he came into the room was the skirt riding high on the woman bending over his bed. The back of her thigh was exposed up to the elastic leg band on white cotton panties. Slender, dark legs, and a tight rear end awoke Sam's groin with a surge. He watched, waiting for her to turn around. But she didn't. She struggled with something on the far side of the bed, tugging hard. The motion bounced the skirt higher.

He quietly closed the door and turned the deadbolt. He unzipped his jeans and pulled out his erect penis. Then he tiptoed over until he stood right behind her.

She tugged at the sheet once more, and it tore free. Off balance, she staggered backwards, right into the construction worker. She bounced off him and turned around.

He slammed a meaty fist into her face. A tooth broke free from the left side of her mouth and flew across the room. It hit the wall with a clicking sound and fell to the carpet. She stumbled backward, banged into the bed, and tumbled to the floor. Sam was on her in an instant. He forced her onto her back, his right fist flying while his left hand jerked her skirt up.

She screamed, even though the left side of her face was numb from the pounding. She pushed at his hand on her skirt. With her other arm, she tried to shield her face, but his battering ram fist pounded her arm until it snapped. Tears flowed freely from her eyes. She couldn't believe what was happening.

One last smash to her cheek and things went fuzzy. She fought to clear her head, only vaguely aware of hearing the "Hawaiian Wedding Song" playing in the background while someone ripped her underwear from her body. A hand pressed against her throat. Her vision blurred even more. Her chest heaved, a vise tightening as she struggled for air.

Then he was inside her, thrusting. All she could feel was pain, as if she were being ripped apart from the inside out. She twisted her hips, trying to buck him off, but her resistance seemed to excite him. He increased the tempo and depth of his thrusting. His face contorted in an animal-like grimace. His thrusting became more violent, deeper, harder. Driving into her very soul.

She gave up her resistance as her brain starved for oxygen. The pain was unbearable. All she could do was try to block it out, to pretend she was somewhere else and that this wasn't really happening. Her body went totally limp, but he continued thrusting.

With an anguished moan, his face turned blood red, veins stood out in his neck like pipelines. Then he stopped, spent.

She felt him relax. Even though he was more than twice her size, adrenaline fueled her strength. Coupled with surprise, it was enough to allow her to push the man off. She scrambled to her feet and bolted for the door.

He moved quickly for a big man, jumping up and grabbing her by the hair. He yanked her head back. She opened her mouth to scream, but he clamped a hand over it and put his other arm around her neck. She dug into his flesh with her fingernails, clawing. Blood oozed across her fingers.

He wrestled her away from the door, back toward the bed. His feet entangled in a pile of clothes on the floor. He stumbled, still maintaining his grip, then fell, twisting forward. Abbie broke his fall as his full weight drove her into the floor. Her head hit at an awkward angle to the right.

The snap of vertebra echoed in the small room, audible over the Hawaiian music playing on the radio. Then she lay still.

Sam got to his feet and stared down at the body of the petite maid. He zipped up his jeans, grabbed his wallet from the nightstand, and fled, leaving Abbie in his wake, eyes closed, mouth half-open in an aborted cry for help.

CHAPTER THIRTY-FIVE

Erin sat in silence, horrified. There was something in Tommy's voice that told her the story was more personal to him than he was letting on. Maybe Abbie was an old girlfriend or something, but the pain on Tommy's face was real and the anguish in his voice audible, even after four years.

"I don't know how he thought he could go off and leave a dead body on his hotel room floor and not raise red flags all across the island," Tommy said. "First he said he hadn't been there all day, a story his construction worker buddies backed up. But we got a DNA match on the semen, so he finally admitted to the sex. He said it was consensual, though, which we knew was a lie. He said she was alive and cleaning up his room when he left. The construction company hired some big gun defense lawyer out of San Francisco to defend him. He got the charges dismissed on a technicality – something to do with a defective search warrant and a right to privacy in his hotel room – "

"Even though it was a crime scene?"

"If it was rape, yeah, it was a crime scene. But if you believed the guy that it was consensual, it was an accident scene. I'm just telling you what happened. On the one hand, you had a *haole* defendant, a *haole* lawyer, a *haole* resort developer pouring millions into the economy and who needed to avoid scandal, and a *haole* judge. On the other hand, you had a Hawaiian maid. The script gets predictable after that. So the guy walks out of court and, the next day, he's back on the job, like nothing ever happened."

"What did Manu do?"

"Well, a couple of days later, Manu sees the guy at a bar drinking with his buddies. Not just coincidence, though. We think Manu'd been stalking him . . ."

*****

A group of *haole* construction workers gathered at the bar in a dark club. Cheesy Hawaiian décor pegged the place as a tourist trap, with fake palm trees in the corner, pictures of hula girls and surfers on the walls, and a longboard over the mirror behind the bartender. The lighting was poor, a smoky haze compounding the darkness.

Manu entered and stood at the doorway for a moment to allow his vision to adjust. He spotted Sam Marcus at the bar in the midst of his buddies, holding court. Manu walked to a table nearby and sat, his attention glued to the man in faded jeans and green tank top. A few of the other workers spotted Manu, but Sam didn't. He kept his mouth running, unaware of the danger that lurked behind him.

"I'm telling you," Sam said, "them little hula girls'll flat put out. They give it away like candy on Halloween. 'Specially that one over at the hotel."

Manu exploded from his chair. Utilizing a perfect football

form tackle, he rammed his head between Sam's shoulder blades and smashed him against the bar. Sam's face slapped forward into wood as the edge of the bar crammed into his belly. Manu grabbed the back of Sam's hair and banged his head against the bar. Then again. And again. And again.

Glass shattered as beer mugs flew in all directions. Slivers dug into Sam's cheek and forehead, gouging his nose, which broke with the first impact. Blood trickled from the cuts and oozed from his nostrils.

Sam's buddies flinched at the initial assault, dumbfounded that Manu had attacked a man who was surrounded by allies. As Manu repeatedly battered their co-worker's face into the bar, they finally sprang into action. Two of them grabbed Manu from behind and two more grabbed his arms, but even the four of them couldn't overpower the enraged Hawaiian.

A grizzled construction veteran about half Manu's size pulled a switchblade from his pocket. With the press of a thumb, he flicked open the blade and jammed it into Manu's back. But it was as if Manu didn't feel it. He just kept banging, banging, banging.

The man withdrew the blade and plunged it in again. Lower this time, kidney level. He pushed with all his strength, driving the blade as deep as it would go. He twisted the knife, turning the blade within Manu's back.

Manu let out a roar, like a wounded animal. His feet slid out from under him and his hands released their grip. Then the floor rushed up to meet him.

*****

"So not only did the guy walk for killing his wife, but Manu ended up doing a year himself for assault and battery, and spent a month of it in the prison hospital."

Erin pushed her dessert plate aside, the pie half-eaten, her appetite history. "That's why he gave his son to Tutu Kela, isn't it? Because he was in prison."

Tommy nodded. He grabbed Erin's pie and took a bite. "That's one of the times when I hated being a cop. I'm the one who arrested Manu. Problem was, he didn't have the money for a *haole* lawyer from San Francisco."

"It probably wouldn't have mattered. The way you described it, he attacked the man from behind in front of a bar full of witnesses. The *reason* he did it is why he only got one year instead of more. But regardless of the reason, he broke the law."

"I don't get how you lawyers can do that."

"Do what?"

"Put guilty people like Sam Marcus back on the streets – on a technicality, no less – while someone like Manu does time."

"We're just doing our jobs."

"Defending the guilty?"

"Defending the Constitution."

"I guess that's why Manu says it's not his Constitution. Maybe he's got a point." Tommy pushed the empty plate back toward Erin. "Anyway, that's the story."

He motioned for more coffee, and they sat silently as the waitress poured. Erin contemplated what she had heard. It put Manu in a whole new light for her and answered some questions about his motivation. It also proved he could be violent under the right circumstances. Had those circumstances been met with Charlie? She wasn't sure anymore.

After the waitress left, Erin said, "Tutu said you grew up with Manu."

"I've known him my whole life. I was best man at his wedding." He paused, then added, "Abbie was my little sister."

CHAPTER THIRTY-SIX

Harry looked up from his perch behind the front desk as Erin and Tommy entered the lobby. Erin smiled at him, and he smiled back, but there was no joy in his smile. He refused to make eye contact with Tommy, who nodded in his direction.

Tommy escorted her up the stairs and down the walkway until they reached her room. She fished her key from her pocket.

"You gonna be okay here tonight?" Tommy asked.

"I'll be fine. Harry said he'd watch out for me."

Tommy stifled a laugh. "What's he gonna do? Sit on 'em if they come back?"

She cut him a look that stabbed his heart. "He's been good to me."

"I know, I know. I'm sorry." He shuffled his feet, as if trying to figure out how to redeem himself for his brief flash of jealousy. "You got my home number? You know, if you need me?"

He took a business card from his shirt pocket and wrote his number on the back. "Call me anytime, day or night," he said as he gave it to her. "I'm ten minutes from here."

She put it in her pocket. They stood facing each other for a moment, saying nothing. She sensed that he desperately wanted to kiss her, and she wanted him to. At least she thought she did. But she wasn't sure, so she waited for him to make the first move.

"Okay, well, you got my number if you need me," he said.

Another awkward moment passed. It was clear he wasn't going to kiss her – too afraid. Time for Erin to end it.

"Thanks for dinner, Detective. And thanks for talking with me."

"You're welcome. And I keep telling you, it's Tommy."

She reached for the door lock but the point of her key missed. Inexplicably, she dropped it. The click of plastic and metal on the hard concrete seemed to reverberate throughout the hotel. Her heart pounded.

She squatted to pick up the key, barely aware that Tommy had already bent over to reach for it. She suddenly became aware of his scent, aftershave mixed with perspiration, a tangy yet sweet aroma. Both their hands grabbed the key at the same time. She looked into his eyes, which peered deep into hers. Together they rose to a standing position. With his hand over hers, he guided the key into the lock and they both turned. The door clicked open. She pushed it in and stepped into the doorway.

This was the moment. Did she invite him in or not?

A vision of Chris flashed across her consciousness. Then a vision of Charlie, lying cold and lifeless on a coroner's slab. The answer was clear: Not yet. Not while she still had things to do, things that required her full and professional attention.

He must have read it in her eyes because he released her hand and stepped back. "I'll see you later, yeah?" he said.

"Okay."

Then he turned and walked away. Erin watched him as he

moved down the walkway toward the steps.

She went inside and closed the door as –

He turned and looked back.

*****

Tommy emerged from the stairwell and entered the lobby. Harry looked up, making eye contact this time. He seemed relieved that Tommy had been gone just a few minutes.

"You make damn sure nothing happens to her," Tommy said.

"You, too, bruddah."

Tommy stopped walking, eyes locked with Harry's.

Then he nodded slightly and walked out.

Kanaka Blues

CHAPTER THIRTY-SEVEN

The Na Pali Coast on Kauai's north shore is one of the most dramatic sights in the Hawaiian Islands. Mountains tower over the ocean, broken up into parallel curtains that stretch 1,600 feet high. From a distance, it appears as if a giant hand had clawed at the green mountains, leaving deep valleys between the curtains that reached successively farther into the blue waters crashing at their base.

Accessible only by foot or boat, the region once harbored ancient Hawaiian civilizations and sufferers of Hansen's Disease, or leprosy. The lepers fled there to avoid the government boats that unceremoniously dropped them into the waters off the Kalaupapa peninsula on the north side of the island of Molokai – the infamous leper colony to which Father Damien de Veuster devoted his last years before succumbing to the disease, himself.

The moon had already reached its zenith, spotlighting the dark waters slamming onto a pristine white beach that formed the webbing between two fingers of Na Pali's curtains. A towering man in a chief's headdress and a warrior's raiment marched along the beach, as if patrolling against an approach by sea. Nearby, another large man slept on the sand, uncovered, watched over by a thousand stars.

233

Kamehameha the Great approached the sleeping Manu. He watched silently for a moment as the big man's chest heaved with each breath.

"*Malama pono, Manu,*" he said. "Preserve that which is good."

*****

In Hilo, another very large man kept a vigil. Harry patrolled the passageway outside Erin's room, each step a lumbering shuffle. Inside the room he guarded, a soft breeze rustled the pages that Erin had salvaged from the attack. Although it was well past midnight, she had scattered them across the bedspread. On her knees beside the bed, the sliding glass door open behind her, she studied them, making notes, her excitement growing with each discovery. What caught her attention now was Charlie's genealogical chart and Tutu Kela's letters.

She went to the dresser and picked up Tommy's card. Without a thought as to the time, she grabbed the phone and dialed the number on the back. Tommy answered after three rings.

"Detective," she said. "I need to talk to you. Can you come over here?"

There was a brief hesitation, then a sleep-fogged voice said, "I'm on my way."

*****

Fifteen minutes later, Tommy pulled his Jeep under the porte-cochere at the Seasurf Hotel, jumped out, and barged inside. Erin hadn't said what she wanted to talk about, but the excitement in her voice was unmistakable. He had thrown on a pair of jeans and a T-shirt, slipped into his running shoes, clipped his gun holster to his belt, and bolted. Now, as he entered the lobby, he looked for Harry at the front desk, but it was vacant. He knew the unwritten rule at tourist hotels was to never leave the front desk unattended; his danger sensors pinged.

He pulled his gun from its holster and held it at his side as he approached the stairwell. He paused on the first step, inclined his ear, and listened. Nothing.

His brain told him to move slowly, but his heart told him to hurry, lest Erin be in danger as she had been that afternoon. Opting to follow his heart, he took the steps two at a time. As he neared the top, he became aware of a shuffling, thumping noise around the corner. He paused at the head of the stairs and peered around. Down the way, just outside Erin's door, he saw the hulking shadow of Harry pacing.

With a sigh, he reholstered his gun and stepped onto the second floor. Harry saw him coming. His visage darkened.

"What you doing here, bruddah?" Harry asked.

"Why aren't you at the front?"

"If I'm at the front, too many ways to get in here without going by the desk. If I'm here, no way to get to her room without going by me."

Tommy nodded. Maybe he had misjudged the fat man.

"You can go back down now," Tommy said. "I got it from here."

With what could only be called a grunt, Harry lumbered past. Tommy waited until he had breached the stairs before knocking on the door.

*****

Erin jumped up from her knees when she heard the knock. She loped across the room and opened the door to greet Tommy.

"Boy, you got here fast," she said.

"It sounded important."

"Come on in." She ushered him to the side of the bed where she had been kneeling. She spied a twinkle of amusement in his eyes as he took in the sight of documents spread across the top of the bed.

"You been reading these all night?"

"I do my best work at night. Sometimes I feel like when the rest of the world is sleeping, I can make up ground."

She went to the coffeemaker on top of a tiny apartment-sized refrigerator and poured a cup. "Coffee? It's the nectar of the gods."

He laughed. "I hope it's Kona."

"What else?" she said as she poured him a cup. "You take it black, right?"

"If it's the nectar of the gods, why pollute it?"

"Point taken." She handed the cup to him, then opened two packets of sugar and emptied them into hers. "Even the gods can use a few pointers on sweetening up their nectar."

She returned to the bed and knelt. He knelt beside her.

"Okay," he said, "what am I looking at?"

"There are two things here. One of them I need your help on. Let's cover that one first."

"Okay."

She grabbed a piece of notepaper that she had set aside on a pillow and pulled it over. "I found this tucked into some papers Charlie left at Tutu Kela's. It's his handwriting. Looks like a to-do list."

"In black ink."

"Noticed that, did you? A couple of things on here have got my attention. The first thing is something I've seen before, but I have no idea what it means. 'Trace Western Pacific.' That mean anything to you?"

"No."

"He also wrote 'Western Pacific' on a genealogical chart I found in Honolulu, so it must mean something to him. Then, about halfway down the list, it says 'Audit BNH/Keala.'"

Tommy whistled. "You think Professor Cain thought Keala was raiding the trust fund?"

"Makes you wonder, doesn't it?"

"If Keala or any of the trustees had their hand in the till, they'd want to squelch an audit before it got off the ground."

"But if it never got past a to-do list, how would Keala know?" Erin asked.

"Good question. Do you know whether the professor ever acted on this?"

"No, but I talked to Keala in Honolulu. If he thought Charlie was on to him or any of his buddies at BNH, he'd figure I knew about it, too."

"Which could explain what happened here today. If any of the trustees are dirty, they'd have to be sure there wasn't a paper trail already in the professor's hands, or now in your hands."

"My thoughts, exactly," Erin said.

"I'll get some of our accountants poking around and see if there's anything to it. If there is, we'd have a more concrete motive than just someone being afraid they wouldn't get re-elected to the Bureau."

"Good. Now here's the other thing." She pulled the genealogical chart over in front of them. "Charlie put this together. I reconstructed his work as best I could, and I think it's accurate." She traced a line on the page with her index finger. "If you follow Manu's ancestry back, you find out his great-great-great-grandmother on his mother's side was Francis Stewart, born in England in 1806. That's as far back as I can go on the chart."

"That doesn't do much good, then. He's got to be able to trace his ancestry back to the 1778 cut-off date to even qualify as a native Hawaiian."

"Ah, patience, Grasshopper."

He looked at her, one eyebrow raised. "Grasshopper?"

"Sorry about that. Too many old *Kung Fu* re-runs."

"Oh, I got the reference. I just didn't figure you for a *Kung Fu* kinda girl."

"What did you think? That I was more of a *Dallas* or *Dynasty* re-run type of girl?"

"No, but – "

"And just FYI, calling a woman a girl can get you neutered in some circles. Especially in Texas. Not that I'm an 'I am woman, hear me roar' kinda girl. Just a word to the wise."

He scrutinized her face, as if searching for the deeper meaning behind what she had said. Her broad smile and laughing eyes belied any seriousness.

"You really like yanking my chain, don't you?" he said.

"Gotta admit I do. Anyway, back to what I was saying."

She shifted closer to him as she stretched to reach another line on the chart. She felt him lean her way. His shoulder brushed against hers. She kept contact as she talked.

"Now stay with me. This is where it gets tricky. In 1836, great-great-great-granny Francis Stewart gives birth to a daughter named Lillian in London. And in 1861, right about the time we're fighting amongst ourselves in the good ol' U S of A, Lillian marries great-great-grandfather, Charles. Then they move to Hawaii in 1866."

"Way too late."

"But, my impatient friend, she gives birth to a daughter in Hawaii in 1870. Little Alexandra. She grows up and marries a ship's captain and moves to California in 1894. Doesn't stay there long, though. In 1898, just after Hawaii was annexed by the United States, she returns to the islands. Care to guess why?"

"Sunny beaches?"

"She comes back because her grandmother, Francis Stewart, writes her a letter and begs her to return to Hawaii to – "

Erin searched out and found a brittle yellow page in the scattered stack of Tutu Kela's letters. Holding it gingerly by its edges, she read, "Quote, 'to fulfill the legacy of your great-great-grandfather Alexander.'"

She put the letter on the bed and leaned back on her heels. "Okay, now let's see how well you really know your Hawaiian history. Kamehameha the First, the Great, had twenty-two wives and fourteen children."

"You're not going to ask me to name them, are you?"

"I ought to. But, no, you only need to know one of them. In 1801, he sent his favorite son on a goodwill trip to the Orient."

"I know about that. He left on the trading ship *Perseverance* for Canton Province. Then he boarded an English ship and was never heard from again."

"And his name was?"

Tommy stared at the papers on the bed for a moment, his face a study in concentration.

"This is the sixty-four thousand dollar question, Detective. Show me what you're made of."

A look of realization settled in on Tommy's face. "Jesus Christ!"

"Nope, different king, different time. This one's name was Alexander Stewart. Here's where we get off into a bit of speculation, but speculation that makes some sense. Suppose Alexander Stewart actually made it to England. And suppose he got married there and had a little girl named Francis."

"Do you really think – "

"I think that's what Charlie thought. Do you think it's just coincidence that granny Francis Stewart writes about Alexandra's good old ancestor Alexander?"

"If Professor Cain thought that, then the papers we found at Manu's place are fakes. They say Manu can't trace his ancestry back to 1778 when in fact – "

"Manu may well be a living, breathing, provable descendant of Kamehameha. Charlie obviously figured that out, but someone doesn't want the world to know. Someone who might stand to lose a lot of power and influence if that becomes known."

She paused, emotion choking her voice. "Someone who was willing to kill, and still is, to keep that fact quiet, and who would frame the very man whose identity he wants to conceal."

"I think the money angle makes more sense," Tommy said. "If Manu's a real descendent of Kamehameha, I'm not sure I see how that really threatens anyone."

"A couple of ways. First, if Charlie recommends approval of the Hasegawa Bill, Manu can make a good argument, at least to the Hawaiian people, that he should be their leader. He'd be in direct conflict with BNH and every other sovereignty group. If Charlie recommends against passage, same thing. Based on what I've read and seen since I've been here, symbolism is incredibly important. As a symbol, Manu's a threat to someone either way."

"So you think this is about Manu and not about money?"

Erin shook her head. "It's always about money, but I think someone's found a way to deal with both issues. I think Charlie learned something else that we haven't found yet – maybe it's ripping off the trust fund or something – but whoever's behind it is playing the Manu angle to set up him up as a fall guy. If they can silence Charlie and frame Manu at the same time, it takes care of two problems at once."

"And now you've become part of that problem."

CHAPTER THIRTY-EIGHT

After showering and dressing in her trademark jeans and T-shirt, Erin loaded Charlie's chart and Tutu Kela's letters into her briefcase and left her room. The sun was already high on the horizon, shining brightly on a remarkably cloudless day for this part of the island. Who knew when the rains would come, though? Erin had already seen how clear and sunny could transform to cloudy and rainy in the time it took to draw a deep breath.

When Erin entered the lobby, she heard the clatter of silverware and the din of voices as tourists ate breakfast in the adjacent restaurant. Harry was at his post, talking with a guest. The guest left, and Harry smiled when he saw her.

"Morning, Miss Erin. Did you sleep well?"

"Well, but not long."

"You need me to get you a table for breakfast?"

"Not this morning, Harry. I'm going to grab a cup of coffee to go. I'm headed up to Laupahoehoe for a bit, but I'll be back before too long."

"You need something in your stomach." He clapped his hand on his ample midsection. "Take it from a man who knows how to fill his belly."

Erin laughed, the sound light. Harry must have noticed it because he said, "You sound mighty chipper for a woman who got shot at yesterday."

"Like my mom always used to say, today's gonna be a better day. I don't suppose it could be any worse."

Harry threw his head back and laughed robustly. His eyes shrank to dashes as his fat cheeks squeezed them shut. "Come on, let's get you that coffee and some sweetbread for the road."

He eased around the desk and led her into the restaurant. Erin waited while he talked to the hostess, who went off to fill the to-go order. She scanned the restaurant, already filled with guests enjoying island-style breakfasts of eggs, Spam, pancakes, pineapple, and *loco moco*, an island favorite of fried eggs sitting atop a hamburger patty sitting atop a bowl of sticky rice, covered in thick brown gravy. She had seen many of these faces before, most of them white, most of them elderly, most of them probably destined for the tour bus that sat outside under the porte-cochere. She saw only one Hawaiian face, that of a slender man sitting alone at a corner table, reading the newspaper and sipping coffee.

The hostess returned with a paper cup of steaming Kona coffee and a lunch sack containing two slices of Hawaiian sweetbread. Erin shifted her briefcase to her left hand and gripped the sack with two fingers, then took the coffee in her right.

*****

The Hawaiian man in the corner booth waited until the *haole* woman left with the big desk clerk, and then he pulled out his cell phone and hit a speed dial number. "Coming your way," was all he said to an answering voice.

Another Hawaiian man, dressed in an aloha shirt and gray slacks, sat behind the wheel of a rusted gray Jeep Wrangler on the side street that fronted the hotel. He hung up his cell phone, turned the key to start his engine, and waited. After a few seconds, he saw the *haole* woman emerge from the hotel, a briefcase and paper sack in one hand, a paper cup in the other. He put his foot on the brake pedal and shifted into drive.

*****

Harry stood at the entryway and watched as Erin put her coffee on top of the rental car, unlocked the door, and tossed her briefcase into the back seat. She placed the sack on the passenger seat then grabbed the coffee from the roof. She looked back and gave him a smile and a wave as she slid behind the wheel. After a few seconds, she backed up, turned out of the parking lot, and headed toward downtown Hilo.

Harry was just starting to walk back to the desk when he saw a Jeep Wrangler pull out of a line of parked cars in front of the hotel and follow Erin to Banyan Drive, then turn the same way. Coincidence? He didn't think so. He squinted and tried to pick out the license plate number but to no avail.

He moved quickly to the front desk, picked up the phone, and dialed. "Detective Kanahele, please."

"He's not on duty yet," a female voice answered.

"Can you give me his home number? It's important."

"Let me patch you through to his cell."

As Harry waited for the detective, he saw the Hawaiian man from the restaurant approach the desk. The man wore his aloha shirt untucked, the usual fashion, so Harry thought nothing of it. Nor did he think anything of it when the man slid his hand under the tail of his shirt. He didn't notice that the hand was covered with a latex glove. The first inkling that anything was wrong came when the man's hand returned to view holding a pistol.

The world seemed to whirl in slow motion as the man raised the gun to hip level, angled slightly up. Harry heard the weapon bark twice before searing pain penetrated his chest. He dropped the phone and fell face first.

The Hawaiian man tossed the gun to the floor and walked casually out the front.

As Harry lay on the tile behind the desk, he was only vaguely aware of screams that seemed miles away. The phone lay just beyond his reach. A man's voice squawked from it.

"This is Detective Kanahele. May I help you?" A pause, then, "Hello? Hello?"

The world stopped spinning and went dark.

CHAPTER THIRTY-NINE

Erin turned off of Highway 19 and headed uphill toward Tutu Kela's Laupahoehoe neighborhood. The sun glinted off the water behind her, dazzling in its brilliance. No clouds had gathered yet, although she saw the dark outline of a squall at sea. Probably heading her way, she thought. What would a day on the Hilo coast be without rain?

She glanced in her rearview mirror and saw a Jeep turn behind her. She thought nothing of it as she continued her climb higher, then turned onto Tutu Kela's street. The same kids she had met earlier played in a yard, enjoying another late start to the school day. Erin slowed as she neared them, rolled down her passenger window, and stuck her tongue out as she drove past.

Giggles and squeals erupted. Elika yelled, "Hey, y'all!"

"Y'all, yourself," Erin called back.

At Tutu Kela's, she pulled to the curb, reached into the back seat for her briefcase, and got out. Tutu Kela was already waiting at the front door.

"Aloha, Miss Erin."

"Aloha, Tutu."

"I have coffee waiting."

"Sounds wonderful."

Tutu led her inside and closed the door.

*****

The Jeep Wrangler stopped a few houses back and watched as Manu Pokui's mother escorted the *haole* woman with the briefcase inside. He glanced over and saw a group of kids playing. One of them, a tall girl, seemed to be staring right at him.

He took his foot off the brake and eased forward, passed the Pokui house, then turned around at the end of the road. He killed the engine and waited.

*****

Tutu led Erin to the same couch she had occupied before. A tray of coffee sat on the coffee table, and Erin helped herself. Tutu sat in her rocker and smiled.

"What can I do for you today, Miss Erin?"

Erin took the bundle of letters out of her briefcase and set it next to the tray of coffee. "First, thank you for letting me take these."

"I hope you found what you were looking for."

"Tutu, does Manu know he's a descendant of Kamehameha?"

Tutu's face clouded. "How you know this?"

"From your letters and from Charlie's research. Does Manu know?"

"If he does, it's not from me."

"Why wouldn't you have told him?"

"It's enough he knows he's Hawaiian."

"But why not tell him? Half the Hawaiian population claims to be descended from Kamehameha, but Manu really is. Why keep that from him?"

"There is no monarchy in Hawaii anymore. No entitlement just because you are royalty. Everyone is equal. That's the way it should be."

"The American democratic ideal."

"It is not the American way; it is God's way."

Erin sipped coffee and looked at her. She saw resolve in Tutu's eyes. She was quickly learning that no one was as they seemed.

"Tutu, I find it hard to believe you kept this from Manu just because you didn't want him to feel entitled. What aren't you telling me?"

Tutu said nothing.

"Tutu, I'm a lawyer. I've spent my career reading faces, and I'm pretty good at spotting liars. I'm also pretty good at knowing when someone's hiding something."

Tutu met Erin's gaze evenly. After a while, she rose from her rocking chair and disappeared into the rear of the house. Erin sat on the couch and waited.

Tutu returned a few minutes later carrying a small box of dark koa wood, adorned with carvings of ancient Hawaiian scenes – the warrior Kamehameha, an outrigger canoe on the ocean, a village of thatched-roof huts.

Tutu Kela sat on the couch next to Erin. She held the box in her lap, gnarled arthritic hands clasped on top of it. She waited silently, as if debating whether to open it. As if debating whether to open some deep dark secret.

"Miss Erin, are you a Christian?"

This was a turn in the conversation Erin didn't expect.

"Yes."

"Do you know the story in *The Bible* of baby Jesus and King Herod?"

"I learned it in Sunday School."

"Do you believe it actually happened, or do you believe it's just a story?"

Erin sat frozen, unsure how to answer because she was unsure of what she believed anymore. She believed in God, but was the God she believed in a God of love or simply a capricious superior being who liked to meddle in his subjects' lives and bring sorrow?

As if she could read her mind, Tutu Kela said, "You have experienced great sorrow in your life."

Erin nodded dumbly.

"And now you doubt God. You wonder how God could allow such sorrow. You wonder how God could allow your Mister Charlie to be taken."

Erin felt the tears well up inside. She had no control over them as they spilled out and down her cheeks.

"And how he could allow Manu's Abbie to be taken," Erin said. And Chris, she thought.

"There is evil in this world, Miss Erin. Evil comes from free will. But there is also good. God has to work with all of it, but he can make something good of evil if we'll let him. You're here now, and that's good. You're trying to help my people, and that's good."

Erin let that sink in. "Yes," she said.

"Yes, what?"

"Yes, I believe the story in *The Bible* actually happened."

"As do I. When King Herod heard of the birth of Jesus, a new king, he felt threatened. So he sent out an edict to find the child, because he wanted to kill him. It's an old theme throughout history. The same thing happened in the Old Testament with baby Moses and Pharaoh. Those who feel threatened always want to destroy those whose existence threatens them."

The box's hinges creaked as Tutu lifted the lid. Inside were black-and-white photographs, their edges curled with age. She thumbed through the photos and lifted one out. Holding it between trembling fingers, she showed it to Erin. It was of a young Hawaiian woman, not more than twenty- or twenty-five-years-old, holding a baby while standing in front of a sugar cane field. Even in the faded photograph, Erin could see she was a Polynesian beauty, with long black hair to her waist.

"That is Lehua-nani. Her name means beautiful lehua blossom. The child is Pu'uwai-hao-kila. His name means heart of steel. They have been gone many years now."

"Who were they?" Erin asked.

"Lehua-nani was my mother. The child was my brother, Pu'uwai. Even though he was just a baby, he truly had a heart of steel, with the same warrior's blood flowing through his veins as flowed through the veins of Kamehameha the Great. I was five-years-old when they died. When they were murdered."

"Murdered?"

"My father was stabbed and our house was set on fire and burned to the ground with my mother and Pu'uwai inside. Only I escaped, and the only thing I was able to take with me was this box of photographs and the letters it contained. The letters you read."

"But why?"

"Because there were those who wanted power for themselves, but who would never have the loyalty of the Hawaiian people if they knew a successor to King Kamehameha the Great lived among them."

"People who felt threatened." The words of the old expression ran through her head: *Uneasy lies the head that wears the crown.*

"Yes."

"*Haoles?*"

"That, I don't know. Friends took me in and raised me as their own in Waipio. They never told anybody that I survived the fire or who I really was. I felt safe. For all these years, I felt safe for myself and for my boy. But only because I kept my secret."

"Then Charlie came along and opened it all up."

"I didn't know that then. But if what you tell me is true, then yes, he opened it all up. And now, many years after my mother and my brother died, there are still those who feel threatened. Maybe for the same reasons, maybe for different reasons. I don't know. I only know that Mister Charlie has died."

"And Manu is in danger."

"And you, too, are in danger, Miss Erin."

"Tutu, I need to find Manu. He needs to turn himself in to the police. To Tommy. The police can protect him."

"Tommy thinks he killed Mister Charlie."

"Not anymore."

A noise from the kitchen drew their attention, the sound of a door opening and closing, followed by the voice of a boy.

"Tutu, who's here?"

David appeared at the door, his eyes bright and alert, his resemblance to Manu uncanny. The resemblance to Tommy was even more uncanny. The boy had his mother's features.

Erin smiled. "You must be David."

He stared at her, unsure of himself. "Yes, ma'am."

"You look like your father."

David's face took on a look of earnestness – brow furrowed, lips set. "You know my papa?"

Erin glanced at Tutu Kela, hoping she read the signal. "I'm his lawyer."

David looked to his grandmother for confirmation. "Is that right, Tutu?"

Tutu kept silent, pondering the question. Erin held her breath.

"Run fetch your grandfather, *keiki*," Tutu said at last. "He needs to take Manu's lawyer to see him."

CHAPTER FORTY

Harry's blood gleamed in the overhead light's reflection. Tommy gripped his hands together in perfect CPR position and pressed against the massive chest, hoping against hope that the pressure was sufficient to penetrate untold layers of fat and stimulate the man's heart. Each compression squeezed blood out of two holes that were now obscured in red fluid. Harry's eyes rolled back into his head; his labored breathing sputtered.

"Don't you die on me, fat boy," Tommy growled under his breath. "Just hang in there."

Harry seemed to be trying to focus. Sirens blared nearby, the sound drawing closer. He opened his mouth as if to speak.

"Don't say anything," Tommy said. Sweat beaded on his brow and coursed down his cheek.

Harry curled a beefy fist around Tommy's wrist. He opened his mouth again.

Tommy stopped the compressions. He looked at Harry, who managed to lock gazes.

"Miss Erin," Harry gasped.

"What?" Tommy leaned close and placed his ear just inches from Harry's mouth.

"Miss Erin." The effort to speak even those words drained

life from Harry. "They follow her."

A chill cut through Tommy. "Where?"

"Lauapahoehoe."

Hands grabbed at Tommy's shoulder and pulled him aside. "Let us take it from here, Detective," a paramedic said.

Tommy kept his gaze locked with Harry.

"Go," Harry said. He coughed, and blood pooled in his mouth, swished out the corners, and down his jaw. He squeezed tighter on Tommy's wrist. "She needs you."

Then his grip eased, his eyes closed, and his mouth went slack.

Tommy jumped to his feet and raced to the Jeep.

*****

The Hawaiian man in the rusted gray Wrangler watched as the boy with schoolbooks under his arm ran out of the house and down the street to meet up with his friends. A few moments later, the *haole* woman – without the briefcase – and an old man exited the Pokui house and walked to the woman's car. He waited until she turned around and drove away before he got out of his vehicle. He closed the door quietly and walked across the street, cut between two houses and around to the back of the Pokui house.

*****

Tutu Kela rinsed the coffee cups and placed them back in the cramped cupboard beside the stove. She filled the pressure cooker with rice and water and turned it on, then set about preparations for the meals she would cook that day. She had just put another pot of water on the stove and turned the burner to high when she heard the creak of the screen door behind her.

"David, I – "

She stopped in mid-turn at the sight of the strange Hawaiian man who stood in the doorway.

"What you doing in my house? You get out."

"Where are the papers, grandmother?"

The man spoke in a quiet tone, one that sent shivers through Tutu. But she was determined not to show fear.

"Out," she said, her voice rising. She hoped the crescendo masked the quiver. "You get out of my house!"

He stepped forward, looming over her. The closer he got, the more she realized just how big he was. He was well over six feet tall and easily exceeded 200 pounds, all of it raw muscle. There was hardness in his body and hardness in his eyes, as well.

She backed up until she touched the stove.

"The papers, grandmother. I want the papers."

He grabbed her arm, his grip grinding the bones in her wrist. She opened her mouth to scream, but he clamped his other hand over her face.

"You will tell me where the papers are," he said, "or you'll wish you had."

* * * * *

The kids down the street chattered and ran through yards,

trying to delay the start of school as long as they could. Elika's mother appeared at the front door.

"School time, *keiki. Now.*" She clapped her hands for emphasis.

There were a few protests but complete obedience, notwithstanding. David picked up his books laying on the sidewalk and walked beside Elika.

"What you got for lunch today?" Elika asked.

"Ahh, I forgot my lunch." He turned and sprinted toward his grandmother's house, calling over his shoulder, "Wait for me."

With yet another excuse for delay, all the kids halted in their tracks and waited for the return of their friend.

As David ran between houses to the kitchen door in back, he heard his grandmother's voice.

"You get out now! I call the police."

He ran to the back door and peeked through the screen. All he could see was the back of a very large man grabbing Tutu. The man swiped a pot of water off the stove, then grabbed the back of her head.

*****

The man forced Tutu's head toward the orange hot burner on which the pot of water had percolated. She fought for all she was worth, but age, arthritis, and her assailant's superior strength overwhelmed her. He held her cheek just inches from the burner. The heat licked at her face.

"Where are the papers?" he asked.

Then she saw him: David's terrified face, eyes large, staring at her through the screen door.

With the last of her strength, she formed one word on her lips: *Run.*

The pressure on her head increased, the gap between her face and the burner narrowed.

Then searing pain.

She screamed.

*****

Tutu's scream freed David from his trance. He bolted from the door as fast as his legs would carry him.

Out of the corner of his eye, the Hawaiian man glimpsed movement. He turned just in time to see David disappear around the corner. He threw Tutu to the floor, concentric circles burned into her cheek, and raced out the door.

David had a fifty-foot lead, but the man's long strides quickly made up the gap. Ahead, Elika waited with the other kids. Would they be in danger if he led his pursuer to them? Or would there be refuge there? Thinking quickly, David made up his mind. He planted his left foot and cut ninety degrees across the street.

"Help," he screamed.

*****

Elika looked up at David's cry. She saw him first, then the large man running after him. As David cut across the street, the man followed his move. Elika picked up a large lava rock, its edges jagged. She stepped to the edge of the street just as the man grabbed David's arm and jerked him to the ground. Elika threw as hard as she could.

It slammed into the side of the man's head. He stumbled then turned to look at her, as if unable to believe what had just happened.

"Run, David," she yelled, then bent to pick up another rock.

The other kids picked up lava rocks of varying sizes and began throwing. In the distance, but fast approaching, came the sounds of sirens.

The man released David, who broke away to join his friends.

CHAPTER FORTY-ONE

Alex Pokui steered the old fishing boat along the Hamakua Coast of the Big Island. Erin stood at his side, admiring the beauty of the coastline. Who wouldn't want to be the king of this land? Erin had done her research since she had been there and knew that men had killed for these islands before. Even King Kamehameha killed many as he led his warriors in the fight to unify the islands. He wasn't known as Kamehameha the Great merely for his peacefulness. On Maui, the bodies of his enemies fell so thick that they blocked up the waters of Iao Stream. The battle became known as the battle of Kepaniwai – the damming of the waters. On Oahu, his army drove hundreds of the opposing force over the Nu'uani Pali, where they fell a thousand feet to their deaths. And at Kealakekua Bay, he killed Captain Cook and a number of his men from the ships *Discovery* and *Resolution* as Hawaiians tried to keep the *haole* invaders from their shores.

"Who is that?" Erin asked.

She pointed at the sleek speedboat that bobbed on the waves about fifty feet offshore of Waipio Valley. Blue trim ran its length from nose to tail. Two Hawaiian men stood inside, one at the wheel, the other at the bow.

"They take you to Manu," Alex said.

Alex cut the motor as he aimed straight for the speedboat. The fishing boat continued to glide, easing its way forward. The man in the bow threw a foam rubber fender over the side to brace for impact.

"Give me your cell phone," Alex said.

"Why? I'm not going to call anyone and tell them where I am. My guess is, I won't even know where I am."

"Just give it to me."

"You're expecting a lot from me, aren't you?" Erin asked. "I'm supposed to just blindly trust you, is that it?"

"You want to see Manu, you give me your cell phone and go with them. You don't want to see Manu, I'll take you back and you can go on your way."

Erin's mind churned. She understood Alex's wariness. After all, he didn't know her or her motivations. Even though Tutu vouched for her, he had to make up his own mind. But the real question, as far as she was concerned, wasn't whether Alex trusted her; it was whether she could trust him.

As the fishing boat softly nudged the speedboat, she made her decision. She handed her cell to Alex, then swung a leg over the side and stepped into the other boat.

CHAPTER FORTY-TWO

Tommy laughed when he saw the scene. David sprinted their way, followed somewhat blindly by a big Hawaiian. His running was hindered by having to hold his arms up to fend off flying rocks as he ran the gauntlet of *keiki* lining the street. The man spent more time protecting himself than paying attention to his surroundings. How else to explain that he apparently had not heard the sirens nor seen the procession of police vehicles headed straight toward him?

Montgomery slammed on the brakes just shy of hitting David's pursuer head-on. The Jeep skidded to a halt, screeching sideways in the street. The man threw on his own brakes when he finally recognized that his real peril was no longer flying rocks. He spun around and raced headlong back into the fusillade as Tommy jumped out and hit the ground running.

Montgomery jumped out of the driver's side, ran to David, and scooped him up in both arms. David's tears flowed over his breathlessness. He hugged Montgomery and buried his face in the detective's shoulder.

"He hurt Tutu." David could barely speak over his sobs. "There was nothing I could do to help her, so I ran."

Montgomery carried him back to a trailing squad car and put him in the back seat. "You did the right thing, David. We'll take care of Tutu."

He turned to the driver. "Stay with him."

Then he joined the chase.

*****

Finally clear of the kids, the man accelerated, but Tommy had the momentum. They approached Tutu's house and had just pulled even with her front yard when Tommy left his feet. He swung his right arm like a shepherd's crook. His forearm caught the man just below his knees, causing him to pitch face forward, unable to throw his arms up in time to safeguard his landing. The man plowed forward on the rock street, skin peeling back with each inch of skid.

Tommy popped to his knees and bounced onto the man's back. With both hands, he pressed his face into the rocks.

"Who sent you?"

The man grunted but said nothing.

"*Who?*"

Still nothing.

A uniformed officer reached them quickly. With a practiced hand, he yanked the Hawaiian's arms behind his back and cuffed him while Tommy scrambled to his feet and raced to Tutu's house. He crossed the yard in just a few strides, then opened the unlocked door and burst inside.

"Tutu?"

He stopped and listened.

"Tutu?"

No answer.

He knocked over a small footstool as he headed for the kitchen, the likeliest place to find her most days. And there she was, lying on the floor, not moving. A circular burn pattern marked the side of her face. Bile rose in his throat. He had to fight to keep it down, to not contaminate the crime scene.

He rushed to her, sat with his back to the stove, and cradled her head in his lap. The skin on her cheek sizzled, red and raw.

"Tutu, can you hear me?"

Her eyelids fluttered, then opened. A wave of relief rushed through him.

"Tutu, are you okay?"

"Tommy," she said, her voice weak. "I knew you'd come. You're a good boy."

"I'm here, Tutu. I'm here."

She tried to sit up, but he held her down.

"You lie still. Wait for the ambulance."

"Where is David?"

"He's fine. Joey has him."

She nodded, her fears momentarily calmed.

"What about Erin, Tutu? Did she come see you today?"

"She's such a beautiful girl. You two would make a good couple."

"Where is she? Where is Erin?"

"She went to see Manu. Alex took her."

"Where, Tutu? Where is Manu?"

"Na Pali," she said. Then her eyes rolled back in her head, and she slipped into unconsciousness.

Kanaka Blues

CHAPTER FORTY-THREE

The blue-trimmed speedboat island-hopped from Waipio to Maui, where it stopped to re-fuel in Kahului. Erin stood silently on the dock as the two Hawaiian men filled the tank and ran routine checks on the boat.

"You want something to eat or to use the ladies room?" Ricky Kealoha asked.

His partner, Kekoa Maunupau, stared at Erin from the driver's seat. Of the two, Ricky was the friendlier. Which wasn't to say he was friendly, just that he was at least willing to talk to her and take care of some of her creature comforts. They had made it clear from the moment they picked her up at Waipio Beach that they neither trusted her nor agreed with the decision to take her to meet with Manu Pokui. Still, they were good soldiers in Manu's sovereignty army, and when he gave an order, they obeyed.

"I could use the ladies room," she said. "And maybe grab something to eat, too. Can I get y'all anything?"

Ricky looked at Kekoa, who turned and gazed seaward. He obviously wasn't taking charity from this *haole* woman. Ricky looked back at Erin and shrugged.

"I'll go with you, maybe grab something," he said. "I got to pay for the fuel, anyway."

261

He walked beside Erin up the dock toward a small building that doubled as the office for the harbor and a gas station/ convenience store. Inter-island airplanes circled over Kahului harbor, lined up for the airport nearby. A tourist helicopter hovered over the airport as another lifted vertically and whisked away up the side of the cloud-covered volcano that gave birth to this island centuries ago – Haleakala, the "House of the Sun." Maui had been next on her honeymoon itinerary with Chris. A sunrise trip to Haleakala's summit was only one of their plans that was never carried out.

"You look sad," Ricky said. There was a surprising touch of tenderness in his tone.

"I've only been to Maui once, but it's got all kinds of bad memories for me."

"When were you here?"

"Just a week ago, to identify Charlie Cain's body."

"Mister Charlie was a good man."

"You knew him?"

"Met him once. I liked him."

They fell silent until they reached the small store, where Erin excused herself and went to the ladies room. When she finished, she splashed water on her face, hoping the cool would chase away the heat of impending tears.

She picked up a soft drink and a bag of chips while Ricky paid for the gas. "That, too," he said, indicating Erin's purchases. The transaction done, they returned to the boat.

"Thanks for paying," Erin said.

"No problem, sistah."

Out to sea, a helicopter circled, probably waiting for clearance to land at the airport. Kekoa stood at the helm of the boat, ready to leave.

"He doesn't say much," Erin said.

"He's the Hawaiian John Wayne," Ricky said, then laughed. "Or maybe like *your* Calvin Coolidge."

The emphasis on *your* was not lost on Erin. "I'm not the enemy, you know."

"That's what the *haole* missionaries said before they stole our land, banned our hula, outlawed our language, and put our queen in prison. You'll understand if we take what you say with a grain of salt."

She nodded, "Point taken."

At the boat, Ricky helped her in then stepped in behind her. Kekoa already had the engine idling. He gunned the throttle and took off to open sea.

Erin looked back toward shore, wondering if she had made a mistake. They had no reason to trust her, and the feeling was mutual. If anything happened, no one knew where she was or where she was going.

She gazed skyward at the circling helicopter. It sure seemed to be taking its time landing.

*****

Police pilot Walter Takai held his bird low and steady, skimming along the Big Island's Hamakua Coast at sixty miles per hour. Montgomery held binoculars to his eyes and scanned the coastline as Tommy hit re-dial on his cell phone. He listened for a moment, then said, "Erin, damn it, call me. It's urgent."

He hung up. "She must have it turned off."

"There," Montgomery said, excitement in his voice.

Tommy grabbed the binoculars from him and looked in the direction of his partner's pointing finger. He quickly zeroed in on the aging fishing boat that he knew so well, moving south along the coast.

"That's Alex," Tommy said. "He's on his way back, so he's already handed her off."

He lowered his binoculars and tapped Takai on the shoulder. "They'll stay north. Get the hell over to Maui, then cover all the bays and landings."

"Why don't we just go to Kauai and wait?" Montgomery asked.

"Because she's vulnerable the entire way. Besides, we've got no guarantee that's where they're really headed. Our best bet is to try to follow their route."

"You think Tutu would lie to you?"

"No, but I think Manu's buddies would lie to her. They figure if she doesn't know where he is, she can't tell anyone. Even if someone tries to burn it out of her."

*****

A small Zodiac boat pushed inland toward the same beach on Kauai where Manu had slept, guarded by the warrior king. Jimmy Cho, a wiry Chinese/Hawaiian, stood at the helm, clothed in baggy khaki shorts and a bird-of-paradise-adorned aloha shirt. A 9 mm Glock handgun was tucked in the waistband of his shorts. Two 30.06 rifles with scopes lay on the floor of the Zodiac.

He stood steady as the Zodiac bounced from trough to trough in the rugged waters that pounded the beach. As it shallowed, the ride grew smoother. He beached the craft just astern of a copse of thickly-bunched lehua trees. As the Zodiac stilled, a figure slowly emerged from those trees.

Manu trotted to the boat, his huge feet kicking up trails of sand as he went. He swung one leg over the side of the boat, then the other. Jimmy Cho took his hand in a firm clasp, and they hugged briefly.

"You sure about this?" Jimmy asked.

"I'm sure."

"But you don't even know this woman."

"Tutu said I can trust her. That's good enough for me."

"All right, brah. It's your neck."

Jimmy used an oar to push back from the beach and cranked the motor into gear. He swung the craft around and headed to sea.

Manu picked up a rifle and leaned against the side of the Zodiac. Spray from the waves sprinkled his face as he set out to meet with the *haole* lawyer.

Kanaka Blues

CHAPTER FORTY-FOUR

Hanalei Bay is a picture postcard perfect oval on the north shore of Kauai, bounded on the east by the magnificent Princeville Hotel and on the west by the beginnings of the world famous Na Pali coastline, anchored by the mountain known to musical fans as Bali Hai in the movie version of *South Pacific*. The peaceful town of Hanalei borders the bay, white sand beaches embracing the waters.

A concrete pier extended into the water at the southeast corner of the bay, near the mouth of the Hanalei River. Kekoa aimed the speedboat for the pier just as, across the bay, a Zodiac boat aimed for the same destination. Even from a distance, Erin recognized the massive figure standing at its bow: Manu Pokui. She could almost imagine a warrior's headdress on him and a spear in his hand instead of a rifle. She couldn't tear her eyes away. As they drew closer, she saw that his eyes were trained on her, as well. Both boats reached the pier at the same time.

"Aloha, bruddah," Jimmy Cho said. He tossed a rope to Ricky, who tied the two vessels together.

Erin walked to the front of the speedboat, next to Manu. "Hello, Mr. Pokui. Thank you for seeing me."

"Miss Hanna, I understand you now think you're my lawyer."

"I know you didn't kill Charlie. And I know who you really are. What more could you want in a lawyer?"

The words seemed to startle Manu. For just an instant, uncertainty flashed in his eyes. Then his face resumed its stoicism.

"And just who do you think I am?"

"You're – "

Suddenly a helicopter swooped down from behind a mountain. Before anyone could move, a burst of automatic weapons fire raked the water, then the pier, then the speedboat. It looked as if Kekoa and Ricky had touched a live wire as their bodies jerked. Mists of red spray coughed from their torsos.

Manu grabbed Erin by her left arm and yanked. Her feet left the floor of the boat, and she nose-dived into the Zodiac. She sprawled face down, only vaguely aware of a heavy weight on her back as Manu shielded her with his body. Bullets zipped into the rubber sides of the Zodiac but mercifully failed to find its bottom.

Jimmy Cho pulled a gun from the waistband of his pants but barely got his arm parallel to the water when bullets riddled his body. He toppled over backwards. Erin heard the splash as his body dropped into the bay. His gun landed on the floor next to her head.

Manu scrambled to the motor and fired up the Zodiac. The helicopter swung in a wide arc over the bay, lining up for a second deadly pass. Manu turned the Zodiac around and headed toward deeper water, directly into the path of the helicopter. He grabbed a rifle and knelt beside the motor. A man with an Uzi in one hand leaned out of the chopper. Manu raised his rifle, trying to line up on his moving target.

Two gunshots barked. A crack exploded on the chopper's windshield. The gunman ducked back inside as the craft dipped down and off to the side erratically.

Manu lowered his gaze, shocked to see Erin holding Jimmy Cho's gun aimed at the sky.

"Go," she said calmly.

He looked at her, frozen.

"Don't argue with a woman holding a gun," she said. "Just go."

"Yes, ma'am."

He revved the throttle, shifted into gear, and accelerated away from the pier, across the bay. He had no sooner gotten up to full speed when three more speedboats rounded the Princeville Hotel point. Erin looked back, then called to Manu.

"You know them?"

Manu looked over his shoulder. He squinted, trying to make out the men in the boats.

"Never seen 'em before."

A cracking sound emanated from behind them, then a bullet zipped past Manu's ears.

"They ain't the cavalry," he said.

She held her arms out to maintain balance and stumbled across the boat until she knelt on the other side of the motor from Manu. She leveled the gun over the back of the Zodiac, sighted down the barrel, and squeezed off a round.

The lead speedboat lurched sharply to the right, then went airborne and flipped twice. Its occupants dropped into the bay as it hung momentarily upside down. It hit the surface and skidded about fifty yards before it came to a stop, floating right side up. Empty.

"Where'd you learn to shoot like that?" Manu asked.

"You forget I'm from Texas."

"Remind me not to piss you off."

By now the helicopter had gotten back on track, lined up, and followed the other speedboats.

"Get us the hell out of here," she said.

*****

The Zodiac skirted the coast along Haena State Beach Park, where a ragged tent city had been set up on the sand. Its residents had no idea that their champion was in the rubber raft that motored by offshore, fleeing for his life.

The remaining speedboats slowly closed the gap as Manu grudgingly gave ground to the sleeker, faster pursuers. The helicopter followed just above, keeping Manu and Erin in sight but staying out of range of Erin's weapon. Each time the Uzi-bearing gunman stuck his head out, she fired a round and chased him back in. Even though she knelt just feet away from Manu, she had to shout to be heard over the wind.

"I'm almost out of bullets," she said.

"Take the handle."

Erin stood and gripped the tiller. The helicopter immediately swung out to the side and accelerated, moving up beside the Zodiac. It appeared to be trying to take advantage of the change of drivers.

Manu grabbed one of the rifles from the floor of the boat, shouldered it, and fired. The shot went wild but it did the trick. The chopper dipped suddenly and banked away, causing the gunman to swing out of the hatch. For an instant it appeared that he would plummet to the ocean, but a hand grabbed his arm and pulled him inside. The chopper then fell back into its original place above the speedboat, following at a safe distance.

Erin glanced at Manu and smiled grimly. He flashed her a *shaka* sign. "Hang loose."

A sound wafted their way from shore. To her left, Erin saw a line of Kauai police cars barreling along the winding road on the coast, lights flashing. A second helicopter appeared above the ridgeline that fronted Mount Waiale'ale. The helicopter swooped down toward the coast as if guarding the parade of squad cars. *Kauai PD* was painted on its side.

"Hope they know we da good guys," Manu said.

The pursuing chopper swung over near the shore. The gunman fired off a burst at the police helicopter, which dipped then pulled up sharply.

"They do now," Erin said, looking back over her shoulder. "The boats are slowing down."

"They're just maintaining their distance. They figure we've got to beach sooner or later. That's when they'll come after us."

"Who are they?"

"Don't know."

"Why are they after you?"

He looked at her for a moment. She saw just a flicker of a smile. "Who said they're after me?"

"You always this nonchalant when people with guns are chasing you?"

He shrugged. "I've had worse right behind me."

Now Erin smiled. Tommy had told her about Manu's foot race with lava in the Kilauea crater.

"They're about to reach the end of the road," Manu said.

"Who?"

"The cops."

Erin looked to shore. Sure enough, the police caravan reached Ke'e Beach, where the road played out. One by one, the cars braked to a halt. Their flashing lights faded in the distance as the Zodiac made a big turn westward around the Bali Hai mountain and headed toward the Na Pali Coast.

"Never thought I'd be sorry to see cops stop chasing me," Manu said.

*****

The police helicopter ascended until it was maybe a hundred feet above the pursuing chopper. Its pilot, Police Sergeant Will Thompson, had flown combat missions in Iraq, so this was nothing new to him. In the passenger seat, Police Corporal Steve Hideki held a semi-automatic rifle in his lap, cocked and ready for action.

Thompson settled at an elevation directly above his enemy, then dipped in a steep dive. Hideki tightened his seatbelt and leaned out the door, rifle at the ready. As they neared the lower craft, Thompson banked right. Hideki squeezed the trigger and ripped off a couple of rounds. The first two shots passed harmlessly by, but the third found its mark just in front of the rear rotor.

"Knock, knock," Thompson said.

The other chopper peeled off to the left, leveled out, and sought higher elevation.

"Watch him," Hideki said. "He's going to try to get above us. Pull up beside him and I can get a shot at the pilot."

"Don't worry. My plan is to always keep you between me and that Uzi."

"Roger that." Hideki laughed. "Damn helicopter drivers."

"To protect and to serve."

For several minutes, each helicopter tried to get the elevation advantage over the other as they gradually leapfrogged higher. While their pilots jockeyed, the gunmen sprayed the air full of bullets, some passing perilously close to whirling rotors. The buzz of gunfire forced each pilot to take evasive maneuvers until finally Thompson got the police helicopter on the tail of the other, about thirty feet separating them.

"Get closer and I'll put a riff in his tail rotor," Hideki said.

"Stay ready."

Thompson throttled forward. Hideki leaned out to the side, weapon steady in his hands. Suddenly the chopper in front lurched upward. Caught off guard, Thompson overshot his position, and his quarry disappeared from view. He pressed his face into the windshield, eyes peeled upward.

"I can't see him."

Hideki grabbed the side of the door and leaned out as far as he could. He rolled his shoulders until his upper body was horizontal to the ocean and looked skyward.

"He's right over us." Then panic set in. "And diving."

A flurry of thuds hit the roof of the police chopper. They weren't nearly as frightening, though, as the pinging sounds of bullets ricocheting off the rotor blades. Thompson fought to pull away, but found himself unable to control the bird. It launched into a lurching, jerking motion, like a bucking bronco, and tossed the two men around inside the cabin.

Thompson spoke calmly into his microphone. Much more calmly than he felt. "Mayday, mayday, mayday."

*****

Erin watched as the police helicopter spun out of control, spiraling downward. As the Zodiac rounded a curve, she saw a splash of foam when it slammed into the ocean. The other helicopter leveled off and resumed the chase, just behind the pursuing speedboats.

"Looks like we're on our own," she said.

Manu glanced over his shoulder. He nodded grimly, then turned the Zodiac sharply toward shore. For the first time, Erin felt a surge of panic course through her body.

"What are you doing?" she asked.

"They want us to beach? Well, I'm beaching."

"Are you nuts?"

"Never claimed I wasn't. But if I'm gonna die, I want to do it on my turf."

"Well, it's not mine."

He looked at her. "Sorry, but I can't get you into a courtroom to die."

*****

The Zodiac nosed ashore on the same beach where Manu had been picked up by Jimmy Cho. He slung one rifle over his shoulder, grabbed the other in his hand, and took Erin by the arm. They jumped out of the Zodiac and sprinted as best they could in the loose sand. Ahead lay thick rain forest that sloped upward and inward to the Kalalau Valley, a deep inward vee protected on both sides by almost sheer thousand-foot green walls of foliage.

Behind them, two speedboats glided across the surf, then shot forward onto the beach next to the Zodiac. Two men scrambled from each boat, armed with Uzis and semi-automatic pistols, and waited while the helicopter descended. Its rotors kicked up a sandstorm, and tiny granules of sand pelted their faces. In one accord, they turned their faces until a man wearing creased khakis and a tailored blue oxford button-down got out. The sun highlighted slivers of gray in his well-manicured beard.

"Keep close," he told the pilot. "Don't lose them."

The helicopter lifted off again, and Joseph Keala addressed the men on the beach.

"Make sure they don't come out of the trees alive."

CHAPTER FORTY-FIVE

Like the point on a flying wedge, Manu's bulk cleared a path through the overgrown vegetation. Erin stumbled along in his wake. A low hanging branch slapped against her face. She put her hand to her cheek and felt blood. So this is where it ends, she thought. Gunned down in a jungle on an island in the Pacific, thousands of miles from home, with a Kamehameha wannabe.

The ground started to slope upward about a quarter mile in. It was a gentle rise at first, then it became more dramatic. The vegetation bunched together more thickly, and the combination of undergrowth and incline slowed them markedly. Erin stayed as close to Manu as she could, counting on his bulk to clear the way. Suddenly they burst into a clearing. Looking back, she saw that it afforded a clear view, over the trees, of the beach and the ocean. Both speedboats were still grounded. There was no other craft in sight. The police, wherever they were, had yet to arrive.

Manu halted at the edge of the clearing, which was about ten yards in diameter. He looked around, then up the mountainside. Then he looked skyward.

"What are you looking for?" Erin asked.

"The helicopter."

"It should be behind us."

"Unless he flew around to the overlook and plans to – "

It swooped into view from behind the mountain, almost in a nosedive straight at them.

"Get in the trees," Manu yelled.

He pushed Erin back as the gunman ripped off a burst. The bullets kicked up rock chips and dirt around them.

Manu crouched behind a tree, his body blocking Erin. He leveled his rifle, sighted down the barrel, and fired off a shot just as the helicopter pulled up. The bullet flew by harmlessly beneath it. From behind and below came the sounds of crashing through the underbrush. Erin knew what that meant: men with guns, dangerously close. They were, in effect, surrounded.

"Get to the other side," Manu said.

He grabbed Erin by the arm and slingshot her into the clearing. She accelerated to a sprint before the helicopter could line up another burst of gunfire. Manu followed, and they regrouped on the mountain side.

"Now what?" Erin asked. *Please have a plan*, she thought. *Because I'm fresh out.*

A shot ripped into a tree trunk just beyond them. Manu whirled and fired off a round with his rifle. A man dropped at the far side of the clearing, face forward into the sunlight. Erin hadn't even seen him in the shadows of the jungle until he fell.

A fusillade of shots commenced from behind the dead man and to both his left and right. His friends had arrived, and they were pissed.

Manu pushed Erin deeper into the jungle. "There's a switchback trail about a quarter mile farther," he said. "That'll get us above them where I can get a clear shot."

If we live that long, Erin thought.

They paused at the start of the switchback trail. While it led up the mountainside, it also led out of the cover of trees. They still heard the whir of the helicopter as the pilot and gunman waited for them to expose themselves. They would be open targets, like sitting ducks in a shooting gallery.

"Where does this go?" Erin asked.

"Into Waimea Canyon. If we can get there, I can get us out of here."

"And if we can't?"

"I think you already know the answer to that."

"So what are our options?"

"You're the lawyer; you tell me."

Erin thought for a moment. "I think the psychologists call it fight or flight."

"I've heard that."

"What are our chances if we fight?"

"Slim and none."

"And flight?"

Now it was Manu's turn to think a moment. "There's a ledge about a couple hundred yards up. If we reach it, we've got a chance. It's at least a good place for an ambush."

"And if we don't reach it?"

Manu's face said it all.

He un-slung the second rifle from his shoulder and handed it to her. He pointed to a boulder at the edge of the trail.

"Take cover there. As soon as you see the chopper, start

shooting. If I can get about fifty yards up, I'll have a better angle. Then maybe I can keep them off of you until you can get past me and to the ledge."

Erin moved to the boulder, knelt, and brought the rifle to her shoulder. Manu started up the switchback trail, before abruptly stopping. They made eye contact.

"Is it true what Travis said? At the Alamo?" he asked.

"You mean 'victory or death'?"

He smiled. "You know, you Texans really are insufferable."

Then he resumed climbing the trail.

*****

Joseph Keala's helicopter hovered at the edge of the trees, kicking up dirt in the clearing. The pilot watched as Manu left the cover of a large boulder and sprinted toward a switchback trail. He tapped his gunman passenger and pointed.

"There."

The gunman placed his Uzi on the floor and retrieved an M-25 sniper rifle from the rear seat. "Hold 'er steady."

The pilot swung the craft around and lined up the passenger door for a shot. The gunman leveled the rifle, braced it against his shoulder, and sighted down the scope. He centered the Hawaiian's broad back in the crosshairs.

He caressed the trigger, increasing the pressure.

A shot caromed off the side of the chopper just inches from his head. He jerked back, squeezing off a wild shot. His bullet kicked up dirt on the switchback trail just above Manu's head.

The gunman pulled back and sought cover inside the cabin. He peered through the open doorway, searching for the source of the shot. He saw nothing but trees, boulders, and dirt. Then out of the corner of his eye, movement. Just beside a large boulder at the foot of the trail. He squinted, unable to believe what he saw: the barrel of a rifle aimed squarely at his head, the *haole* woman sighting through the scope.

"Go, go, go," he yelled. "Pull up."

The pilot yanked back hard on the stick. The chopper rose vertically as a rifle shot echoed. A stinging sensation burned into the gunman's thigh. He looked down, stunned. Blood trickled from a hole in his pants leg.

"I'm hit. The *haole* bitch shot me."

*****

Manu hopped from rock to rock, the trail slick with run-off from recent rains. He kept the rifle slung over his back so he could use both arms for balance. His head seemed to rest atop a swivel as he turned it side to side, watching his step, watching Erin down below, and watching the armed helicopter over the trees.

Just above him was a ledge, protected by a rock overhang. From there, he would have a good vantage point to hold off the attackers until the *haole* lawyer reached him. Then they could leapfrog higher and deeper into the valley. A few leaps and they would be on level ground. From there, he knew of hiding places the pursuers could never hope to find.

He placed his hands on the ground and scrambled on all fours up the trail. He switched back 180 degrees at the turn, the ledge now in sight ahead of him. From below, he heard sounds of gunfire. Mud kicked up around him as shots came close, but they were never a serious threat. He saw that the helicopter bounced up and down, obviously dodging the *haole* lawyer's shots, just enough to keep the gunman inside from finding his mark.

He reached the ledge and scooted under the overhang. From there, he had an unobstructed view of the clearing below and also had a good angle on the helicopter. He saw that the lawyer had her sight trained skyward, firing off the occasional shot. He smiled. That was all the advantage he needed.

He knelt at the edge of the ledge, unslung his rifle, and raised it to his shoulder. He lined up the chopper's motor in his sights. One well-placed shot and it would no longer be a factor.

Just as he began to squeeze the trigger, he caught movement below in his peripheral vision. He dropped the rifle from his eyes and looked over the ledge. One of the foot pursuers was moving along the valley wall directly behind the lawyer. The man didn't have a clear shot at her, but he was only steps away.

Manu leaned over the ledge and took aim, but the cliff wall was too jagged and its outcroppings successfully shielded the man from him.

Just beyond the ledge, a boulder rested precariously on the trail. It was a place where the trail disappeared behind the boulder, where one had to squeeze between it and the cliff wall to pass. The man sneaking up on the lawyer would be directly beneath it in just a few seconds.

Manu dropped his rifle and raced to the boulder. He squeezed into the gap between the valley wall, then placed his back against the stone. He put his feet against the wall and pushed. Muscles groaned, tendons and sinews creaked, as he pressed with all his might. Veins popped in his neck, and his face turned red with the effort.

And suddenly he found himself lying flat on his back on the edge of the drop-off, the boulder already gone from sight.

His eyes drifted to another boulder twenty feet away.

*****

Erin heard it first, then she felt it. Gravel and loose rocks cascading down the mountainside, bouncing far out. A few smaller rocks scattershot at her. One nicked her cheek.

A voice yelled behind her.

She spun, shocked to see a man with a weapon, frozen to his spot about a first down's length behind her. His head tilted back, a look of terror on his face. Suddenly he disappeared beneath an asteroid crashing to earth. The massive stone wiped him off the path, then crashed through trees. She looked up to see the source of the boulder.

For a second, she thought she must be nuts. Either fear or adrenaline or weariness was wreaking havoc with her brain, because her rational mind told her she couldn't be seeing what she saw.

King Kamehameha the Great stood with his back braced against a second boulder on a ledge about fifty feet above. He wore a feather-laden headdress and full battle gear. The boulder he pushed against dislodged and crashed down the mountainside. It hit the side of the cliff, bounced outward, and hit the clearing below just as two men emerged from the trees. They both disappeared amid frantic screams, followed by silence.

Erin looked back up the mountainside, but there was no Kamehameha. Just Manu Pokui standing on a ledge where the boulder had been.

She shook her head. Was she going crazy?

CHAPTER FORTY-SIX

Walter Takai swung his police helicopter around a point on the Na Pali Coast. Up ahead lay the Kalalau Valley. Tommy saw two speedboats on the beach and a helicopter hovering over the trees, dipping and bobbing erratically. A sharp cracking sound echoed, unmistakable as a rifle shot.

Tommy grabbed his own rifle. "Get us there now."

Takai brought his chopper hard on the tail of the other, which suddenly spun around as its pilot realized that he was under attack. Now they faced each other, head on.

Tommy raised his rifle and leaned out the doorway; his opponent raised his weapon and leaned out as well. The respective pilots struggled to keep their crafts level so their passengers could get off shots.

The Plexiglas on the other chopper suddenly cracked, jagged lines marching outward. Tommy saw a splotch of crimson on the pilot's face. The chopper jerked downward and rolled over onto its side. Tommy's opponent pitched out headfirst, one hand still gripping his weapon. His scream could barely be heard over the roar of engines.

The helicopter dipped, rose, then dove nose down into the rain forest.

*****

Manu lowered his rifle. He watched the helicopter disappear from the sky, then looked over the ledge at the *haole* lawyer. She looked up at him. As they made eye contact, she held out her hand, palm down, and wagged it, as if to say, "Ehh, not bad."

In spite of himself, Manu laughed. Anyone with that kind of cool under fire, with that kind of sense of humor – well, she couldn't be all bad, *haole* or not.

By his count, they had taken out the four gunmen from the speedboats, but that left a fifth man, the one who had exited the helicopter when it landed on the beach. Things were different, now, though. The cavalry had arrived, probably waiting on the sand for Manu to chase his prey to them. He determined not to disappoint.

He sprinted down the switchback trail, letting gravity have its way. He wasn't worried about falling, just getting down as quickly as he could. From his vantage point, he saw the fifth man fighting his way through the trees, in the direction of the beach. Probably going for one of the speedboats, probably prepared to kill whomever might stand in his way.

Manu reached the clearing at top speed. The lawyer followed him into the trees.

*****

Panic had set in on Joseph Keala. His courage waned as his henchmen died around him, and now his tank was bone dry. When the helicopter slammed into the trees just fifty yards away, he knew his only chance was to reach the boats on the beach.

He tore through vegetation that threatened to ensnare him. The ground sloped sharply downward as he neared the beach. One stumble and he'd go head over heels. Trees thinned, the white sand and blue Pacific visible ahead as a blur. He heard the crash of runners behind him, following the trail he had blazed, keying on his sounds. His heart raced, his chest seized, his eyes blurred with sweat. His career was over, no matter whether he escaped or not. The only question left unanswered was whether his freedom was also over.

He glanced over his shoulder and saw the big man behind him. His once formidable lead had dwindled to barely twenty feet. He gasped for breath, ducked his head, and burst out of the jungle onto the white sand.

Directly into the waiting arms of Detective Kanahele. Behind him, two police boats were just beaching. Uniformed cops swarmed out. The police helicopter had landed nearby, and Detective Montgomery sat in the passenger seat, a rifle trained on Keala.

Out of breath, out of room, and out of fight, Keala flopped on the sand. The detective unhooked handcuffs from his belt, stepped over the prostrate Keala, and cuffed his hands behind his back.

"Joseph Keala, you're under arrest for the murder of Charles Cain."

"I had nothing to do with that," Keala said.

Just then, Manu burst out of the trees. He lumbered to a halt as Kanahele hoisted Keala to his feet, and a uniformed officer led him away.

Tommy and Manu faced off with each other. Sweat coursed down Manu's face, his breathing labored.

"Howzit, bruddah," Tommy said.

"Howzit."

"It's over now, bruddah. It's over."

CHAPTER FORTY-SEVEN

Erin stumbled out of the trees, shocked to see police scattered across the beach and Joseph Keala being led off in handcuffs. She was even more shocked to see Montgomery putting handcuffs on Manu. She bent over, hands on her knees, and fought for air. When she caught her breath, she looked at Tommy.

"Is that really necessary?" she asked.

"He's still under arrest for the eviction on the beach. And for the escape."

She ran over to Manu. "Don't say anything. You've got Fifth Amendment rights, whether you want them or not."

Manu looked at her, his face a puzzlement of disbelief. Then a broad smile emerged. He looked over his shoulder at Tommy. "You heard my lawyer. I'm not saying nothing to you."

Tommy smiled back. "You listen to your lawyer."

Montgomery led Manu away as Erin peeled off and turned back to Tommy. Relief was etched on his face.

"You okay?"

"I'm fine. Now."

"You've had quite an adventure since you've been here. You've been shot at, hit in the face with doors, and chased up a mountain on the Na Pali Coast. You don't find that in most of the travel brochures."

She looked back at the mountain behind her, up to the ledge where she had seen Kamehameha the Great. She opened her mouth to say something, then closed it and shook her head.

"What?" Tommy asked.

"Nothing. You wouldn't believe me anyway."

They walked together toward the police helicopter.

"So how do you like our islands, anyway?" Tommy asked.

"Go out to Hawaii, everybody said. Lie on the beach, sip a few Mai-Tais. You'll love it."

They laughed together, their voices in harmony. Tommy stepped closer. His arm touched hers as they crossed the sand. When they got to the helicopter, she froze at the doorway. He must have sensed something was wrong by the look on her face.

"You sure you're okay?"

She shook her head, unable to speak. The thought of entering another helicopter seized her heart with dread. She realized how ridiculous she must seem. She'd just had a life-or-death chase with automatic-weapon-firing bad guys and now that it was all over, she was too frightened to board a perfectly safe helicopter.

"Can we take one of the boats back?"

"Yeah, to Hanalei. But you've still got to get back to Hilo somehow."

"I'll take a plane."

"You got a problem with helicopters?"

"I was in one that had trouble staying up." She bit her lip to still its tremble. "Just in case you've ever wondered about this scar on my forehead. And the last one took me to Charlie. I'm about helicoptered out."

There was a softness in Tommy's face that eased her fear. "That's okay," he said. "Besides, believe it or not, I've never seen Na Pali by boat."

*****

Erin sat in the back of the boat, with Tommy beside her, mercifully silent. The wind felt good on her face, cooling the heat of fear that had assaulted her on the beach. She sensed that Tommy was dying to ask about the helicopter flight and her scar. After all, she had laid a helluva teaser on him.

"It was on my honeymoon," she said softly.

He barely heard her over the roar of the motor and the rush of the wind. He leaned closer, his head just inches from hers. "What?"

"I said it was on my honeymoon. Two years ago."

He looked at her. The word "honeymoon" formed on his lips, but no sound came out. She knew what he was thinking: Honeymoon means husband.

"Off the coast where the lava flow is."

Realization settled in on Tommy's face. "I remember that. I was part of the search team. We found – "

"My husband's body."

He leaned back and folded his arms across his chest. "I didn't know that was you."

"I didn't see any need to tell you before."

As they rounded the bend to Hanalei Bay, she turned toward

Tommy, who stared straight ahead, as if still having trouble digesting her bombshell.

"Were you following me?" she asked.

"Excuse me?"

"I asked if you were following me. How did you know where I was?"

"Harry called from the hotel. He saw someone follow you when you left this morning."

Tommy paused.

"What aren't you telling me?" Erin asked.

"Someone shot Harry to shut him up."

Erin shook her head and hugged herself. She suddenly felt cold. A shiver coursed through her.

"Is he okay?"

"He was alive when I left, but I haven't heard anything since. I'll call and find out when we get to Hanalei."

Erin looked back at him for a moment. She sensed there was still more to the story.

"What else aren't you telling me?"

"They hurt Tutu."

It felt as if all the air had dissipated in her lungs. "Hurt her how?"

"She's okay. She just wanted to make sure we found you before they got to you."

"Hurt her how, Tommy? I want to know."

He paused, debating how much to tell her. "They burned her face on the stove. The guy who did it stopped when he saw David."

"David." She turned that over in her mind. "Is he okay?"

"He's fine. We got there and grabbed the guy before he could do any more damage."

The boat throttled back as it crossed Hanalei Bay and eased next to the shot-up pier. Police teams still worked the scene, but the bodies had been removed. All that remained to testify to the bloody shoot-out were chipped concrete and a blue-striped speedboat with blood in the bottom.

An officer tied off the boat, then Tommy helped Erin out.

"Take me to see Tutu, Tommy. Then I want to go see Harry."

CHAPTER FORTY-EIGHT

The bandage covered the entire right side of Tutu's face. Second degree burns, the doctor said. Not serious enough to require skin grafts. Mostly they would just be painful for a while. The question of scarring was still open.

Alex and David sat with Tutu on the couch in their living room, man and child each squeezing one of her hands. Erin sat in the koa rocker, consumed with guilt, while Tommy stood behind her, hands on the back of the chair.

"It's not your fault, child," Tutu said. "These people wanted to hurt my boy, my *keiki*. You were just trying to help him."

The idea of anyone referring to the giant Manu Pokui as a child seemed absurd to Erin, but she knew that a mother's love always saw her son as a little boy.

"But if I hadn't come here –"

"It's God's way, child. If you hadn't come here, we wouldn't know who hurt Mister Charlie. And we wouldn't know who tried to hurt my boy. But now we do. Now Manu is safe."

Erin stood and went to the couch. She dwarfed the tiny Hawaiian woman as she leaned over and put her arms around her. Tutu released her husband's and grandson's hands and hugged

Erin. Tears flowed from both of them.

"Thank you, child, for what you've done."

Erin straightened and wiped her eyes. Her face flushed red.

"You are always welcome in my home, Miss Erin."

Erin looked at the end of the couch and, for just a moment, felt as if she could see Charlie there, again. He took off his glasses and nodded at her.

*****

Tommy wheeled his Jeep into the parking lot of the Hilo Medical Center on Waianuenue Avenue. He and Erin had not spoken much since reaching the pier at Hanalei, not on the drive to Lihue nor on the plane flight back to Hilo. Erin figured she had given Tommy some things to think about, and he was now not sure what his relationship should be with her. He apparently decided on professional – cop/witness – rather than personal.

Erin let Tommy do the talking as they tracked down Harry's surgeon, a wizened Japanese man with a striking shock of white hair.

"One of the bullets collapsed a lung," the doctor said, "but we got that patched and reinflated, and he seems to be breathing all right on his own. The interesting thing is his weight."

"His weight?" Erin and Tommy echoed in unison.

"He's morbidly obese. He'll be lucky to live another ten years with the pressure that weight is putting on his internal organs. But the irony is that the bullets had trouble penetrating the fat. Between that and the pectoral muscle on his left side, the second bullet stopped just millimeters from his heart." He laughed and shook his head. "It's not something that I'd recommend, but in this case, being fat saved his life."

Tommy chuckled. Even Erin couldn't help herself and laughed out loud.

"Can we see him?" she asked.

"Sure. Just don't stay too long. It'll tire him out. We're gonna keep him here a few days to watch that lung, but he should be fine."

They followed the doctor's directions and soon found Harry's room. He still looked pale, connected to various monitoring devices, and had an oxygen tube in his nose. His eyes brightened as he saw Erin enter, with Tommy close behind. Erin stifled another laugh as she saw how Harry's massive bulk dwarfed the bed, giving him the appearance of a beached whale.

"I hear I have you to thank for saving my life," Erin said.

"Any fool knows how to use a telephone," he said. His words came out in gasps because of his labored breathing.

Erin went to his bedside and took his giant hand in hers. Her hand disappeared inside his meaty grip.

"Don't try to talk," she said. "We're not going to stay, but I wanted to see you and say thank you."

She leaned over and kissed him on the cheek. "And do that."

"If I'd known that was how to get a kiss from you, I'd have gotten shot sooner."

She laughed gently. "I'll come back and see you again real soon. Right now, you take care of yourself and get better."

She took her hand back and stepped away from the bed.

Harry looked past her at Tommy. Tommy nodded slightly at Harry, who nodded back, unspoken messages delivered with each nod.

CHAPTER FORTY-NINE

"You haven't said much since I told you about my other helicopter trip," Erin said.

Tommy squeezed the steering wheel tightly, eyes on the road. He ventured a sideways glance at her before turning onto the Bayfront Highway. The sun was starting to set, and the moon had already emerged, spotlighting the waters of Hilo Bay.

"I didn't know what to say," he said. "I can't imagine how you must feel, and I didn't want to say anything stupid."

"What makes you think you'd say something stupid?"

"Precedent."

When they reached the hotel, he pulled under the porte-cochere, killed the engine, and shifted in his seat to face her. She waited for what he had to say. It seemed to take forever in coming, as if he had to work up the courage to speak.

"Sometimes I see a kind of sadness about you, and I wonder what it's about. Now I know, and I understand. And I'm glad you trusted me with that."

Now it was Erin's turn to struggle for words. After about a minute, she said, "And you thought you'd say something stupid."

"Like I said, there's precedent for it. Listen, you hungry?"

"Yeah, but what I really need is a shower. Running gunbattles in the jungle really work up a sweat."

She read disappointment on his face, so she quickly added, "If I hurry, will you wait? I hear they make good pancakes at that place up the street."

"Yeah. Take as long as you need. I'll be right here."

*****

Jim's House of Pancakes was nothing more than a glorified diner, but it lived up to the billing it received in the travel guides Erin had read before her honeymoon, though she and Chris never made it here. A friendly waitress brought the tall stacks of pancakes they ordered, but Erin wasn't prepared for the thickness of the individual pancakes nor for the ultimate height. Tall apparently meant TALL. This was a Texas-size stack.

Tommy watched in amusement as she slathered on gobs of butter, then drowned the stack with maple syrup, pouring between the pancakes as well as on top. When she realized that Tommy wasn't preparing his plate, she looked up and saw him staring at her. He wore a smile that could easily have been confused for a smirk.

"What?" she asked.

"Just wondering if this is how they do it in Texas."

"Yeah. And they're not rude enough to comment on it."

"Sorry."

She smiled at him. "I guess I'm hungrier than I thought."

Tommy took his knife and scraped a thin sliver of butter from the small side bowl and spread it on the top pancake. Where Erin's butter gathered in thick clumps, Tommy spread his so thin as to become nearly invisible. He dripped just enough syrup on top to barely moisten the surface. He cut into his first bite, then stopped with his fork halfway to his mouth as he realized that Erin was staring at him.

"What?" he asked.

"Just wondering if this is how they do it in Hawaii."

"Yeah. And they're not rude enough to comment on it."

She laughed and shoveled a huge bite into her mouth.

"Yeah, that's real lady-like," he said.

"Lady-like's for women who deprive themselves." She chewed vigorously and swallowed. "Ladies wouldn't order pancakes in the first place. They don't know what they're missing."

They both ate with gusto, avoiding any serious talk until they finished. Tommy poured each of them another cup of coffee, then pushed the pot aside.

"What's next for you?" he asked.

"I need to call Senator Lawrence and bring him up to speed. After that, I'll present my report and then I guess it's over for me."

"What will your report say?"

"Mostly just what we found out about Manu. I'll try to piece together the rest of Charlie's notes and see if he had any recommendations to make, but there wasn't much that I could tell."

"I guess the Bureau for Native Hawaiians may have seen its last days."

"Not necessarily. Just because Keala got greedy doesn't mean the BNH isn't a good thing. I know some bad lawyers, even some crooked lawyers, but I'm not ready to chuck the whole legal system because of it."

"Keala says he had nothing to do with Professor Cain's death," Tommy said.

"What did you expect him to say?"

"I don't know. We have him dead to rights on attempted murder of you and Manu. He didn't deny any of that. So why deny killing the professor?"

"He's probably smart enough to know that killing Charlie, who was over here on business for the U.S. Senate, is a federal crime. Does Hawaii have the death penalty?"

"No."

"Well, there you go. The feds do."

"I suppose. I made some calls earlier. We're already looking into BNH's trust accounts. In fact, the U.S. Attorney's gotten involved and served a federal subpoena on their financial records this afternoon. My guess is we're gonna find Keala had his hand in the till. He couldn't have known that was already in the works by the time he flew off to Kauai. He was probably hoping to take you out before you could stir it up. Too late for him."

"Yeah. That's probably why he went after Charlie, too. To head that off."

"You ever gonna come back?" Tommy asked. "Or have we just added to your trunk full of bad memories?"

She thought hard about the question, then said, "I don't know."

CHAPTER FIFTY

Smartly dressed in a gray pinstripe suit, Erin opened massive oak doors and entered a packed meeting room at the U.S. Capitol in Washington, D.C. A gray-haired man wearing a dark suit, sitting in an aisle seat about halfway down, turned and looked at her as she passed. There was something familiar about him, but Erin couldn't place it. With her eyes, she sought out Senator Lawrence, the chairman of the Senate Committee on Indian Affairs, sitting in the middle of fourteen men and women on a raised dais. To his left sat Senator James Hasegawa, the senior senator from Hawaii whose bill had set in motion the events of the past few weeks. Senator Lawrence smiled at her, his eyes twinkling even in the bright lights. His friendly face put her at ease. Her breathing relaxed as she took her seat at the table.

"Ms. Hanna, thank you for your appearance here today," Lawrence said. "We've all heard of the events that took place in Hawaii. From the safety of our offices in Washington, it's hard for us to fully understand the risks you faced – risks we caused you to face. For your strength and courage, we're in your debt."

"Thank you, Senator."

"Do you have an opening statement you'd like to make?"

"Yes, I do." She placed her notepad on the table, scanned the top page briefly, and then totally ignored it as she spoke from memory.

"Captain James Cook first stepped foot on Hawaiian soil on January 21, 1778. Less than one hundred years later, the population of native Hawaiians had been reduced by ninety percent, killed off by the white man's diseases to which they had no immunities. But at least the Hawaiians had their land, their kingdom, and their identity as a people. Until, that is, in its frenzy of manifest destiny, the United States determined that Hawaii, with its strategic Pearl Harbor, should be American territory. And so, with the aid and support of United States troops, American revolutionaries overthrew the Kingdom of Hawaii, imprisoned her queen, and set up a provisional government.

"Five years later, in 1898, the United States annexed Hawaii as its own territory. President Grover Cleveland told a joint session of Congress, 'Hawaii is ours. As I look back upon the first steps in this miserable business, and as I contemplate the means used to complete the outrage, I am ashamed of the whole affair.'"

When Erin paused, there was total silence in the chamber. Nary a cough nor a murmur to be heard.

She looked down the row of senators, making and briefly holding eye contact with each.

"Well, Senators, I'm ashamed, too."

*****

When the Committee broke for lunch, Erin pushed her way through a group of reporters as Senator Lawrence came off the dais. He took her by the arm and led her to a nearby cloakroom. Senator Hasegawa waited inside, talking with the gray-haired man Erin had seen in the aisle seat. When she entered, Hasegawa excused himself and approached. The man turned and sought out another senator to buttonhole.

"Erin, this is Jimmy Hasegawa," Lawrence said.

Hasegawa took her hand, his grip firm but gentle. "Miss Hanna, I thought you'd be interested in an update on what's going on back home. Joseph Keala and his co-conspirators have been formally indicted for fraud and embezzlement. He's also been charged with assault, attempted murder, and half a dozen other crimes. There's also a special federal grand jury being impaneled, and he's looking at about a dozen federal charges, as well."

"I didn't hear you mention a murder charge in all that."

"There's no evidence to tie him to Professor Cain's death."

"But you know he did it."

"You're a defense lawyer, Erin," Lawrence said. "If they charged him with Charlie's murder, you could pick that apart blindfolded. There's absolutely no evidence that puts Keala or any of his people with Charlie the night he disappeared. They've got him good and tight on enough other charges that he'll never see daylight again. Sometimes you've just got to be satisfied with what you can get."

Erin nodded slowly. She knew, intellectually, that Lawrence was right, but emotionally was another matter. And she was surprised to find herself becoming, at least on an emotional level, a pro-death penalty convert. If she ever found the man or men who killed Charlie, she felt as if she could push the plunger on the chemicals herself.

"I won't keep you," Hasegawa said. "I just wanted to meet you personally."

Hasegawa dipped his head in Lawrence's direction, almost a bow, and walked off.

Lawrence put his arm around Erin and pulled her close as they walked back to the meeting room. "You done good, Erin. I'm just sorry you had to go through all that."

"You couldn't have known."

"Doesn't make me feel any better, though."

"I'm sorry I couldn't give you any recommendations," Erin said. "I don't know what Charlie was thinking there, and I didn't feel comfortable making it up as I went along."

"Yeah, but you gave us a new respect for the people who'll be affected by whatever we do. In the long run, that's better than any recommendation. And you helped get rid of some people who didn't need to be where they were in the first place."

"I suppose that counts for something." She rubbed her eyes, fighting exhaustion. "By the way, who was the guy Hasegawa was talking to when we came in?"

"Ted Hotchkiss. He's a lawyer with one of the big D.C. firms." He snorted. "I use the term lawyer loosely. He's a damn lobbyist. He represents the tourist and resort industries. He's to the Hawaii developers what Jack Abramoff was to the American Indian casinos."

"And he's got Hasegawa's ear?"

Lawrence shook his head. "His ear, but not his heart. Why?"

"He just looks familiar, is all."

"I'm sure you've seen him someplace. Maybe even while you were in Hawaii. He gets around."

"And we all pay the price."

Kanaka Blues

CHAPTER FIFTY-ONE

Back in Dallas, Erin drove to Charlie's tidy house in a University Park neighborhood just a few blocks north of the SMU campus. Charlie usually walked to school, wearing his rumpled hat and carrying his battered briefcase as he traversed the sidewalk along Hillcrest Avenue toward the school. Erin often saw him as she wheeled her Camry into the faculty parking lot. She'd honk, he'd wave, and it always got her day off to the right start. Now, as she drove north along Hillcrest, she knew she'd never see him again. There would be no honks, no waves, and no right starts to her day.

She turned on his narrow street of post-World War II brick homes, tiny, cramped, and worth a small fortune on today's real estate market by virtue of being located in the prestigious Park Cities area – a combination of the exclusive Highland Park and its wannabe neighbor, University Park. She cruised down the street almost at idle speed and pulled to a stop in front of his home. She killed the engine and sat for a moment. She rested her head on the steering wheel, summoning up the reserves deep inside to allow her to enter his house for perhaps the last time.

She wasn't sure why she was there or what she expected to

find. His creditors and friends had been notified of his death, and his mail had been forwarded to the office he still kept at SMU even though he was retired, so it was unlikely there would be messages on his answering machine or anything in his mailbox. Maybe she simply wanted to be in his surroundings once more, to soak up his essence, maybe even to capture some of his intellectual strength.

She sat up straight and shook her head. It sounded nuts to her. Maybe she would take Senator Lawrence up on the offer he made after the hearing to foot the bill for a short vacation before throwing herself back into her work. Her emotional well-being balanced on a precarious perch, and maybe time off was just the thing to keep it balanced instead of tumbling like one of those well-placed boulders Manu used to target the bad guys.

Or was that King Kamehameha who pried those boulders loose?

She smiled and shook her head again. Yep, she definitely needed some time to re-fill her emotional well.

She cranked the car and took one last look at Charlie's house, with its well-maintained yard of thick Saint Augustine grass, a neat garden of seasonal flowers on either side of the front steps, and freshly-painted green shutters bordering the windows.

And a hanging screen on the window at the far left of the house.

Not at all like Charlie to leave a screen dangling. Of course, Charlie had been away for some time, but she had been charged with watering his plants, taking in his mail, and checking his answering machine. She thought back to the day of Charlie's funeral, the last time she was here, and tried to recall whether the screen was loose then. She was sure she would have noticed a hanging screen, just as she did now. It would have leaped out at her as an oddity on the front of his otherwise perfectly-in-order house.

She turned off the car again, got out, and went to the window where the screen hung by one corner. She saw scrape marks along the edge of the windowsill that she immediately recognized as the work of someone who had pried it off. She also saw that the latch on the inside of the window was open, scratch marks again leaving telltale evidence of tampering. Whoever went in this way had been either careless or unconcerned, which might mean they knew that the homeowner was already dead.

She hurried to the front door and let herself in with the spare key Charlie had given her. The inside of the house looked just as it did the last time. It smelled musty and was decorated much like you would expect a grandparent's house to be, full of antique furniture Charlie inherited from his mother and never bothered to replace or update. Charlie didn't have much of value. He never went in for fancy gadgets, TVs, stereos, or the like, and all the artwork on his walls came via garage sales or inheritance. A burglar could take one look through a window and realize this wasn't a house worth the time, effort, or risk of a break-in.

Unless you were looking for something specific. In Charlie's case, that meant the object of the break-in, if indeed there had been one, would have been his office in the second bedroom just across the hall from the master. The room with the hanging screen.

Erin headed directly there, her footsteps echoing on the hardwood floors. She stepped into the room and knew instantly there had been a search. All desk drawers and filing cabinets were in varying degrees of openness, either pulled partly out or simply not closed all the way, books pulled off of shelves and hastily returned, envelopes ripped open on the desk, and papers scattered on the floor.

Someone had been searching for a document, or documents, but what? This break-in occurred after Charlie's death, maybe after his burial, even. That meant that anything that was taken from his apartment or hotel room in Hawaii, or that was in the file folder Harry saw Charlie carrying, did not contain what the searcher sought. She had read all the notes and documents Charlie squirreled away in his locker at the University of Hawaii, none of which contained any explosive information. In fact, even his genealogical charts made little sense until read in conjunction with Tutu Kela's letters. But it was the conclusions someone hoped to cover up, not the letters themselves. And whoever attacked Tutu and followed Erin on the Big Island already knew that those letters had not traveled to Dallas, Texas.

So what was this intruder looking for? Was it something not connected to Charlie's death or his assignment in Hawaii? After all, Charlie had not been home in weeks. How would something relevant to his work in the islands end up at his home, or why would someone think that in the first place?

Of course, Charlie had written her a letter that awaited when she returned to her office following his death. Maybe he mailed something else, something he felt needed the additional safeguard of being an eight-hour plane ride away. And perhaps the more important question was whether it – whatever *it* was – had been found.

She pulled her cell phone from her purse and keyed Professor Tanaka's number.

"Professor, this is Erin Hanna."

"Ahh, Miss Hanna, so good to hear from you. I watched your testimony before the Senate on C-SPAN. Charlie would have been proud."

"I hope so."

"'That's my Erin,' he would say. But I know you're not calling just to hear my congratulations."

"No, but I appreciate them anyway. I was calling to see if you knew whether Charlie had subpoena power while he was investigating in Honolulu."

Tanaka was silent, as if the thought had never occurred to him. "I don't know," he said at last.

"So you don't remember seeing him with any documents that came with a subpoena?"

"No. As far as I know, he never subpoenaed anything. Or he never told me if he did."

"Okay. Thanks, Professor."

"Will I see you in our fair islands again soon, Miss Hanna?"

"Maybe. You never know."

*****

After leaving her cell number and Charlie's house in the hands of the University Park police, Erin called Senator Lawrence, who was in a meeting. She went to the law school to check both her mail and Charlie's, but that proved fruitless. She left instructions with the faculty secretary to notify her immediately if anything arrived in the mail or other delivery service from Charlie or simply from Hawaii, then left for home.

Sleep tugged at her consciousness as she pulled out of the parking lot and south on Hillcrest. Exhaustion had been a constant companion since she first received that early morning call that she had come to think of as the "whozit?" phone call. Her cell rang, shaking her back into a vague state of alertness. She grabbed it off the passenger seat and looked at the caller I.D.

"Let me ask you something, Senator," she said. "Did Charlie have subpoena power as part of his investigation?"

"And hello to you, too," Senator Lawrence said.

"Sorry. Just a little preoccupied right now."

"But to answer your question, yes, he had subpoena power. He would have had to go to federal court to get one issued, probably through the U.S. Attorney's office in Honolulu. They knew he was over there working for us."

"Did he ever exercise it? I didn't find anything in his notes that he couldn't have gotten on his own, which makes me think that he either didn't subpoena anything or else something's missing."

"I don't know, but I can find out. I'll have someone in Senator Hasegawa's Honolulu office check with the court." Lawrence paused. She heard the ambient noise of traffic and knew he was on the road. "Why are you asking? I thought this was all wrapped up."

"Just following up on a hunch. You know me; I'm never satisfied."

He laughed. "I call it thorough. It's what makes you such a dangerous lawyer."

She paused briefly, then asked, "Is your offer still open to pay for a vacation? I want to go back to Hawaii. To the Kona Coast Cottages."

For a moment she heard nothing but the sounds of car engines and an occasional horn honk. Then he said, "Isn't that where you went on your honeymoon?"

"Yeah."

"Are you sure that's a good idea?"

"I've been thinking about it ever since I left Washington and, yeah, I think it's a good idea. It's the last place I was ever really happy. Maybe it's finally time to let Chris go and say good-bye. What better place?"

"You're sure?"

She bit her lip, choking back what she knew would be a sob if she let it go. "I'm sure. So if you find out whether Charlie subpoenaed any documents, get word to me at the Cottages. Let Professor Tanaka know, too. I'll touch base with him while I'm over there."

"I thought you were going there to rest."

"I won't be able to rest unless I know for sure. Maybe I can put my mind at ease once and for all."

Kanaka Blues

CHAPTER FIFTY-TWO

Erin stepped off the plane at Kona International Airport to a mid-afternoon blast of hot, dry air more suitable to a desert than an island. She retrieved her suitcase from the open-air carousel under a thatched-roof covering, secured a white convertible from the rental agency, and headed north from the airport on the Queen Ka'ahumanu Highway. Ten minutes later, she turned off toward the ocean at the joint entrance to the Hualalai Resort and the Kona Coast Cottages, built on the cooled lava flows of the volcano Hualalai, which last erupted in 1800-1801.

A mile-and-a-half later, she arrived at the lonely entrance gate to the Cottages, set atop a lava field with no neighbor around for at least a mile. Erin rolled down her window as the gatekeeper stepped out, clipboard in hand.

"Aloha, ma'am," he said. "You staying at the resort?"

"I'm checking in. Erin Hanna."

He ran his forefinger down the clipboard and stopped near the bottom. "Yes, ma'am. Just take this road to the circle at the end. Park in the circle and someone will be waiting for you at registration."

He raised the arm blocking the road and she drove through. She kept her window down and enjoyed the warmth of the dry air that swirled her hair around her face. An ache in her heart reminded her that Chris wasn't beside her as he had been two years earlier. Then again, she was here this time to say good-bye. Not to banish him from her memory, but to finally make room in her life for someone else. Who that would be, she didn't know. Maybe Tommy Kanahele. She hadn't told him she was back on the island and didn't yet know if she would. But she knew that she no longer wanted to be alone.

Entering the Kona Coast Cottages was like stepping out of a time machine, both as a visit to the simplicity of ancient Hawaii – no radios or televisions in the rooms, and cell phones forbidden in public areas – as well as to the more recent history of two years ago. After checking in at the front desk, a porter loaded her bags into a golf cart and off they went. Memories flooded Erin as they drove down a dirt road. Barely more than a wide path, it wended through tropically landscaped acreage that intruded on the roadway from both sides. A sweet fragrance of plumeria filled the air, reminding her of those early morning walks she and Chris had taken at first light, ambling the grounds with no purpose other than being together in paradise.

To her left was the gift shop and, behind that, the fishponds that they had circled dozens of times, hand in hand. To her right, the various gathering places for guests: the beach activities center, the Polynesian-style dining room, the main swimming pool, and beyond, the blue Pacific lapping at the beach of Kahuwai Bay. The porter deposited her at a cottage on the beach at the south end of the property. He carried her bags inside, accepted his twenty-dollar tip with a smile and a *"mahalo,"* then was on his way in search of another new guest with cash in hand.

Erin stood on the lanai and gazed seaward. The resort's glass bottom boat hovered over the nearby reef. Across the bay to the north, snorkelers floated atop the water in twos and threes. A few well-done guests lay on lounge chairs on the salt-and-pepper beach. There was no sound save for the rustle of palm leaves and the gentle splash of the surf, the kinds of sounds engineers had captured on "sleep machines" and sold by the millions to harried city-dwellers on the mainland.

She opened her suitcase on the king-sized bed, complete with Hawaiian quilt of green and soft pink designs. A mini-refrigerator stood in the corner, with a coffee-grinder and maker on top. She opened a package of Kona coffee beans, ground sufficient for one cup, and turned on the maker. She planned to slip into shorts and T-shirt and sit on the lanai with a steaming cup of Kona, then take a stroll around the eighty-three acres of resort grounds. But first she would check her messages on her cell phone.

She turned the cell on and saw that she had one message. It was from a University Park, Texas, police detective named Swofford telling her they found fingerprints on Charlie's desk at his house. She dialed the number left on the message and soon had the detective on the line.

"We ran the prints through our database," Swofford said, "but we got no matches. We know they're not the professor's, though."

"Will you do me a favor and send them to Detective Tommy Kanahele on the Big Island of Hawaii?"

She fumbled in her purse for Tommy's card, gave Swofford the number, and hung up. She filled a cup with coffee and went out to the lanai. She sat facing the water, angling for the breeze blowing in, and luxuriated in its caress of her face. Should she call Tommy and let him know she was there? She sipped coffee and pondered her options.

*****

By the time Erin returned from an hour-long walk on the grounds, the sun was starting to set. She splashed water on her face and ran a brush through her hair, then hustled over to the main dining room for dinner. The Hawaiian hostess showed her to a table on the lanai, just steps from the beach, where she enjoyed a dinner of mahi-mahi and a glass of iced tea while watching the sun set. As the last light faded, leaving behind wisps of pink clouds on the horizon, Erin returned to her cottage, a long, hard sleep on her agenda.

When she reached the cottage, she found a legal-sized envelope clipped to the message board next to the lanai. It bore her name on the outside. She carried it inside, sat on the edge of the bed, and took out its contents: a handful of documents that had been faxed to her, care of the Kona Coast Cottages. She read the message on the cover sheet first:

Ms. Hanna, Senator Hasegawa asked that I send these to you. These are bank records produced by Hawaii National Bank to the U.S. Attorney's office in response to a subpoena from Professor Cain. As far as I can tell, this is all the material Professor Cain subpoenaed to date. I also sent a copy to Professor Tanaka.

It was signed by Coby Howell in Hasegawa's Honolulu office.

Attached to the cover sheet was a copy of a subpoena and photocopies that showed wire transfers from Hawaii National Bank in Honolulu to the Bank of Japan in Tokyo. The account at Hawaii National from which the transfers were made was in the name of a company called Western Pacific Resorts. The transfers totaled over two-hundred-fifty thousand dollars.

And the account in Tokyo to which the money was transferred was in the name of Yukinobu Tanaka.

Erin scrambled to her suitcase and retrieved her laptop. She stuck her cell phone in her pocket and raced from her cottage to the business center adjacent to the gift shop. It wasn't much of a business center, just a row of three chairs against a wall with ports for plugging in computers and connecting to the Internet, but it would serve her purpose.

As she waited for her computer to boot up, she turned on her cell phone. As it came to life, a loud tone announced she had a message waiting. She dialed her mailbox and listened to the voice of Tommy's partner, Detective Joe Montgomery: "Miss Hanna, we ran some fingerprints that the police in Texas sent us and came up with the name Luke Tanaka. Does that mean anything to you?"

She dialed Montgomery's call-back number. He answered quickly.

"Detective, this is Erin Hanna."

"Miss Hanna, believe it or not, it's good to hear your voice. I take it you got my message."

"I did. And things are starting to make sense. Here's what I've got so far."

She quickly filled him in on the wire transfers to an account in Yukinobu Tanaka's name in Japan. "You got any background on Luke Tanaka?" she asked. "The same last name can't be just a coincidence."

"He's hooked up with Japanese gangs here in Hilo and in Honolulu. He's pretty small time. Just some penny ante stuff on his record, but he does have a father named Yuki who teaches at the law school at the university."

Erin's computer was up and running, connected to the Internet. While Montgomery talked, she clicked away on the keyboard. She ran searches in government and legal databases with the precision of an expert.

"We tracked Luke Tanaka to Dallas, all right," Montgomery said. "He flew in the day after Professor Cain's funeral, then right back to Honolulu the next morning. The ticket was in his name, but it was paid for by a credit card belonging to Yukinobu Tanaka."

"Tanaka had to have been looking for the records Charlie subpoenaed. He had no way of knowing Charlie had left them with the U.S. Attorney."

"What was he trying to hide?"

She linked from database to database as she ran her search, then struck gold.

"Bingo!"

"What?"

"It takes a little doing, but Western Pacific Resorts is ultimately controlled by Theodore Hotchkiss."

"GQ."

"What?"

"Never mind. Just go on."

"He's a lobbyist for a group of resort developers. I saw him just this week in Washington, talking to Senator Hasegawa."

A memory kicked in for Erin. The first time she met Tanaka, a nice-looking gray-haired man had nearly bumped into her as she entered the law library. She now knew that it was Hotchkiss. Had he been at the library to meet with Tanaka?

"What would he be paying this professor for?" Montgomery asked.

"Professor Tanaka was working closely with Charlie on his investigation. Hotchkiss may have been paying him as a spy, or maybe even to influence Charlie's report. Charlie must have found a connection between the two, and that's why he subpoenaed the bank records."

She looked at the subpoena in the batch of faxed documents. "It's dated the day Charlie disappeared."

They both fell silent. Montgomery exhaled deeply. "You think this professor killed Charlie?"

"Not personally. But I bet he found out about the subpoena and set it up. Maybe he used his son and his gang friends." Now Erin exhaled deeply. "Is Tommy around?"

"No. He took the day off to get ready for tomorrow."

"What's tomorrow?"

"We've got to serve a court order to evict some folks from a beach in the morning. A judge let Manu out, so we figure he's gonna be in the middle of it. Tommy was trying to track him down to see if he could head off a fight tomorrow."

"If you hear from him, will you let him know what's going on?"

"Sure. Where are you?"

"I'm at the Kona Coast Cottages."

"I'm coming over there to stay with you. I'll call Honolulu PD on the way, get them started on the professor. I'm down the road in Kailua right now, and I can be there in less than twenty minutes. Tommy would kill me if I let anything happen to you."

"Detective, there's no reason to do that. I'm perfectly safe. No one knows I'm here."

*****

While the Kona Coast Cottages had a secured front entrance, the adjacent Hualalai Resort did not. Anyone could enter the Hualalai grounds and, from the beach, access the Kona Cottages grounds next door undetected. That's exactly what Luke Tanaka, a nasty-dispositioned young man with bulging muscles and the acne and rage that went hand-in-hand with the steroids that produced them, was doing as Erin and Montgomery talked. Two equally nasty-dispositioned Japanese men followed him.

Luke pulled a Glock 9 mm from the pocket of his windbreaker and screwed a silencer onto the barrel.

CHAPTER FIFTY-THREE

With her laptop tucked under her arm and her head down, Erin rounded a curve in the narrow road and headed toward her cottage. She stopped when she saw shadows between it and its adjacent neighbor. They could have merely been other guests out for a walk, but there was something about their movement that set her nerves on alert. It was the furtive way they moved, staying near the cottages and avoiding clearings. She didn't know if it was Montgomery's paranoia rubbing off or her own internal alarms, but she knew instantly that the shadows were there for her.

She turned and headed back the way she had come.

A soft spitting noise sounded behind her. She heard the angry buzz of a bullet fly past her head. It hit the trunk of nearby palm tree with a loud *thunk*.

She broke into a run.

A splatter of stars on the black palette of sky overhead, augmented by flickering torches that were lit at sunset, illuminated Erin's way as she churned dust on the path. She hung close to the side of the road, hoping to blend her shadows with those of the foliage that encroached on the right of way.

Another bullet spun angrily by, rippling palm fronds as the road turned sharply right. A few steps ahead lay a fork. She bore left. A shot *thunked* into a tree trunk behind her, where she would have been had she not turned.

She knew that the men chasing her must somehow be connected to Hotchkiss, but how did they know where she was? It couldn't have been blind luck. Of all the resorts in all the islands, why come here? Then it hit her: She had told Senator Lawrence to have Hasegawa's office let Professor Tanaka know about any subpoenas Charlie may have obtained. They also likely let Tanaka know where Erin was staying.

In the faint light, she saw an ice station ahead at another fork in the path. She remembered this one: left meant the more populous areas of the resort, right took her behind the gift shop and toward the fishponds. Her heart said to bear left, toward crowds, but her mind overrode her heart. *People doesn't mean safety*, it argued. *It means innocent bystanders.*

She planted her left tennis shoe and cut sharply right. She jettisoned her laptop into a hibiscus bush and pulled her cell phone from her pocket. She pressed a button to light up the screen and held it close to her face as she scrolled through her call log, found a number, and pressed the call button.

*****

Montgomery slowed on the winding road that led to the Kona Cottages entrance. He kept his speed steady at fifty miles per hour, fast enough to screech his tires but slow enough to stay on the pavement.

His cell phone rang; he snatched it up from the passenger

seat.

"Hello?"

"It's Erin." Her voice sounded distant, breathless. "Some guys are chasing me. With guns. Do you know where the petroglyph field is at the resort? It backs up to the main road."

"Yeah. I'm just coming up on it, in fact."

"Wait there. I'll lead them to you." She paused. For a moment he heard the beat of running feet, the sharp exhales of heavy breathing. "And call for back-up."

*****

Erin stuck her phone into her shorts pocket and poured all her energy and concentration into running. She peeled her ears, listening. They were still back there, but they didn't sound any closer.

The path took her between a row of cottages that bordered the large fishpond. She hoped she didn't run into any late-evening strollers. She also realized that, with the curving path she trod, stray bullets could easily enter any of a number of those cottages. She switched from hoping to praying that the guests were all at dinner or somewhere over in the common areas.

Another bend or two and she was on a straightaway that allowed her to pick up more speed. It also made her a bigger target. A buzzing noise like a swarm of bees filled the air around her. She bent at the waist and ducked her head, veered to the right side of the road, and vaulted a low wooden fence. Just ahead lay the petroglyph field. Its wooden boardwalk meandered through a smooth lava flow filled with ancient carvings that told Hawaii's history in the most rudimentary of forms. Stick figures of men in boats, fishing and fighting. And now, hundreds of years later, men were still fighting in this field.

The uneven surface of the lava flow made walking difficult, much less running. It did the same for the men behind her, so Erin stumbled to the boardwalk with about the same lead she had maintained from the start of the chase.

She scrambled onto the boardwalk and ran toward the end. She vaulted over the railing and landed hard on yet more lava rock. Her right ankle turned as she hit ground. An electric shock ran up her leg and disappeared into her hip. She grimaced and bit back the pain, swallowing the nausea that bubbled in the pit of her stomach, and struck out for the unseen road no more than a couple of football fields away. Her run was reduced to a hobble. She was now in the open, clearly silhouetted on the lava field.

A burning sensation dug into the back of her left arm. It took a moment for her to realize this was not a nerve jolt from her ankle but the sting of a bullet passing through the fleshy part of her arm. Blood oozed down both sides.

Nausea bubbled up again in her throat. Her breath fled; her head swam. She stumbled, struggled for balance, and fell. Her cheek slapped hard against the lava.

*****

Montgomery knelt in front of his car, its lights out. He held his gun in his hand as he scanned the lava field for signs of movement. Nothing.

He went to the fence that bordered the field and climbed over. Then he heard it: footsteps on wood. Then a scuffling sound, followed by footsteps on rock. Behind those, more sounds of footsteps on wood.

Then flashes of light. His trained cop eye knew them for what they were: muzzle flashes.

He saw a shadow approaching. A staggering, stumbling approach.

The flying hair. He knew it was Erin.

He raced toward her.

She stumbled sharply, then collapsed.

*****

Erin was vaguely aware of someone approaching, but from the front, not the rear. She looked up as Montgomery knelt beside her.

"Erin, are you hit?"

"My arm. It's no big deal."

She heard hissing sounds followed by the *chink* of bullets gouging into lava.

As sounds of sirens wafted toward them, Montgomery steadied his gun with both hands and sighted at the muzzle flashes on the boardwalk. A shot slammed into his chest. He spun away and landed face first. His gun clattered onto the rocks beside Erin.

She crawled to him but he lay motionless.

"Got 'em both." Luke Tanaka's voice carried on the night

breeze.

Three sets of feet jumped from the boardwalk onto the lava, and began their approach. She held her breath as she inched her hand toward Montgomery's gun. She tried as best she could to appear motionless as she hooked her index finger in the trigger guard and dragged the weapon closer.

She turned her head and looked back at three approaching silhouettes. It appeared as if two held their guns at their sides, apparently confident their prey had been stilled. The middle silhouette held his hand extended forward. Ever ready. On alert.

Erin pulled the gun into her palm and let her hand wrap around the grip. Her finger slipped over the trigger.

Waiting.

They drew closer, speaking in whispers.

"Anybody moving?"

"No, brah. Not anymore."

The voices were close now, no more than ten feet away.

Now five feet.

"We better make sure," Luke Tanaka said.

Erin saw the shadow of an arm raise and point at her.

She rolled over onto her back, swung Montgomery's gun up, and fired.

CHAPTER FIFTY-FOUR

As the ambulance departed with Erin and Montgomery, a coroner's wagon arrived to cart off the three bodies Erin had left behind with the police. Paramedics bandaged her arm and strapped a walking brace onto her ankle. On the ride to the hospital, she held Montgomery's hand and spoke to him in low tones while the paramedics stabilized his breathing. He never lost consciousness, apparently more in pain than in danger.

After ensuring that Montgomery was in stable condition and that her own injuries were properly treated, Erin left the hospital against the doctors' advice to catch the last flight of the day to Oahu. She was met at the Honolulu airport by a police officer, who transported her to a substation in Manoa Valley, near the University of Hawaii. Fifteen minutes later, she stood in a small room with two detectives, Sato and McKee, and looked through a one-way mirror at Professor Tanaka. He sat alone at a small table in an interrogation room, eyes downcast. His posture and general appearance diminished his size, making him appear even smaller than he was.

"Did he ask for a lawyer?" Erin asked.

"He just asked for you," Detective Sato said.

"Did he say anything at all?"

"Nope. Just asked for you, then clammed up."

She took a deep breath. The wound to her arm throbbed, as did her ankle. She found it hard to believe that this little man, whom she had come to like and even to associate with Charlie, was most likely responsible for all this death.

Killing Luke and his friends was self-defense, a fact she knew intellectually beyond a doubt, but the emotional scar of taking lives was something she wondered if she'd ever get over. While part of her felt sorry for Tanaka, part of her hated him for what he had done.

"I'm ready," she said.

Sato opened the door, and she entered the interrogation room alone. Tanaka looked up as she came in and sat across from him. He lowered his eyes again and dipped his head in a small bow.

"Miss Hanna, I'm glad you came."

"I can't be your lawyer."

"I have no desire for a lawyer. I wish only to clear my conscience."

"All right. I'm listening. Just so you'll know, though, the police are listening, too."

"I understand."

She leaned back in her chair and crossed her arms. For the first time, he seemed to notice the bandage on her bicep.

"You are injured."

"Compliments of your son."

He lowered his eyes again. "He shames me."

"You shame yourself, Professor. Tell me why you did it."

"First, please know that I never wished harm to come to

Charlie. I only wished to influence his report and his recommendations. As I am sure you know, money corrupts. I find, to my great shame, that I was susceptible to its charms."

He met her eyes again, and Erin saw the pain on his face. She wasn't sure if it was because he was sorry for what he had done or simply sorry that he had been caught.

"How did you get sucked into this?" she asked.

"Initially, I was just asked to monitor Charlie's investigation and report back. It seemed innocent enough, and I was well paid. Later I was asked to exert whatever influence I had on Charlie. I even leaked information that Charlie was leaning against the Hasegawa Bill."

"Why would you do that?"

"I hoped it would create a groundswell and maybe rub off on him."

"You obviously didn't know him very well," she said.

"Maybe not, but I tried to use everything I had at my disposal. All I knew was that it was in my benefactor's interest that the Hasegawa Bill fail."

"Your benefactor? Professor, this isn't *Great Expectations*. We're talking about bribes."

"A bribe implies I was being asked to do something dishonest or corrupt. Lobbyists pay money to government officials all the time to influence them. It's entirely legal. And I wasn't a government official. I was merely a lowly law professor who was helping a colleague with his research. I was paid to put forward a point of view. That's all. I never dreamed – "

His voice broke off.

"You never dreamed what? That someone with millions to lose might do something to stop the threat Charlie posed? Did you really never dream that, or did you simply shut your eyes to the possibility?"

He sat silently, squirming under Erin's intense gaze. She let the tension fill the air until he found it unbearable.

"Perhaps you're right. Perhaps I should have known. When I finally allowed myself to accept what I had done, it was too late. Charlie had disappeared."

"When was that? After Charlie confronted you about your relationship with Hotchkiss? How did he find out?"

"He saw us together at the law school. And Mr. Hotchkiss knew that he had seen us."

"You also knew what Charlie had found out about Manu Pokui. You told Hotchkiss, who was petrified of what that might do to galvanize the Hawaiian population. He saw the perfect opportunity to get rid of Charlie and frame Manu at the same time. He even blew up his own client's construction site. Did he use Luke to do all that?"

The words seem to slam into Tanaka with great force. It was as if he honestly never considered whether his thug son might have been on Hotchkiss's payroll, as well.

"You'll have to ask him," he said.

"I can't, Professor."

"Why not?"

She stood, unsure what to say. Obviously he hadn't been notified of his son's death. She stared at him for a moment, debating whether to say more. After an awkward silence, the truth dawned. He looked at the bandage on her arm then back into her eyes. Tears formed in his.

She left as he lowered his head on the table and wept.

*****

A crowd of media and on-lookers watched in anticipation as a row of Hawaiians lined up on one side of a beach just south of Hilo, while a row of police stood on the other, in full riot gear. A tent city hung in the balance. Manu Pokui stood in front of his "army." His opposite number was Tommy Kanahele.

"Why you keep doing this, bruddah?" Tommy asked.

"Like John Wayne said, 'A man's gotta do what a man's gotta do.'"

"You got *haole* heroes now?"

A smile played at Manu's lips.

Behind them, a rental car pulled up. Erin got out and pushed her way through the crowd of watchers. Over Tommy's shoulder, Manu saw people moving aside as she shouldered her way to the front, hobbling with a slight limp. His smile erupted.

"You bettah watch out. My lawyer's here."

Tommy glanced over his shoulder and saw Erin. He looked back to Manu. "Just please be careful, bruddah. I don't want you getting hurt."

Tommy turned and walked toward Erin, his eyes never leaving hers. A uniformed cop took his place in front of Manu, bullhorn in hand. "All right now, people," the cop said. "We've got a court order that says you have to evacuate this beach. Please do so peacefully."

A roar went up from the Hawaiians. Manu put his hands on his hips defiantly. Tommy reached Erin and stood next to her as they watched the standoff.

"Joe said I could probably find you here," Erin said. "The doctor says he was lucky the bullet was high. It just hit bone and muscle. Broke his collarbone, but he's doing pretty good."

"Yeah. I haven't been over to the hospital yet, but I talked to him on the phone."

"I'm sorry I got him shot."

"You saved his life is the way he tells it."

Tommy folded his arms across his chest. "Your arm okay?"

"Hurts a little, that's all."

"I shoulda been there."

"I was starting to feel a little like poor ol' Nell on the railroad tracks, always waiting on Dudley Do-Right to come along. It's about time I started looking after myself."

They watched as Manu and the cop with the bullhorn spoke softly to each other. A last minute plea from law enforcement, an expected rebuff from Manu.

He looked at her arm again. "You sure you're okay?"

"Just a little sore. And a little hungry."

"You wanna go get some pancakes?"

"You mean a professional consultation? Cop to lawyer? Talk about the case a little bit?"

"That's not at all the kind of consulting I had in mind. In fact, I thought we wouldn't talk about the case at all."

They continued to watch the standoff for a moment. The two

lines started to close on each other. Erin took Tommy's hand in hers. "Why, Detective, I'd be honored to have pancakes with you."

He squeezed her hand in his. They turned and threaded their way through the crowd as the melee started behind them.

About the Author

Mike Farris is an award-winning screenwriter, literary agent, and entertainment attorney, focusing on the film and publishing industries. He lives in Dallas, Texas, with his wife Susan, who is also an attorney.

Kanaka Blues

If you enjoyed *Kanaka Blues* consider
these other fine Books from
Savant Books and Publications:

Tropic of California by R. Page Kaufman
The Village Curtain by Tony Tame
Dare to Love in Oz by William Maltese
Today I Am A Man by Larry Rodness
The Interzone by Tatsuyuki Kobayashi
The Bahrain Conspiracy by Bentley Gates
Called Home by Gloria Schumann

Scheduled for Release in 2010:
The Jumper Chronicles by W. C. Peever
Mythical Voyage by Robin Ymer
Ammon's Horn by Guerrino Amati
My Unborn Child by Orest Stocco
Poor Rich by Jean Blasiar

If you are an author or prospective author who would like to be
published contact Savant Books and Publications at

http://www.savantbooksandpublications.com

Made in the USA
Lexington, KY
16 July 2010